"What is it, then?" he snapped, irritated beyond measure by the knowledge that this staircase was deserted, and likely to remain so at this time of day. It meant that nobody was likely to catch him if he did yield to the temptation to kiss her.

"How like you not to notice," she snapped back, "that you have just made me the subject of gossip by hauling me out of the room in front of all those..." She pulled a face. "Well, I am sure they are all perfectly respectable people, but they will now all be talking about me. About *us*."

He winced as she scored a direct hit.

But it was her own fault. He'd laid careful plans about how he was going to conduct himself with each and every one of the young ladies who'd be staying at Theakstone Court this week. With rigid propriety. *She* was the one who'd blown his plans sky-high by...by...

By just being herself.

Which made him even more annoyed than ever.

## Author Note

When Napoleon abdicated in April 1814, people all over England celebrated in various ways. Many towns held fetes, where military bands played, and there was communal singing, and fireworks displays. In at least one town (Great Yarmouth) a feast was also put on for around eight thousand "poor" people. Local dignitaries and members of the elite served at the table.

Later in the year, another fireworks display, held to commemorate the hundredth anniversary of the accession of George I of Hanover to the British throne, went spectacularly wrong. Part of the elaborate backdrop—a Chinese pagoda—caught fire, resulting in the death of two men and a number of swans. The crowd there thought the destruction of the pagoda was all part of the spectacle and cheered wildly.

However, I have been at a display where a fire broke out, and nobody there cheered. Instead, the entire crowd surged instinctively away from the fire, carrying me along with it.

And so from these three elements, my opening scene began to form in my mind...

# ANNIE BURROWS

---

*A Duke in Need of a Wife*

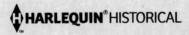

**⬧HARLEQUIN®** HISTORICAL

Recycling programs
for this product may
not exist in your area.

ISBN-13: 978-1-335-63491-7

A Duke in Need of a Wife

Copyright © 2019 by Annie Burrows

All rights reserved. Except for use in any review, the reproduction or
utilization of this work in whole or in part in any form by any electronic,
mechanical or other means, now known or hereafter invented, including
xerography, photocopying and recording, or in any information storage
or retrieval system, is forbidden without the written permission of the
publisher, Harlequin Enterprises Limited, 22 Adelaide St. West, 40th Floor,
Toronto, Ontario M5H 4E3, Canada.

This is a work of fiction. Names, characters, places and incidents are
either the product of the author's imagination or are used fictitiously,
and any resemblance to actual persons, living or dead, business
establishments, events or locales is entirely coincidental.

This edition published by arrangement with Harlequin Books S.A.

For questions and comments about the quality of this book,
please contact us at CustomerService@Harlequin.com.

® and TM are trademarks of Harlequin Enterprises Limited or its
corporate affiliates. Trademarks indicated with ® are registered in the
United States Patent and Trademark Office, the Canadian Intellectual
Property Office and in other countries.

Printed in U.S.A.

**Annie Burrows** has been writing Regency romances for Harlequin since 2007. Her books have charmed readers worldwide, having been translated into nineteen different languages, and some have gone on to win the coveted Reviewers' Choice Award from *CataRomance*. For more information, or to contact the author, please visit annie-burrows.co.uk, or you can find her on Facebook at Facebook.com/annieburrowsuk.

Visit the Author Profile page at Harlequin.com for more titles.

I'd like to give a special mention to Poppy, who inspired the creation of Snowball.

# Chapter One

*July 1814*

It all happened so fast.

One moment, everyone was *oohing* and *aahing* at the cascade of red and gold sparks bursting into the night sky. The next, they were screaming and running as a sheet of flame erupted with a sound that put Sofia in mind of a fusillade of cannon.

Worse still, the bigger people were shoving the smaller, slower-moving ones out of their way. In the panic, a tall man elbowed Sofia right in her eye as he spun away from the exploding fireworks. A split second later someone else deliberately shoved her aside. What with the blow to the face, the shove and the surge of running people, Sofia felt herself beginning to lose her footing.

Already scared, Sofia now faced the terrifying prospect of being trampled underfoot. Fortunately, the man who'd shoved her out of his way had shoved her in the direction of a clump of sturdy-looking bushes. All Sofia had to do was alter her topple into a deliberate dive and she ended up underneath them, rather than under the pounding feet of the fleeing mob.

Her heart was pounding, her limbs were shaking, but she was safe—if a bit bruised and grubby. Still, for once she'd have a jolly good excuse for returning to her aunt and uncle covered in leaves and mud. For once, she could lay the blame squarely at the feet of the beast who'd pushed her out of his way, rather than having to confess that she'd had to dig her dog out of a rabbit burrow, or rescue her from a boggy patch of meadow, or one of the many other mishaps which so regularly seemed to befall her when exploring Uncle Ned's estates.

It took a remarkably short time for the massive crowd which had gathered to watch the fireworks display to disperse.

Still unsure that it would be safe to emerge from her cover, Sofia gingerly raised herself on one elbow and peered out from under the lower branches to see what was going on.

Uncle Ned had bought the most expensive tickets to this event which Burslem Bay's town council had put on to celebrate the peace with France. It had not only included the price of supper, but also the right to stand halfway up the castle mound, ensuring the best view of the fireworks. It meant that even from beneath the bushes, Sofia could still clearly see that the scaffolding on which the fireworks display had been mounted was now well ablaze.

She could also hear someone screaming. She raised herself a bit further and saw, to her horror, right beneath the flaming scaffolding, in the area where the servants and shopkeepers had been standing, a woman with her skirts on fire.

A woman all on her own, desperately swatting at the flames, which were now licking up her sleeves. Sofia had seen something similar in her childhood, when a stray rocket had set a magazine, as well as the men nearest to it, ablaze, so she knew that the woman ought to lie on the ground and roll, not leap about the way she was doing. But this was England in peacetime, not a fortress on high alert. Which meant she could well be the only person here who knew what needed doing.

So Sofia wriggled out from under the shrubbery and began running back down the slope as fast as she could, desperately hoping she'd be strong enough to wrestle the panicked woman to the ground and extinguish the flames before it was too late. Out of the corner of her eye, she noticed two men also running in the same direction—two of the waiters who'd served at supper, to judge from the white shirts they wore, with blue sashes wrapped round their waists. They reached the burning woman first. One of them pushed her to the ground. The other one, who was slightly behind him, and who'd clearly had the presence of mind to grab a champagne bucket on his way, upended the contents over the unfortunate woman, putting out most of the flames at once.

By the time Sofia got there, the waiters had extinguished all the flames and were standing back, breathing heavily and looking a bit sick at the state of the poor woman who lay there moaning and shaking.

Most of one side of her dress had gone and her hair looked as though it, too, had been singed. Sofia wasn't surprised the woman was trembling. Her clothing had caught fire, she'd been flung to the ground by one burly man and then had ice-cold water thrown over her by another. She'd felt pretty shaky herself when she'd been lying on the ground, after two men had treated her rather roughly. And her gown had only been ripped a bit. It hadn't melted away, leaving her legs exposed.

How she wished there was something she could do for the poor woman.

Well, actually, there was. She tore at the fastening of her cloak, and, falling to her knees beside the woman, flung it over her body. It might not be able to stop the tremors racking the poor creature, but at least it would prevent the two men from being able to look at her exposed limbs.

'Don't just stand there staring,' she shouted at them. 'This woman needs medical attention! One of you run and fetch a doctor!'

The two men exchanged a glance.

'I say...' one of them began to protest.

But the other one, who was still holding the empty ice bucket, held up his free hand as though to silence his colleague.

'She's right, Gil. Go and fetch Dr Cochrane.'

As the first waiter hurried off, the other one tossed the ice bucket aside and stepped closer. By the flickering light of the blazing scaffolding, Sofia noted heavy, straight dark brows and a beak of a nose, which gave him a harsh appearance.

'You can leave her now,' he snarled at her.

Snarled? What right had he to snarl at her? And why was he glaring so ferociously?

'The doctor will attend her.'

'When he gets here,' she retorted, 'I dare say he will. But until then, I prefer to stay with her.' She took hold of the injured woman's hand, to offer the poor creature what meagre comfort she could.

'You look to me,' said the waiter with the ferocious eyebrows, 'as though you could do with medical attention yourself.'

At that, Sofia realised that her eye socket throbbed at the point where it had encountered the tall man's elbow. And that she had scratches up her arms from diving under the bushes.

'And you really ought not to have removed your cloak.' As his eyes made a swift perusal over her person, she recalled thinking that muslin was not the best of fabrics to wear when diving under bushes. She was thankful that she'd have an acceptable excuse to give Aunt Agnes for ruining yet another gown.

'Yes, that's probably true,' she admitted when the waiter's eyes lingered over the portion of her tattered skirt through which her knee was poking, 'but right this minute, I believe this lady needs it more than I do.'

'She is not a lady,' he said, somewhat pedantically to her way of thinking.

'What does her station in life have to do with anything? She is clearly hurt very badly and needs both a doctor and a cloak to cover her far more than I do.'

The waiter raised one of his brows, just a fraction.

'That is a very…compassionate thing to say. Nevertheless, I am sure there are people looking for you, people who will be concerned about your welfare. You ought not to be wandering about alone, in the dark.'

'I am not *wandering about alone*. I am kneeling on the ground, tending to a woman who has been badly hurt. And I intend to stay with her until there is some other female who can take my place.'

As though in gratitude, the injured woman gave Sofia's hand a rather shaky squeeze.

'Oh, how I wish I could just take you home with me and nurse you myself,' Sofia said apologetically. 'It must be awful to be in this state and reliant on strangers.' For the second time that night, Sofia felt the unpleasant sensation of childhood memories surging to the forefront of her mind. Only this time it was of the days following her papa's death, when she'd been passed from one harassed officer to another before finally being loaded on to a ship returning to England. Though none of those men had meant to be unkind, nor had any of them really had much idea how to handle a fellow officer's orphaned daughter.

'You are a stranger to her yourself,' put in the waiter, who was beginning to really annoy her.

'Yes,' she shot back at him, 'but at least I am a woman!'

'Look, miss…'

'Underwood,' she supplied automatically.

'Miss Underwood,' he said. 'I promise you that I will ensure this woman has the best possible care. And that as soon as is practical, I *will* procure a female to tend to her.'

'Yes, that's all very well, but until then…'

'And to set your mind at rest, I will also send word of her progress. If you will allow me to know how I may contact you?'

Sofia bit down on her lower lip. The most annoying thing about the waiter was that he was correct. Her aunt and uncle would be getting worried about her once they discovered she'd become separated from them during that stampede. And there wasn't anything more she could do for the injured woman, not really.

'Yes. Very well. We have taken lodgings on Marine View. In Theakstone Crescent.'

The man appeared a little taken aback. He took a breath as though to say something, but never got the chance. Because Uncle Ned came bustling up.

'Sofia! What the devil do you think you are playing at? Your aunt is worried sick about you! Get up off the ground and come here this instant!'

She got up. And under cover of brushing some of the leaves and ash from her skirts, she sidled closer to the waiter. 'I have a little money of my own,' she said softly. 'I would gladly contribute towards the cost of nursing her, if that would help.'

'Sofia!' Uncle Ned grabbed her arm and pulled her to a respectable distance from the waiter. 'Where is your cloak?'

She pointed to the injured woman.

'Great heavens above,' groaned Uncle Ned, rolling his eyes for good measure. Sofia winced, imagining the scene there was going to be when she explained how she'd disposed of a garment she'd only borrowed from her cousin Betty on the understanding she would take the greatest care of it.

Uncle Ned could clearly imagine it, too, for, as he dragged her away from the scene, he muttered, 'Have you no sense?'

Oliver clenched his fists as he watched the man clamp one hand round Miss Underwood's upper arm and drag her away as though he'd just caught her committing some crime. If there was one thing he detested, it was men who used their superior strength against females. Particularly females of their own family.

If it wasn't for the even more badly injured woman lying right at his feet, he'd have gone after Miss Underwood and given her uncle a piece of his mind. Only there *was* an injured woman lying at his feet. A woman whose need outweighed that of the one who'd been able to walk away from the catastrophic ending to the evening.

He bent his gaze in her direction. She'd stopped moaning. Was that a good sign, or a bad one? If only he knew what to do, the way Miss Underwood had instinctively seemed to know.

She had knelt down and held the burned woman's hand.

But then, Miss Underwood was female. As he'd become all too aware when her knee had peeped out at him through a rent in her skirt at that critical moment.

It would probably not prove soothing if he were to kneel down and take hold of the burnt woman's hand. But he had to do something. He gazed round, through the flickering, reddish shadows at the milling crowds. Where was that damned doctor? What was taking Gil so long?

The woman suddenly gave a convulsive shudder.

'The doctor will be here soon, Miss... Mrs...' He broke off, grinding his teeth. He hadn't even thought to ask her name.

'Pagett,' the woman croaked.

'Pagett,' he repeated, in what he hoped was a reassuring sort of way.

She moaned again.

'Be brave,' he said. 'Just a little longer and the doctor will...'

'That's just it,' she whimpered. 'I can't afford no

doctor. Not to pay for treatment of this…' she moved her legs, waved her arms vaguely '…not this much.'

And Miss Underwood had thought of that, as well.

'You must not worry about that,' he told Mrs Pagett. 'I will make sure all your bills for treatment are met. And that you have the nursing you need, for as long as you need it.'

'You?' She frowned up at him. 'Why should you do that?'

'Because it is my duty. And that of the committee who organised tonight's events to take care of you. And,' he added as an afterthought, 'your family, should you be unable to work to support them for any length of time.'

She rolled her head from side to side. 'It's all very well you saying that now. But who's going to listen to what you have to say?'

'Everyone,' he said with perfect assurance. 'Because I am the head of the committee.'

'You are?' She gazed up at him in disbelief.

'Yes,' he assured her. 'I am the Duke of Theakstone.'

## Chapter Two

'And you say the man in question is Viscount Norborough,' said Oliver. 'You are certain of that?'

Perceval, his secretary, opened the document case
he'd brought with him into the study, riffled through
the contents and withdrew a slim ledger.

'The tenants of Number Six Theakstone Crescent,' he
said, holding out the relevant entry so that Oliver could
see it, 'are Lord and Lady Norborough, their niece, Miss
Underwood, sundry servants and a dog. They took up
tenancy on June the first on a three-month lease.'

Oliver leaned back in his chair, frowning as he recalled the rough way the uncle had manhandled his
pretty young niece away from the scene.

He started tapping one finger on the arm of his
chair. He should have insisted she stay put, until she'd
received medical attention.

But then Dr Cochrane had been too busy with Mrs
Pagett to have spared time for Miss Underwood.

And he'd heard mention of an aunt. That lady had
probably done all that was necessary for the minor cuts
and bruises Miss Underwood had sustained.

Wouldn't she?

'What do we know of these Norboroughs, Perceval?'

'Their principal estate lies in Derbyshire. Lady Norborough is the oldest sister of the Earl of Tadcaster. The—'

'No, no, I didn't mean *that*. I mean, what of their character? Their habits? Their history?'

'I shall look into it, Your Grace,' said Perceval smoothly.

It wasn't good enough. Oh, Perceval would dig and dig until he'd unearthed every last secret the couple might ever have attempted to conceal. But it would take time. And Miss Underwood might be suffering who knew what right now.

'It need not be a priority, Perceval. You have your hands full with the investigation into the cause of last night's accident.'

They'd already visited the scene of the fire, hoping that in daylight they would be able to determine what had caused the painstakingly constructed display to explode.

Though he knew nothing of fuses or gunpowder, the men who'd set it all up certainly did and were all equally puzzled by how it could have gone so spectacularly wrong.

'No evidence left,' one of them had said gloomily. 'Ashes, is all.'

'Evidence?' He'd pounced on that word, and all that it implied, with a *frisson* of disquiet. 'Are you saying you think some crime took place here?'

'Sabotage,' one of the other workmen had stated. 'Must have been.'

'Or carelessness,' Perceval had muttered, so that no-body but Oliver could possibly have heard. 'Or drunk-enness. Or incompetence.'

Well, whatever the cause, Perceval would get to the bottom of it.

'In the meantime,' he decided, 'I shall call upon Miss Underwood.' He could not rest easy until he'd seen with his own eyes that she had suffered no last-ing ill effects from the incident. And it *wasn't* because she was pretty, as far as he'd been able to judge from the glow of the burning scaffolding. It was because of her bravery in running towards a woman whose clothes had caught fire, when everyone else had been fleeing in the most cowardly, selfish manner. And the compassion she'd shown in kneeling down and hold-ing the burned woman's hand. And her disregard for the woman's social station when she'd so selflessly donated her own cloak to conceal Mrs Pagett's limbs, even though doing so had meant he'd been able to catch a glimpse of a shapely lower leg through her own ripped skirts.

Perceval tucked the ledger back in his folder and ex-tracted Oliver's diary. 'You are attending an extraordi-nary meeting of the Committee to Celebrate the Peace with France, tomorrow at five.'

'And Marine View is on my way. Efficient as ever, Perceval. I need only set out half an hour sooner.'

'I shall make a note of it, Your Grace,' said Perceval, licking the end of his pencil.

'The Duke of Theakstone,' Babbage intoned from the doorway.

'Duke of Theakstone? Are you sure?' Aunt Agnes

frowned at the butler who'd come with them from Nettleton Manor. 'I wasn't aware we knew any dukes. Ned? Do we? Know this duke?'

Uncle Ned lowered his newspaper. 'Theakstone? Ah. Come to think of it, he's our landlord. Probably come about some problem over the lease, or something of that nature. Show him to the study, Babbage, and I will attend him there.'

Babbage cleared his throat apologetically. 'His Grace gave me to believe he wished to speak to Miss Sofia, my lord.'

Uncle Ned and Aunt Agnes both turned to gape at her. It was Uncle Ned who recovered first. 'Nonsense! Must be some mistake. Sofia don't know any dukes. Keep too close a watch on her, don't you, Agnes? Where would she have met him? Eh?'

'Nowhere,' said Aunt Agnes decisively. 'I can assure you of that.'

And so could Sofia, if he'd bothered to ask her. But that was not his way. Sofia was not, as he was so fond of saying, *his* niece. She was pretty sure he didn't begrudge her house room. It was just that he held the firm conviction that raising girl children was a woman's work. He'd said so, the very first day she'd reached Nettleton Manor, bedraggled and woebegone and half-sure they, too, were going to pass her on to yet another set of strangers. It had been the first time he and Aunt Agnes had discussed her as though she wasn't even in the room. In the years that followed, they'd fallen into the habit of doing it on what felt like a regular basis.

Babbage cleared his throat, reminding them all, tactfully, that they were keeping a duke kicking his heels in the hallway. Not that she could account for a man claiming to be a duke turning up and asking after her. As far as she was aware, she'd never met a duke in her life.

'Yes, yes, show him in here, then,' said Uncle Ned impatiently. 'Must be some mistake. Get it cleared up in a trice, I dare say. Ah, good morning,' he said, tossing his newspaper aside and getting to his feet to greet the man who strolled in. As though he owned the place. Which was what he was claiming, though he couldn't possibly. For this was no duke. This was the waiter from the evening of the fireworks that had gone wrong.

The waiter nodded to her uncle, then made straight for her, his ferocious brows lowering into an expression of concern.

'Your poor face,' he said, stretching out a hand as though he would have stroked her black eye, only withdrawing it at the very last moment, as though suddenly recollecting his manners.

But she felt as though he'd touched her all the same. Which gave her a very odd feeling. She couldn't remember the last time anyone had looked as though they had wanted to touch her with affection. Or concern. Certainly not Aunt Agnes. On first seeing Sofia, she'd shuddered with revulsion before sending her off to be stripped and scrubbed clean by a very junior housemaid. And had held her at arm's length ever since.

*'Try to remember you are a lady born,'* was her most frequent refrain. Which had swiftly supplanted her first maxim: *'You are in England now and must act accordingly.'*

Although last night, after seeing Sofia's ruined gown and not seeing Betty's cloak, she'd bombarded Sofia with just about her entire arsenal of verbal weaponry. And this morning, when she'd arrived at the breakfast table sporting a black eye, far from reaching out to her the way this man had just done, she'd raised her hand to her own brow. 'Just like your father,' she'd moaned. 'Never happier than when he was neck deep in mischief.'

Which was most unfair. Sofia had worked so hard to become a Proper English Young Lady that nowadays everyone within ten miles of Nettleton Manor thought she was a dead bore.

'Has your niece,' said the waiter who was masquerading as a duke, 'received medical attention since the night of the bonfire?' He rounded on her uncle, looking distinctly annoyed.

'It is only a few bruises and scratches, nothing more,' said Aunt Agnes in self-defence.

He then raised one of those eyebrows towards her aunt in a way that would have shrivelled Sofia, had it been directed at her.

For a moment, Sofia thought about telling Aunt Agnes that there was no need to quail under the force of those eyebrows. They might look lethal, but they adorned the forehead of a mere waiter. *Not* a duke.

However, it wasn't often that anyone took her part against her uncle and aunt. And so she remained silent while Aunt Agnes flushed and began to stammer excuses.

'She sees a doctor regularly. She is here for her health, after all. For the sea bathing.'

'Her health?' His voice dripped with such disdain

even Sofia could see how he could pass for a duke. 'Then what was she doing out at night, in the chill air?'

'It's all moonshine, the notion that Sofia is invalid-ish,' broke in Uncle Ned. 'This trip to the seaside is all down to my wife's brother putting a lot of ridiculous ideas into their heads.'

Sofia blushed and hung her head, since Uncle Ned was closer to stating the truth than he knew. And she still felt a bit guilty about the way her Uncle Barty had manipulated them into bringing her here.

'What you need,' he'd said, the last time he'd been over to visit her, 'is to get away from this devilish dull backwater and meet some people other than rustics. Go about a bit. Attend some dances. That will put the roses back into your cheeks,' he'd prophesied. And then he'd proceeded to harangue his sister for neglecting Sofia to such good effect that they'd all decamped to the fashionable seaside town of Burslem Bay, to see if a course of sea bathing might help restore her appetite, so that she'd regain the weight she'd lost over winter.

'Now, Ned, that isn't fair,' said Aunt Agnes. 'Poor Sofia was wasting away…'

Uncle Ned snorted. 'You wouldn't have dreamed of spending all this money on a cottage by the sea if your pestilential brother hadn't started throwing his weight around.'

'But he is as much her guardian as either of us, Ned. Of course he thinks he has a say in her welfare…'

Sofia was beginning to curl up with embarrass-ment. It was bad enough when they argued about her as if she wasn't there. But to do so in front of a stranger, as well?

The so-called Duke gave the bickering couple another look of disdain, before sauntering across the room and taking the chair next to hers.

'You must wish to know how Mrs Pagett is faring,' he said.

'Mrs Pagett?' Lord, but her voice had come out all squeaky. But then he was a bit overwhelming, up close. He exuded so much confidence and vitality.

Just as if he really was a duke.

'The woman whose aid you went to when her dress caught fire.'

'Oh, yes, thank you! How is she? Did you find a doctor for her—?'

'Sofia, really,' her aunt interrupted, roused from her quarrel with Uncle Ned by the sound of Sofia actually conducting a conversation which she was not supervising. 'Remember your manners. Please forgive her, Your Grace. I am sure she does not mean to be so impertinent, peppering you with questions like that.'

'Not at all,' said the waiter-Duke. 'She is merely expressing a very feminine curiosity and concern for someone whose unfortunate accident has clearly shocked her very much.'

Sofia promptly decided she liked him, no matter whether he was a waiter or a duke, or something else entirely. For nobody, apart from Uncle Barty on the rare occasions he could be bothered to visit, had ever defended her from one of her aunt's criticisms, not to her face like that. Not in all the years she'd been living under her roof. The locals had all, without exception, expressed sympathy upon hearing that Lady Norborough had taken in the orphaned offspring of her scapegrace younger brother. And prophesied that she'd have her hands full taming the result of such a scandalous match as he'd made.

Having delivered his set-down, the waiter who claimed to be a duke turned back to Sofia. 'My personal physician is overseeing her treatment. He thought it best to install a nurse in her home, for day-to-day care. He informs me that her injuries are not so severe as you might suppose, given the spectacle she made when her gown caught fire. The damage was confined mostly to her clothes and the lower part of her legs, particularly her right leg. And her hands when she tried to beat out the flames. There is some blistering about the face and the loss of some hair, but I am informed it will grow back. Her hair, that is.'

Sofia shuddered. 'Oh, how awful. The poor woman. But thank goodness you got to her so quickly.'

He dipped his head in acknowledgement of the part he'd played in Mrs Pagett's drama.

'How I wish... I mean, is there anything I can do?'

'Of course there is nothing you can do, you foolish girl,' said Aunt Agnes. 'You are not a doctor. I cannot think how you came to be mixed up in such a squalid scene in the first place.'

Nor had Sofia, to start with. But as she'd lain in bed the night before, she'd remembered how her papa had always used to say she was full of pluck. That nobody nowadays thought so stemmed, she suspected, from the horrible events surrounding her papa's death. By the time she reached Nettleton Manor, she'd been so relieved to finally find refuge that she'd done her utmost to fit in. It had taken a couple of years before she'd been able to stop worrying that her newly discovered family were not going to throw her out if she displeased them. And by then, the habit of behaving with extreme caution had taken deep root.

She still swam, though, and climbed trees, whenever she was sure nobody would find out. And last night, when she'd seen that lady in such awful trouble, she hadn't stopped to think about the consequences. She'd just run to help.

While all this was flashing through Sofia's mind, the Duke had turned to give Aunt Agnes a really blistering look. 'Your niece appears to have a very compassionate nature, Lady Norborough. I am sure her enquiries as to what she could do extended only to visiting to offer comfort, or something of that sort.' He turned back to Sofia. 'Am I correct?'

'Well, no… I mean, I am sure I would not be permitted to actually visit,' she said with regret, darting an anxious glance in her aunt's direction. Visiting the lower orders was one of the things she said Sofia was to avoid at all costs, considering the company she'd kept in her earliest years. 'But I did wonder if I could contribute, financially, towards her care…'

'Now just a minute…' This time it was Uncle Ned who was raising an objection.

'It does your niece credit,' said the Duke. 'However, in this instance, Miss Underwood,' he said, turning to her and gentling his tone, 'the care of Mrs Pagett will be charged to the committee who organised the event. After all, they were responsible for the safety of all those who attended the supper and fireworks. Whatever it was that caused about two-thirds of them to go off simultaneously, instead of one at a time, there can be no doubt about *that*.'

He got to his feet and looked at her aunt and uncle

for a moment or two in the kind of silence that had them all holding their breath.

'I shall call to take your niece for an airing in my carriage, tomorrow. Be ready,' he said, turning to her, 'at three.'

## Chapter Three

For the second time in as many days, Oliver drew his curricle up outside Miss Underwood's lodgings, wondering why on earth he was altering his busy schedule to squeeze in a meeting with her. He'd had no intention of doing more than assuring himself she was recovering properly from the incident at the fireworks when he'd called the day before. He certainly hadn't intended to invite her out for a drive.

But then her aunt and uncle had talked over her so dismissively. Which was so unjust, given the bravery she'd shown in rushing to Mrs Pagett's help.

He hadn't liked the way her uncle had dragged her away that night.

And he hadn't liked the way they'd both berated her for behaviour that to him seemed compassionate and caring.

That was what had prompted him to invite her to drive with him this afternoon—the chance to detach her from their overbearing, disapproving presence, so that he could talk to her freely. About Mrs Pagett.

It had nothing to do with the flare of attraction he'd

felt when he'd seen her sitting in that drawing room, in full sunlight. He met dozens of pretty girls all the time. She was nothing out of the ordinary. It was just that he had a preference for slim brunettes with brown eyes, that was all. The fact that he'd seen her legs through her ripped gown had probably stoked the more primitive side of his nature, too. He had no need to worry that he was developing an unhealthy interest in her.

In fact, by the time he'd driven her through the town and along the seafront he was bound to have discovered some flaw in her personality which would enable him to relegate her to the status of passing fancy.

He tossed the reins to his groom, pressing his lips into a firm, determined line. The girl he'd seen at the fireworks display probably didn't exist outside his imagination, anyway. She certainly hadn't put in an appearance in her aunt's drawing room. That girl had been all polite propriety and butter-wouldn't-melt-in-her-mouth missishness. Even when he'd spoken to her directly, he'd gained the impression she wanted to shrink into the sofa cushions and disappear from view. If he'd come across *that* Miss Underwood at a ball or a supper party, he wouldn't have spared her a second thought. He certainly wouldn't have drifted off to sleep with a vision of her, crouching on the ground, holding Mrs Pagett's hand in his mind. Or gone on to dream about joining her on the ground and giving in to the temptation to run his hand through the rips in her skirts to find the silken skin of her calves.

He mounted the front steps and rapped on the door. Putting this inconvenient fascination for Miss Underwood to bed was what he would accomplish this afternoon. And then he could return to his well-ordered existence where his every move was dictated by duty, honour and reason.

Not emotion or desire.

'Here he is!' Aunt Agnes was practically jumping up and down on the spot. She'd spent all morning deciding what to wear. If there had been time, she would have gone out and purchased an entirely new carriage dress and bonnet. 'Oh!' She clapped her hands to her chest. 'He has come in the most ridiculous vehicle. There can hardly be room for us both in it. I hope he doesn't intend…' She whirled round to look at Sofia with narrowed eyes. 'It is the height of impropriety to go driving, alone, with a single gentleman to whom you are not related.'

'You had better inform him of that fact when he comes in,' said Sofia, tongue in cheek.

'Don't be ridiculous! As if he needs telling. He must have changed his mind about the outing, that is what it is,' she said, trotting over to the mirror and fluffing her hair into place. 'At least he is gracious enough to come and inform us.' She plopped herself down and arranged her skirts only a moment before Babbage came to announce their visitor.

The Duke strode in on the tail end of the butler's words. He glanced at Sofia, where she was sitting on the sofa, Snowball next to her with her muzzle on her lap. 'Good afternoon, ladies,' he said, bowing to each of them. 'Are you not ready?' He shot a rather irritated glance at Sofia. 'I did specify three o'clock and I do not wish to keep my horses standing.'

'Oh, but we thought you must have changed your mind,' said Aunt Agnes.

He whirled on her. 'Why should you think any such thing? Besides, if I had done so I should have sent a note. Well?' He turned to Sofia again.

'I have only to don my pelisse and bonnet,' she said, keeping her eyes fixed firmly on his and pretending not to notice the frantic, yet furtive, way Aunt Agnes was trying to attract her attention. If she wanted to forbid her from going out with him unchaperoned, then she should jolly well have told *him* that it was highly improper behaviour the moment he'd suggested it. Sofia had never been invited to go out for a drive with a gentleman to whom she was not related. And she had no intention of letting such a treat slip through her fingers. Hadn't she promised herself, when Uncle Ned had finally agreed to bring her to the seaside, that she was going to make the most of every opportunity for enjoyment that came her way? And start putting the past behind her?

'Well, hurry along, then,' said her means of escaping her aunt and uncle for an hour or so.

Sofia hurried into the hall and into her pelisse and bonnet. Snowball, who recognised these signs of human behaviour as the prelude to going for a walk, ran around and around in circles, almost tripping the Duke when he came into the hallway himself.

'Here, Snowball,' said Sofia, bending down to scoop her dog up into her arms. 'You do not mind me bringing her along, do you?' Belatedly, she considered that the Duke might not like to have an animal of such dubious heritage perched up on the lap of the lady he was about to parade about the lanes in his curricle. A lady, moreover, who was sporting a rather spectacular black eye.

The Duke looked at the wriggling bundle of fluff in Sofia's arms, then looked into her face, as though his thoughts were following the same path her own had just wandered down. 'Not at all,' he said with chilling politeness. 'Though would the creature not prefer to take a walk? With a footman?'

'Oh, I shall take Snowball out again later for exercise,' she said, airily ignoring his hint. 'This carriage ride is just an extra treat for her. She absolutely loves carriage rides.'

'Indeed,' he said drily, eyeing Babbage in such a way that the butler went and opened the front door for them to exit.

'Oh, yes, you should have seen her during our trip here,' she said, making her way down the front steps. 'She kept her nose to the door the entire time, breathing in all the smells wafting in with her eyes half-shut as though she was in some sort of doggy heaven.'

'Hmmph. Dogs do tend to experience life through their noses,' he conceded as he handed her up on to the seat of the curricle. As he went around to the other side to climb in, Sofia put Snowball down right in the middle of the bench seat. The Duke paused in the act of taking his own seat and raised his left eyebrow.

'So this little bundle of fluff is in reality the chaperon I took such pains to exclude from our outing.'

'A girl cannot be too careful with her reputation,' she said, parroting one of her aunt's most frequent homilies.

'I have a groom to stand up behind, naturally. However,' he said, settling into the seat and taking the reins, 'you are to be commended for not attempting to take advantage of the situation.'

'Take advantage? Whatever do you mean?'

'Most females in your position,' he said, nodding to the groom to let go of the horses' heads, 'would be trying to take hold of my arm under the pretence of being afraid of the motion of the vehicle.'

'We haven't set out yet,' she said, as he flicked the reins and set it in motion. 'That is,' she hastily amended as the groom leapt nimbly up behind, 'there is a little rail here by my side which I can hang on to should you prove to be a careless driver.'

Sofia could tell the Duke did not like the implication that she might dislike the manner of his driving by the way his jaw clenched, but fortunately before either of them could pursue that topic any further, Snowball caught sight of a cat sitting on the window ledge of one of the houses they were passing and let out a loud bark.

'Hush, Snowball,' said Sofia, tapping the dog's nose firmly with two fingers to reinforce the command.

The Duke snorted. 'You cannot expect any self-respecting dog not to bark at a cat.'

'On the contrary. I have trained Snowball to be silent when required.' She'd had to. Aunt Agnes had at first objected so strongly to having the animal in the house that she'd spent hours and hours training her dog into total obedience. 'Now that I have given the command she will not bark again until I give her leave, I promise you.'

'A remarkable animal, then,' he said, glancing down at Snowball. 'A good deal of poodle in the family, I take it?'

'Yes, I think so. I have to have her trimmed regularly or she becomes completely circular in appearance. Like a snowball on legs, in fact.'

'Ah, hence the name.'

'No, when she was a pup, she just looked like a little furry snowball. And it was Christmas. The name just came to me.'

'Her tail has the look of a spaniel, though.'

'Yes, her mother was definitely a spaniel. It was the father who...'

Oh, lord, why had she never seen it before? *That* was why Jack had given her the puppy. Because she was of mixed breed. It had been a cruel joke, referencing Sofia's own background.

Was that why Aunt Agnes had been so cross with him? It certainly explained why her aunt had not shown any great aversion to Snowball after those first few fraught minutes when she'd scolded Jack for being so thoughtless. Why she'd never once threatened to have the dog destroyed, or sold, no matter how many times Sofia had returned from walks dripping wet or covered in mud. She'd scolded her, yes. Said she despaired of ever making a Proper Lady of her. But never, ever threatened to part her from the pet she'd fallen in love with at first sight.

In rather the same way she'd fallen for Jack.

And later, when he'd told her that he'd taken one look at Springer's latest litter and thought of her, she'd assumed he'd meant that he'd noticed how lonely and out of place she still felt in England and had wanted to give her something of her very own, to love her and be with her always.

But all the time he'd been making fun of her mixed parentage.

How...beastly of him. How cruel.

And how stupid of her not to have seen it.

The Duke cleared his throat. 'I did not bring you out here to talk about dogs, however.'

'No, of course not,' she said, distractedly running her fingers over Snowball's crest. In spite of suddenly understanding what Jack had meant the dog to be, she loved her just the same. Snowball was loyal and loving, obedient and clever. 'Good girl, Snowball,' she said.

'Are you feeling quite well? You seem a little distracted.'

Well, it wasn't every day a girl was on the receiving end of such an epiphany. Not that she was going to let it have the devastating effect upon her that the last one she'd had about Jack had done. No, for this was more in the nature of a deepening of a truth she'd already learned.

That Jack was a vile, vile person. And not the romantic hero of her girlish dreams. At all. Oh, yes, he might have told his sisters not to be so beastly to her whenever he caught them out in some petty act of spite. But she'd been mistaken in thinking his motives were the slightest bit chivalrous. It was far more to do with how much he disliked *them*.

'Miss Underwood?'

'Oh, I beg your pardon. I was wool-gathering.' On receipt of this admission, the Duke's lips thinned and his ferocious brows drew down until they almost met one another over the great beak of his nose. Clearly he did not appreciate women wool-gathering when he'd done them the signal honour of taking them up in his curricle. And that after casting aspersions upon his prowess as a driver! 'That is, I was wondering how best to answer your question, without…that is, I hardly know you.'

'I do not wish to hear any details of your ailments,' he snapped.

'No, I don't suppose you do.' After all, nobody else ever did. All she'd had to do that day she'd come home from learning exactly what Jack thought of her was claim to have a headache and feel sick—which was the perfect truth—and they'd left her alone in her room for days.

'I am assuming that it is on account of your poor health that you did not appear in London this spring.'

'What? I mean, why should you have thought I would be in London?'

'To make your debut. I should have thought... I mean, you look to be of an age to make a come-out. And your uncle is the Earl of Tadcaster, is he not?'

'Yes...' Though nobody would think so to look at her today, in one of her cousins' cast-off walking dresses, a bonnet that did nothing to disguise her black eye and a dog of indeterminate heritage sitting at her side. Certainly not the couple of scarlet-jacketed officers who were loitering on the corner where the Duke was slowing down to take the turn down to the seafront.

'To be honest,' she said, turning to look at his profile so that she could pretend she hadn't seen the scornful looks directed at her by those officers, 'Aunt Agnes did use my poor health as a pretext for not taking me to London this year.'

'But not former years?' He glanced down at her, as though assessing her age. 'You look as though you should have made your debut some time since.'

She gasped at his effrontery.

'Why has the Countess of Tadcaster not given you

a court presentation then? She is surely a most suitable person to do so.'

Had he been investigating her background? Or was he just one of those people who knew the intricate web of families that made up the *haut ton* so well that the few casual references to her family, made by her uncle and aunt, had been enough to place her exactly?

'Well, when my father first died, Uncle Barty was a bachelor, so everyone thought it more appropriate for his sister to take me in charge, especially since she already had two daughters.' She'd heard Uncle Barty say as much to the subaltern whose invidious task it had been to convey her to the head of her family. And heard the subaltern subsequently repeat the message to Aunt Agnes. 'And then last spring, when I might have made my debut, Lady Tadcaster was…er…in a delicate condition.'

'Ah, yes. She presented the Earl of Tadcaster with an heir during the summer months, did she not? It escaped my mind. And this year, you were too ill to endure the rigours of a Season…'

'I most certainly was not!'

He crooked one of his eyebrows at her. She pondered the fact that they could crook. They were remarkably mobile, considering that in their resting state they relaxed back into a completely straight line. Not that relaxed was really the correct word to apply to brows which managed to look so aggressive even when they were perfectly still. Or when he was staring at her, pointedly.

She sighed. 'I can see you are going to carry on badgering me until I tell you the truth which is…well, over the winter months, I did fall ill.' Or perhaps it was more truthful to say she'd made herself ill. So stupidly.

It had started with hearing Jack and his friend discussing her in such derogatory terms, while she'd been crouching, hidden, underneath the jetty on which they'd been standing.

'Sorry, I'll have to spend a bit of time dancing attendance on the heiress,' Jack had apologised to his friend, 'since my family expect me to marry her. But don't worry, it won't take much time out of the vacation. I'll only have to toss her the bone of a few moments of idle chat, a smile and a compliment or two and she'll be content to chew on it for days on end, like the mongrel bitch she is.'

'Don't sound as if you like her much, old man,' the friend had said, sounding almost as shocked as she'd felt.

'Like her?' Jack had sounded offended. 'She's as dull as ditch water and about as attractive.'

She wasn't sure how she'd managed to stumble home after hearing that. And she'd shut herself in her room unable to bear the thought of facing anyone, knowing what she knew. Especially not with eyes red from weeping. After only a few days, during which she'd totally lost her appetite as well, she had started to look so ill they'd finally sent for a doctor, who'd bled her and cupped her until she really was so weak that when one of the housemaids had sneezed while lighting the fire, Sofia had caught the infection which had developed into a fully fledged inflammation of the lungs.

'Coming to the seaside was supposed to have a tonic

effect upon me,' she said wistfully, recalling her Uncle Barty's last visit to Nettleton Manor.

'Not surprised you are fading away,' he'd said, shaking his head. 'Stuck out here with no company but such as that dolt my sister married and his infernal relatives. What you want is to get some sea air and go to some assemblies where you can dance with a few men in scarlet coats, eh, what? Stroll along the promenade and flirt with a beau or two.'

That had sounded good. Sea bathing. And having some beaux. *That* would show Jack that there were men who found her interesting. Pretty even. *That* would prove she was *not* pining away. Not that he had the slightest idea his attitude was at the root of her illness. She hadn't told anybody what she'd overheard. It would have been too humiliating. And anyway, what would have been the point?

She suspected that Uncle Barty had only made the suggestion to cause trouble. He never left Nettleton Manor until he'd practically come to blows with Uncle Ned about something—the way he was managing Sofia's fortune, or his treatment of Aunt Agnes, both were frequent grist to his mill. Usually she did her best to stay out of the quarrels which erupted on the slightest pretext. Especially if they concerned her. But during that last visit, she'd seen that he was the one person who could give her the answers to all the questions she'd been reluctant to ask Aunt Agnes for fear of offending her.

'Is it a lot, the money that will come to me when I marry?' she'd asked him, linking her arm through his as they'd strolled down to the rose garden.

'Good Lord, yes. You'll be rich enough to buy an… that is, yes—yes, it is.'

She'd begun to suspect as much, upon hearing how keen it had made Jack to marry her, in spite of what he thought of her. She'd never truly felt like an heiress before that day under the jetty in spite of hearing the word bandied about. In fact, she'd felt far more like a charity case, considering the way her cousins passed down their gowns from the previous Season to her each year when they went to buy new ones.

'And what will happen to it if I don't marry,' she'd wondered aloud, 'or if I die?'

'You ain't going to die, my girl, so stop thinking along those lines.'

'But if I did?'

'Well, in such a case, it would all go back to your mother's family, where it came from,' he'd said. Just like that. His honesty had stunned her, for everyone else had said, in the days when she'd still tried to talk about her parents, that it was better to let sleeping dogs lie.

'You…you know how to contact them, then?'

'Of course I do,' he'd said with a puzzled frown. 'Why should you think anything else?'

'But I thought that all contact was lost when…when Mama married Papa.'

'Ah. Well, it was given out that was the case. On account of them being Catholic and your father refusing to allow you to be brought up in that religion. They had to appear to cut their daughter out of their lives. And you, as the offspring.'

'Mama was a Catholic?'

'What did you think she was?'

'Well, I don't know. I was so little when she died. Papa could not bear to talk of her and Aunt and Uncle won't have her name mentioned. So I thought…well, the only thing I did hear was that she was some sort of…trader.' The only words used to describe her mother's origins had actually been of such a derogatory variety that Sofia had been half-afraid to find out any more.

'No, no, very good sort of people, the Perestrellos. They do own vineyards and their wine graces the tables of the wealthy all over the world. But they come from aristocratic stock. The mismatch was one of religion, not class. Unless you consider her race, which some do, the fools.'

Fools like Jack. Who'd always appeared to be sympathetic to her for being of what he called mixed heritage.

'And if I never marry,' she'd persisted, determined to get the full facts. 'What then?'

'Not marry? Pretty little thing like you?' He'd pinched her chin. 'Course you'll marry. Fellers'll be queuing up to court you.'

'No, but seriously, Uncle Barty, I really want to know. Will I ever be able to have it? Just for myself? To do with as I please?'

'Well, if you reach the age of thirty without getting hitched, then, yes.'

Thirty? She was going to have to wait another eight years before the law considered her fit to take charge of her own money?

'Can't imagine why nobody has explained it all to you,' Uncle Barty had said with a frown. 'Nor why you couldn't have just asked your Uncle Ned…no, actually,' he'd said, making a motion with his hand as though swatting away a pesky fly, 'I can see exactly why you couldn't talk to that dolt. But I shall talk to him, never fear. I mean to tell him how shocked I am by your appearance. Inform him that he clearly hasn't been taking proper care of you. That I very much fear you will fade away altogether if they don't take steps to stop this decline.' He'd chuckled with glee at the prospect of gaining another rod with which to beat his brother-in-law.

But this time, she hadn't crept up to her room to hide until the worst had blown over. Instead she'd gone back inside with Uncle Barty and said, albeit rather timidly, that she rather liked the sound of spending some time at the seaside, if nobody would mind too much. And since it had been the first thing she'd shown any interest in since well before Christmas, Uncle Ned had grudgingly conceded that for once Uncle Barty might have the right of it.

And so here she was, bowling along the seafront, in a curricle driven by a duke, no less, with the wind whipping her curls from her bonnet.

Hah! That would show Jack when he found out, which he was bound to do because Uncle Ned or Aunt Agnes were sure to inform him.

Her lips curved into a smile.

She could hardly wait.

# Chapter Four

Oliver watched a little smile curve her lips and wondered what had put it there. For the first time in his life, he found himself striving to think of some topic that would keep a woman's mind focused exclusively on what he had to say and not on whatever stray thought might pop into her head next.

'I separated you from your relatives so that we may speak freely about Mrs Pagett,' he bit out. It had the effect he'd hoped for since she turned inquisitive brown eyes up at him.

'Oh, yes. Of course. How does she do? But before we get on to that, there is something I need to say first. I am sorry for speaking to you the way I did.'

'What way was that?'

'Well, when I first saw you. I ordered you about. You did look very offended, when I look back on it. I don't suppose many people speak to you that way, do they? Only, the thing is, you see, I thought you were a waiter. You dressed the way the man who served at our table was dressed.'

'That night, I was acting as a waiter.'

'Acting? Whatever for?'

'It was decided…that is, the committee who organised the event to celebrate the Peace with France felt that, um, it would be a good idea for men such as myself to wait on the lower orders.'

'You mean,' she asked, wide-eyed, 'that *all* the waiters were dukes?'

'No. I mean, all the waiters hailed from the better families about these parts.'

'That is very radical.'

'You disapprove? You think men of my rank should always stand on their dignity?' His father would certainly never have demeaned himself by waiting at table. It was one of the factors that had made the experience so very satisfying, showing the world that he was nothing like the man who'd sired him.

'Disapprove? Oh, no. I was just a bit surprised, that is all. Was it…a sort of…oh, I forgot, I'm not supposed to pepper you with questions, am I?'

Normally, he would agree. But Miss Underwood looked so contrite and the way she'd stopped before actually asking her question had piqued his interest.

'Asking me one question is hardly peppering me with them, is it? What did you wish to know?'

'Oh.' She darted him a look of relief. 'Well, I just wondered if the act had some sort of religious significance. You know, like…when Jesus washed the disciples' feet.'

He winced. 'Nothing so noble,' he confessed. 'The decision was taken for purely practical purposes. You see, what with the amount of ale supplied, there were fears from some quarters that there might be…unruliness. That it might all end in disaster.'

'Well, it did.'

'Yes, and I have a feeling that the ale, or some other spirituous liquor, may have played a part in it. There can be no other reason for the fireworks to have all gone up at once like that.'

'Unless someone did it deliberately.'

That was the second time someone had raised suspicions about the causes of the explosion. 'Why would anyone wish to do anything of the sort?' He wondered if he'd been right to so quickly dismiss the rumours that had reached Perceval's ears about a shadowy figure loitering behind the scaffolding not long before the fireworks display had started. He shook his head. 'The town council put on an event for the benefit of the townspeople, paid for by the local landowners.'

'We had to pay for our tickets.'

'You are not locals. Those holidaying in the area were allowed to attend, if they would subscribe. That seemed fair.'

'I suppose it was,' she conceded. 'Mrs Pagett still got hurt, though. And, oh, yes, you were going to tell me how she does.'

'I fear her road to recovery may be a long one. Although this one,' he said in disbelief, 'is not.'

He clearly hadn't been paying enough attention to the route along which he'd been driving because they were at the end of Marine View already. And he hadn't said the half of what he'd meant to say to her.

'Do you attend the assembly,' he asked her as he brought the curricle to a halt at the foot of her front steps, 'at the Marlborough Hotel this evening?'

'Oh, no, the very idea!' Sofia indicated the bruising

on her face with a wry smile. 'I could not possibly go about looking like this.'

'Your view, or your aunt's? No, you need not bother to reply. I believe you would be bold enough to attempt anything, without giving a rap what anyone else were to say of you.'

Sofia's heart skipped a beat. Once upon a time, her papa had praised her for being full of pluck. But her aunt had done her best to suppress that side of her. She'd warned Sofia that, because of her background, she needed to be much more careful in her behaviour than most young ladies. And, determined to please her, she'd done her utmost to stop behaving like a 'hoyden'—she'd curbed her language and followed all the rules, no matter how strange she'd found them.

She'd ended up so repressed that nowadays, in company, she didn't really speak unless she was spoken to, but was more likely to sit quietly in a corner doing embroidery. The only time she allowed her deepest, truest self to emerge was when she was out walking Snowball, deep in the woods, where nobody else was about.

She'd become the sort of girl who cared so much what people thought of her and might say about her that they all found her as *dull as ditch water*.

But this man did not believe so. He'd seen something in her that nobody else had seen for years. And in doing so, he had reminded her of who she'd once been. Before she'd started trying so desperately to please the only people who'd been willing to take her in.

She turned to observe his expression. He looked annoyed. But then those eyebrows made him look slightly annoyed all the time. And why should she wish to

know whether his observation was meant as a reproof
or a compliment, anyway?

And yet, somehow, it did matter.

Perhaps because if there was one person who liked
the real her, then she might find the courage to be herself, instead of the pattern card of virtue her aunt had
tried to make her into. The version of herself that nobody much liked, least of all herself.

'In that case,' he bit out crisply, 'I shall have to take
you out for a drive again tomorrow.'

'What? I mean, why? I mean, I'm sure that is very
kind of you—'

He shook his head. 'I am not kind, Miss Underwood. I will take you for another drive because I have
not had the time today to say all I wished to say to you,'
he said irritably. 'And because it would be impossible
to have any meaningful conversation in the confines
of that house.' He glared up at the drawing-room window, through which Sofia could make out the outline
of her aunt through the net curtains.

Well, in that she could agree with him. She had
never had a single conversation within her aunt's hearing that had been truly meaningful. Or in which she
had dared to express her own opinions. At least, not
after the first month or so of living with her, by which
time she'd discovered that her manners had more in
common with the sort of women who followed the
drum than a Proper Young Lady.

The groom had now reached the horses' heads, so
the Duke climbed down and came round to help Sofia
down. Since it was far too high for her little dog to
jump down, she handed Snowball to the Duke. He
received the bundle of fluff with astonishment, be-

fore bending to deposit her on the pavement with a faint grimace of distaste, though he'd wiped it from his countenance before straightening up to extend his arm to Sofia.

'I cannot think what you can possibly have to say to me,' she said, glancing nervously at the drawing-room window. She'd enjoyed her outing, but she was already bound to get a dreadful scold for going off with this man alone. How much worse would it be if Aunt Agnes discovered he meant to repeat the offence again the next day?

'Mrs Pagett, if nothing else,' he replied, following her line of sight. 'There was not enough time to discuss…' His brows drew into a heavy scowl. 'Next time I call for you, do try to stick to the topic at hand rather than digressing so much.'

'I beg your pardon?' If he was so annoyed with her, why was he bothering to waste any more of his precious time with her? And why hadn't he kept the conversation going in the direction he'd wanted, come to that? She'd felt as if he'd been positively encouraging her to ask questions. But then, what did she know about what dukes considered good conversation? What any single man thought, come to that. She'd only really mixed with people carefully selected by her aunt and uncle. And the only single man they'd thrown in her way had been Jack, Uncle Ned's nephew.

The Duke of Theakstone escorted Sofia to her front door, but did not come in. For a moment, she resented the way he'd abandoned her entirely to the mercy of Aunt Agnes.

Although, she reflected as she took off her coat, even if he had come in it would only have postponed the confrontation, not spared her from it altogether. She had flouted her aunt's wishes and escaped her strict scrutiny. There was nothing anyone, not even a duke, could do to prevent her aunt from lecturing her.

But she was not going to take it lying down like a…a doormat. She would do better to spike Aunt Agnes's guns.

So she entered the drawing room in what she hoped looked like an apologetic manner.

'I do hope you are not angry with me, Aunt Agnes,' she said while her aunt was still drawing breath. 'But the Duke of Theakstone is such a forceful man that when he told me to go and put on my coat, it felt like a direct order. And I didn't know how to disobey him.'

Her aunt regarded her through narrowed eyes for a moment or two before appearing to accept Sofia's explanation. But then, why wouldn't she? Sofia had worked so hard to conform to her aunt's exacting standards that for the last couple of years she'd behaved like a veritable milksop.

Until the day she'd heard Jack mocking her behaviour and she'd begun to wonder why she'd bothered. She could never be anything but the product of a slightly shocking marriage between an Englishman and a foreigner. A Catholic, to boot. And why should she try to shoehorn her personality into the mould her aunt and uncle deemed 'proper', when they were so intent on pushing her in Jack's direction so that he could benefit from the money she would inherit?

Especially since it was the only reason he would consider her as a wife.

'I will have to marry someone, some day,' he'd said. 'So why not her? She may be boring, but at least she's biddable. In fact,' he'd boasted, 'she rather idolises me. I will only have to drop the handkerchief, you know, and she will go into raptures. And then all that lovely money of hers will be mine to spend as I wish. Once she's breeding, I can leave her in the country and have some real fun.' They'd both laughed, then, in a way that had turned her stomach.

Drop the handkerchief, indeed! He'd have to do more than drop a handkerchief. In fact, he could weave and embroider and hem a dozen handkerchiefs and it would make no difference. She was most categorically *not* going to marry Jack. Not now she knew what he really thought of her. Not now she knew he was the kind of man who'd marry a woman for her money, so he could go out and enjoy himself with other women. Because that was what that dirty laughter had been about. She'd spent the first ten years of her life with a father who was a serving soldier and he had most decidedly not lived like a monk once her mama had died. On the contrary, Sofia had lost count of the number of ladies who'd lived with them, ostensibly as nursemaids to her, but who always, always, shared her papa's bed. Nobody, he'd told her, could replace her mama. She need never fear that he would ever call another woman his wife. But they needed somebody, didn't they, to take care of them?

Take care of them? Hah! The moment she'd heard her papa was dead, Maria, his latest lady friend, had promptly ransacked their billet for anything of value before leaving to secure another 'protector'.

Which was yet another reason, she sighed as she went to take her place on her usual chair, that she'd taken such pains to become whatever her aunt and uncle wanted her to become. She'd been so grateful they'd taken her in and told her she must consider Nettleton Manor her home, that she would have cut off all her hair and dyed her face blue if they'd so much as hinted it would guarantee her safety.

'Did His Grace say something to upset you?' asked Aunt Agnes with a slight frown.

'Upset me? The Duke? No.' On the contrary, he'd reminded her of who she really was. Or at least, who she had once been...and could become again if only she could summon the courage to stand up for herself a bit more.

'Well, you look a trifle out of sorts.'

Which was the effect that thinking about Jack always had on her, these days.

'What did you discuss, Sofia?'

'Oh, Snowball, at first,' said Sofia, bending to stroke her faithful dog's ears. 'And the state of my health and why I hadn't had a court presentation,' she said, darting a swift glance up at her aunt from under her eyelashes, to see what effect that statement might have.

'Those are all rather personal questions. No wonder you are upset.'

'Yes, but then dukes probably think they can say what they like, to whomever they wish.' He'd certainly had no compunction about giving Aunt Agnes a set-down.

A smile tugged at her lips as she recalled the moment. Oh, but it had felt so good to have someone rush to her defence. Even if it had been totally unnecessary.

'Why are you smiling like that?'

'Oh, well, because he said he would be calling to take me out driving again tomorrow,' she said as meekly as she could.

'Without consulting me?'

Sofia shrugged. 'He's a duke. I don't suppose he is in the habit of consulting anyone about anything before doing exactly as he wishes.'

'And he wishes to take you out in his curricle again,' said Aunt Agnes with amazement. As if there was no accounting for taste.

Rather than explain that he'd practically reprimanded her for obliging him to waste yet another afternoon on her, Sofia shrugged again.

And smiled.

## Chapter Five

Oliver clenched his teeth, went down the steps, across the pavement and climbed back into the driver's seat.

Dammit, the girl had done it *again*. Diverted him from his original plan. He'd known exactly what he'd wanted to say while tooling her round the lanes and along the seafront this afternoon. It shouldn't have taken more than ten minutes. But somehow the time had slipped through his fingers like water and before he knew it he was drawing up outside her lodgings having barely touched on any of the items on his agenda. An agenda which he'd drawn up, he reflected as he flicked the whip to set his horses in motion, as a means of passing the time profitably during an outing he'd never meant to take in the first place.

He reached the end of Theakstone Crescent and turned left to take the road up the hill away from the bay, eyeing the neat rows of lodging houses with mixed feelings. Normally he felt a good deal of family pride at the visible proof of the way his grandfather had transformed the fortunes of the people living in what had merely been a mean little fishing village by developing Burslem Bay into a seaside resort. But today, there was also an undercurrent of disquiet. If his grandfather hadn't wanted more for his guests to do at his nearby hunting box, when there was nothing left on the moors to shoot, Oliver might never have met Miss Underwood. She didn't mix in the same social circles, even if her grandfather was an earl.

Which was probably why she had no idea how to behave, when presented to a duke. No other female would have handed him a dog, as though he was a mere footman. Or prattled on about the first thing that came into her head as though he was just *any*body.

Although, to be fair, she had apologised once or twice when she felt she'd crossed a line. She appeared to know that she ought not to be so familiar with him, but simply couldn't help herself.

He thought about that for several hundred yards.

And then recalled the slightly anxious way Miss Underwood had glanced up at the front window, as if she could sense somebody watching her.

His brows drew down as he went back further still, to the aunt's reaction to his decree Miss Underwood was to go out driving with him, alone but for a groom. He'd been too annoyed when he'd deposited her on her front step to notice it, but now that he was going over the scene again, he could see that she'd been bracing herself for a scold.

He supposed he should have gone in with Miss Underwood, and... He drew in a sharp breath. Wasted even more of his afternoon on her behalf? No, it was as well he hadn't felt the urge to shield her at the time.

It was bad enough that she made him act out of character as far as she had done. He held to that opinion until he was clear of the town. But once he'd reached the open moorland which surrounded Burslem House and there was no traffic upon which to focus his mind, he slowed his horses to a sedate trot, to give himself more time to work out what, precisely, it was about Miss Underwood that made him act so unlike himself, every single time they met.

It wasn't as if she exerted herself, especially, as far as he could tell. She didn't pout, or preen, or simper, or flutter her eyelashes at him, like the eligible debutantes with whom he'd been mingling during the Season. She didn't hang on his every word, but spoke to him in a frank and open manner that was...actually, it was rather refreshing, in a way, to come across a female who didn't appear to have any idea how to flirt.

Or no wish to flirt, as far as he could tell.

Or at least, not with him.

Her mind clearly kept wandering far from him. He'd almost been able to see the thoughts flitting across her face.

And he hadn't liked it. Any other woman would have been hanging on to his every word. Making the most of the situation to...to sink her claws into him. Because every other female of his acquaintance knew he was on the hunt for a bride this Season.

Her slight air of distraction, of being untouchable, had made him want to do something to make her take notice of him. *That* was why he'd invited her to drive out with him again, he saw now. He wasn't falling under some sort of subtle female spell. She'd simply roused a very basic male urge to hunt, to conquer, that was all it was.

His mouth relaxed from its grim line as he drove

through the stone pillars marking the start of the drive up to Burslem House. Because he'd finally understood why he'd invited her to drive out with him again. He wasn't going soft. On the contrary, her apparent lack of interest had piqued him; she seemed so unattainable that he was rising to the challenge she represented.

By the time he pulled the curricle to a halt before the front steps, he was no longer frowning. Because he'd formulated a plan.

His groom jumped down and went to take the horses' heads. His butler opened the door before he'd reached the top step. His head footman took his hat, coat and gloves, and then an under-footman opened the door to his study where a third, more junior servant was engaged in pouring him out a tankard of fresh ale. Perceval, who'd been sitting at his own desk, working through a pile of correspondence, got to his feet, ready to attend him.

Oliver took a pull of his ale and let out a sigh as his life resumed its orderly pattern, with everyone knowing their duties and performing them like clockwork.

Except...

He put down his tankard. 'I have been having some thoughts about the house party we are to hold at Theakstone Court next week.'

Perceval blinked.

Oliver turned and walked round his desk. He didn't like the reminder that normally, at this point, he would have been asking his secretary if there were any urgent matters that had cropped up while he was out that needed attending to before they got down to the vast amount of estate matters to which he devoted this hour of the afternoon.

He sat down, steepled his fingers under his chin and leaned back in his chair. Now that he'd decided to take a bride, he'd worked out that the most obvious way to determine which of this Season's crop of debutantes would best fit the role would be to invite a select few to his principal seat. During the week they would stay there, he would be able to observe them more closely than he'd been able to do in town.

Because, on the face of it, there was little to choose between the handful of the most eligible, in the eyes of society. They were all well born, with perfect society manners and the usual feminine accomplishments. Which was just the trouble. He had no idea what lay behind the façade of good manners…if anything at all. At times he suspected they might all be just empty shells.

At least Miss Underwood was transparent. She said whatever popped into her head without thinking. Even when she *was* thinking, he could practically see her thoughts flitting across that expressive little face. Some people, he reflected, might describe her as a breath of fresh air.

'I wish you to add another family to the guest list.'

'At this late date?'

Oliver raised one eyebrow in affront.

'The staff at Theakstone Court are well able to make the necessary arrangements in time. Or they should be,' he concluded repressively.

'Your Grace has possibly not taken into consideration the time required to contact the family in question, as well as awaiting a response from them before notifying Mrs Manderville,' said Perceval apologetically.

'Are you implying that anyone would be likely to turn down an invitation to spend a week at Theakstone

Court?' Most people would give their right arm to receive such an honour. 'Especially not once I inform them of what is at stake.'

'Then you would wish me to send the invitations to the, ah, fortunate young lady and her family at the same time as I notify Mrs Manderville to make rooms ready for her family's arrival?'

'That would be the most efficient course to take,' said Oliver, wondering why his secretary had not thought of that in the first place.

'And the, ah, young lady in question?' Perceval went to his desk and dipped his pen in his inkwell.

'Miss Underwood. She is eligible,' he added, when Perceval's pen hovered in mid-air for long enough to let a drop of ink splash on to the blotter. 'As you yourself pointed out, she is the niece to the present Earl of Tadcaster as well as being the granddaughter of the former holder of that title.' And more to his taste, physically, than any of the other, better-born young ladies he'd considered taking as his Duchess. She might have many flaws, but at least he wouldn't find it a chore to produce the necessary heir, were she to become the bride in his bed.

Nor was she likely to bore him, the way the other candidates for the position already did.

What was more, he'd already discovered that she had a compassionate nature. True, all the other girls on his list had a reputation for being caring, but he hadn't actually seen any of them rushing to the aid of an injured woman of the lower classes. Nor had they any idea what it was like to be torn from the only family they'd known and sent to live among strangers. Which would mean she would know exactly how his own little daughter felt. The daughter whose existence he'd only recently discovered.

In fact, he couldn't imagine why he'd only just decided to consider Miss Underwood as a potential bride. The others might fill the role of Duchess more smoothly, but she was exactly the kind of woman he'd hoped to find to become a mother for Livvy.

Yes, no matter what the rest of the *ton* might think of his choice, in many ways she was exactly what he was looking for.

## Chapter Six

'You will never guess what that Duke of Theakstone has in mind with regard to Sofia,' said Uncle Ned as he lopped the head off his boiled egg at breakfast the next morning. 'He's taken the queerest notion into his head to consider looking her over to see if she'd make him a suitable bride.'

Sofia struggled to swallow her mouthful of tea, rather than spraying it all over the tablecloth. Suitable bride? It couldn't be true.

*'Sofia?'* Aunt Agnes appeared as shocked as Sofia felt.

'I know.' Uncle Ned shook his head with a bemused air. 'Thought he must be castaway when he said it, but see, here,' he said, tossing a stiff cream card across the table to Aunt Agnes. 'The invitation came first thing.'

Invitation?

Aunt Agnes let out a little shriek. 'Theakstone Court! He's inviting us all to spend a whole week with him at Theakstone Court.'

'Yes, he's inviting a whole gaggle of girls with their families for the week to see how they manage there.'

What kind of man invited a whole gaggle of girls to his house, to see how they *managed*, rather than courting and proposing to just one woman? Why…why… he was going about it as though he was conducting a week-long interview for paid employment.

'Of course, you will write and send our regrets, and so forth,' said Uncle Ned, applying himself to his egg.

'What? Why?' Aunt Agnes looked at him as though he'd lost his mind.

'Well, naturally we shan't go,' retorted Uncle Ned.

'Why ever not?'

Yes, why wouldn't Uncle Ned let her go there? Typical. Whenever she…

She took her teacup in both hands and took another sip, guiltily aware that until Uncle Ned had said she *couldn't* go, she hadn't actually *wanted* to go to Theakstone Court. It was only when he started telling Aunt Agnes it was out of the question that she was remembering all the other things she had wanted to do and not been allowed. The entire trip to Burslem Bay had been a series of disappointments. Uncle Barty had painted a picture of the kind of seaside holiday which would have been the perfect tonic. But Aunt Agnes hadn't let her attend any assemblies, so she hadn't danced with any dashing men in red coats, let alone acquired a coterie of beaux.

'Waste of time,' said Uncle Ned, waving his butter knife in Sofia's direction to emphasise his point. 'Sofia's going to marry Jack. Been settled for some time.'

Oh, no, it hadn't. Jack hadn't proposed. They were not officially betrothed. The two families had just always assumed that one day Jack would *drop the handkerchief…*

'Yes, but nobody needs to tell the Duke of Theak-stone, do they?' said Aunt Agnes in a conspirato-rial tone. 'And it's not as if Sofia's going to have her head turned by the prospect of a coronet. She dotes on Jack.'

Dotes? Hah! She might have done, once, before the scales fell from her eyes. She reached for a slice of toast to stop herself from blurting out the truth—that the prospect of being leg-shackled to an oaf like Jack filled her with revulsion. And, since she'd put the piece of dry toast straight into her mouth, there was a good chance that if either of them noticed the little grimace she made, they'd put it down to lack of butter. Not that they ever did pay her much heed once they'd embarked on one of their squabbles.

'And you need not fear that a man like the Duke of Theakstone is likely to choose our Sofia over all those other girls you say he's invited.'

They both turned to look at her in that rather pained way that was their habit. In attempting to avoid catch-ing anyone's eye, she managed to brush her hand against her teacup, spilling its contents into her saucer.

'See? A man of his rank is bound to want a truly elegant female to preside over his homes, not a…well, a…someone like Sofia. I am sure there can be no harm in accepting his invitation.'

Sofia watched the tea stain spreading along the fi-bres of the once snowy-white tablecloth, rendering it a muddy brown. She didn't have a burning desire to become a duchess. But hearing her closest relatives, the aunt and uncle whose approval she'd tried so hard to gain, declare the unlikeliness of such a thing ever happening, filled her with an all-too-familiar feeling of failure, made worse by the belief that Aunt Agnes was correct. She could *never* become a duchess. If even a callow boy like Jack could only stomach the prospect of marrying her because he would be compensated by getting his hands on her fortune, she was never going to win what sounded like a competition, against better-bred, better-trained girls, to win the regard of a sophisticated, attractive man like the Duke of Theakstone.

'See, even Sofia knows it, don't you?' Now it was Aunt Agnes's turn to wave her butter knife in her direction. 'There can be absolutely no danger to your plans... I mean, for Jack and Sofia's future happiness, in accepting the invitation. And much to be gained. I mean, a week at Theakstone Court, Ned! Can you imagine what Mrs Chalfont will say? Or General Benning, when they find out?'

'Hmm...' Uncle Ned took a thoughtful pull at his ale. 'I do hear that there's some very fine country round the Court. No shooting at this time of year, but the fishing is supposed to be excellent. And I must say, this place is cursed flat.' He glanced out of the window. 'Nothing but a pack of invalids and elderly spinsters wanting you to play whist and wittering on about their quack medicines.'

And so it was settled. She and Uncle Ned and Aunt Agnes were to spend a week at Theakstone Court so that the Duke could decide she wasn't good enough to become his Duchess.

How ever was she going to contain her excitement?

With modestly downbent head, she left the breakfast table and went to her room to prepare for her morning dip.

* * *

Life definitely had a way of pushing you in directions you would really rather not go, she reflected later, as the two burly women ducked her beneath the waves and held her there for several seconds, reminding her that once again she had no escape. No choice. She never had. Her very earliest memories were tinged with the helpless feeling of being uprooted whenever Papa's marching orders had come.

Her mood had not improved by the time the Duke came to take her for the promised drive in his carriage. What was more, instead of feeling rather pleased at doing something rebellious in going out with him alone, she was inclined to add him to her list of people who pushed her around without once consulting her. Fancy speaking to her uncle about his intentions, rather than making them known to her! And handing out an invitation to his stupid Duchess decision-making party without even asking her if she actually *wanted* to be his Duchess.

He angled her a perplexed glance as she heaved herself, with resignation, into his curricle, and pulled Snowball on to her lap. 'Are you not feeling the thing today, Miss Underwood? You seem rather subdued.'

'The thing?' She sighed. The thing that was the matter with her today was actually no worse than it had been the day before. It was just that she felt more conscious of being stuck in her personal version of limbo. The stay in Burslem Bay had actually started to revive her spirits, in spite of not dishing up the beaux Uncle Barty had predicted. Simply getting away from Nettleton Manor had been enough to break her out of the depression that had dogged her since she'd stopped assuming her whole future would revolve around Jack.

It was just that the conversation at breakfast had brought it all back with a vengeance—what was she to do with herself, until she came into her money, if she didn't marry Jack? Not that she could share such a personal matter with a man she barely knew.

And he was still waiting for a response from her. 'I am just a touch blue-devilled, I suppose,' she said, taking a measure of comfort in using a phrase Aunt Agnes would consider vulgar.

'Perhaps I have some news that might cheer you up,' he said, without showing by so much as a flicker of his eyelid that he disapproved of her choice of vocabulary. 'I have instructed my secretary to include you on a very exclusive guest list. You should be receiving the invitation to attend a select house party at Theakstone Court today.'

'Oh, yes, I know all about that,' she said morosely. 'It came at breakfast.'

The look he directed her way was most definitely affronted this time.

'And it has not pleased you?'

Pleased her? No, at no point today had she felt pleased about the invitation. Though how could she explain her reaction to what he clearly felt should have sent her into raptures? 'It is just...' She kept her eyes fixed firmly on the gleaming backs of his matched greys. 'I mean, Uncle Ned said...' As she recalled what Uncle Ned had said, followed by what Aunt Agnes had said, she felt something very like a brownish stain seeping across her soul.

'I sincerely hope,' bit out the Duke, affront flowing from him in waves, 'that he explained that all the other families I have invited are in possession of a daughter who has attracted my notice, for one reason or another.'

'Yes,' she admitted glumly. And they would all outshine her so much that she couldn't see what point there was in her going, except to provide Uncle Ned with a week's fishing and Aunt Agnes with the chance to boast of her stay at Theakstone Court to the principal families in the region of Nettleton Manor, when they returned.

'And you are not flattered?' Now he looked positively annoyed.

She supposed she ought to explain…

She shook her head. 'I… I cannot… I mean…my feelings upon the matter are…'

'Oh, please,' he said with heavy sarcasm, 'do not hesitate to express your feelings. My own, I do assure you, are immune to anything you might say.'

It had nothing to do with his feelings. She just could not confide in a man who she'd only met a matter of days ago. And his arrogant assumption that he was the cause of her dilemma made her see red. 'Very well,' she said, flinging up her chin. 'For one thing, I find it extremely hard to believe you can seriously be considering me as…as…well, as your wife, when we hardly know each other.'

'That is the whole point of inviting you to Theakstone Court. So we may get to know each other better.'

Oh. That was a fair point, actually. 'Yes, but what can you hope to discover in a week? Or I about you? I mean, in a week, you could easily conceal all sorts of vices from me.' After all, Jack had successfully done so for years and years and years. If she hadn't been swimming in the lower lake and if Snowball hadn't barked a warning so that she'd just had time to duck under the jetty and hide, and Jack hadn't chosen to dismount and water his horses at that particular spot, she might never have learned the truth about him.

'Vices?' His voice turned extremely chilly. 'You suspect me of concealing vices from you?'

'Well, that's just it. I don't know, do I?'

'I should think you might be able to judge me by my actions. As I did you. We were the only people at the Peace celebrations, barring Lord Gilray, who ran to help Mrs Pagett. Everyone else fled the scene to protect themselves.'

Which was another good point. She'd even admired him for having the presence of mind to collect the ice bucket on the way.

'Yes, that's true. But even so...'

'Ah, here we are,' he said, reining the curricle to a halt. 'Your lodgings.'

Sofia blinked up at the façade of Number Six. How on earth had they fetched up here so soon?

Because, she realised on her second blink, he hadn't taken her all the way to the seafront. He'd turned the curricle up a side street the minute she'd started expressing reservations about his character. And brought her straight back here.

Oh, dear, she really did owe him an apology. He did seem to be a decent man, who'd done nothing to deserve her harsh remarks.

But while she was searching for the words to explain herself, without going as far as confiding in him about the way Jack had deceived her, which would have been too humiliating, he'd climbed down, reached up to seize her by the waist and deposited her on the pavement.

'I... I...'

He turned his back, plucked Snowball from the seat, thrust the dog into her arms and climbed back into his curricle.

'I'm sorry,' she said miserably as he put his horses into motion. Even though he could not possibly have heard.

She trudged up the front steps, feeling even more of a failure, and even lonelier than she'd felt since the day she'd heard Jack describe her to his London friend.

She buried her face in Snowball's soft fur as she made her way up to her room, where she draped herself along the window seat.

Oh, well, she reflected as she gazed down over the rooftops sloping down to the seafront. It wasn't as if she'd wrecked her chances with him. He'd never have proposed marriage. For she was not the kind of girl a duke would choose. She was *dull as ditch water*. Tainted by birth. And the only thing that might have tempted him—her money—he could know nothing about, because as sure as eggs were eggs Uncle Ned would have kept that juicy titbit from him. Because he wanted her to marry Jack.

'Oh, Snowball, what am I going to do?'

Snowball licked her chin in a sympathetic manner, but did not provide Sofia with any inspiration. But then, Sofia had already spent hours, and days, and weeks, trying to come up with a plan she could present to her uncles to which they would agree. So how likely was it a dog could do any better? And anyway, time after time, when she started to form a plan that she thought might content her, she would run up against the strictures imposed upon women. She couldn't just set up house somewhere, on her own, not without causing the kind of talk that *all* her family would hate. But neither could she bear the thought of staying with Aunt Agnes and Uncle Ned once they'd learned she had no intention of falling in with their plans for her and Jack.

Going to live with Uncle Barty and his new wife would be acceptable in the eyes of society, but although he was always criticising Uncle Ned, it had never crossed his mind to invite her to go to him instead. Because, basically, he didn't want her. Had never wanted her. But especially not now, when he was so keen to fill his nursery. She flushed as she recalled the times she'd caught him pinching his rosy-cheeked wife on the bottom.

No, she couldn't go to live with Uncle Barty. She would just be swapping one awkward situation for another.

She'd briefly toyed with the idea of seeking out her mother's family, but they weren't likely to welcome her with open arms, either. Especially since they were all Catholic and she'd been raised Church of England. They'd want to convert her, she expected. And she'd no wish to waste any more of her life trying to turn herself into somebody her family would approve of. If she wasn't good enough just as she was, then…then…

She sighed again and buried her face in Snowball's side. Even when she came of age, Uncle Barty and Uncle Ned would still try to oversee her business affairs.

Which meant they would oppose every single thing she ever wanted to do with her inheritance, no doubt.

'Do you know,' she informed Snowball, 'I'm beginning to think I would be better off if I didn't have any money. At least then people would accept it if I went off to seek employment as a governess, or a companion, or something like that. At least then I might acquire some self-respect.'

Snowball let out a yip. As if to remind her that things hadn't come to such a pass, quite yet.

'Quite right, Snowball,' Sofia agreed. 'I have plenty to be thankful for. I have a roof over my head,' she observed, remembering the time between her papa's death and Aunt Agnes taking her in, when it had started to look as if she'd never have anywhere to call home. 'And food to eat all the time.' Another thing that had, occasionally, been in short supply before she'd come to live in England. 'And no business feeling sorry for myself. Something will turn up.' That was what Papa had always used to say. And if it didn't turn up, he'd go out and make something happen.

Could she be as brave? As resourceful?

Only time would tell.

## Chapter Seven

Unfortunately, the dreary daily round she had to follow did little to provide inspiration. After breakfast,
she was taken to the shore for her dunking, then hauled
out of the water and into the changing hut to dry. Aunt
Agnes then escorted her to the tea room next to the library for a hot drink. After which they would go into
the circulating library to see if any new books had come
in. If it wasn't raining, they walked back to their lodgings, for the exercise, avoiding the promenade along
which officers from the militia took their own daily
stroll. If it was raining, Aunt Agnes hired a hack. Sofia
spent afternoons sitting in the parlour pretending to do
embroidery, occasionally glancing up at the window to
watch either the rain trickling down the panes, or the
dust motes dancing in the beams of sunlight stealing in.

After dinner, Uncle Ned and Aunt Agnes would
get ready to go out to whatever assembly, card party,
or supper to which they had been invited. While she
got ready for bed.

'We made a mistake taking you to that supper and
fireworks display,' Aunt Agnes explained, the first

time they went out and left her. 'It was too much for you in your fragile state of health.'

What she really meant, Sofia suspected, was that they did not want to risk her meeting anyone who might tempt her away from Jack. The Duke turning up to take her out for a drive had been enough of a shock, though they'd quickly been able to explain him away. For why would a man like that look twice at someone like Sofia? And then the way he'd deposited her on the front step after that last outing had reassured them that he posed no threat. Particularly since he'd been conspicuous by his absence ever since.

She was gazing out of the window one fine, sunny afternoon, wishing she had been more tactful, wishing she'd done things differently, wishing he would give her a chance to apologise for her behaviour; but most of all, wishing she could just go out for another drive with him along the seafront, with the wind whipping her curls across her face and his large, solid body at her side.

But the curricle which drew up, just as though she'd summoned it by wishing, did not belong to the Duke. Though the driver was far more familiar.

And far less skilful with the ribbons.

Jack.

She drew back from the window, her stomach churning. Thank goodness she'd seen him arrive. By the time he strode into the drawing room she would have managed to school her features to show nothing more than polite interest in his arrival, rather than glaring at him like a harpy who was barely holding back the urge to rake her claws across his self-satisfied face.

It helped that he greeted Aunt Agnes first. While he

was shaking hands with her, Sofia had leisure to study him, now that her eyes were fully open to his faults.

He didn't look any less handsome. She could actually see why she'd been so absurdly grateful whenever this good-looking, elegant youth had deigned to grant her a few moments of his time. However, now that she'd spent some time with the Duke, she could see that Jack wasn't as elegant as he thought. The Duke would never wear a waistcoat that gaudy. Nor would he wear his shirt points so ridiculously high.

'Oh, look who is here, Sofia,' gushed Aunt Agnes, finally deigning to include her in the proceedings. 'Is this not a lovely surprise?'

'Is it?' Jack blinked. 'Oh. Ah. Yes. Had a few days' leisure and thought I'd pop over and see how poor Sofia was faring,' he said to Aunt Agnes in the manner of a rather poor actor reciting his lines. 'And—Good God!' he exclaimed, flinching the moment he turned and looked at her face, properly.

Sofia had forgotten, until that very moment, that the bruises round her eye socket were starting to show streaks of green among the purple and black. Everyone else had grown so used to them that they didn't react at all. But Jack managed to make her feel as though she was disfigured.

'Was going to ask if you'd like to take the air with me. Come out for a drive. But obviously, you won't want to go anywhere with your face...' He trailed off, making a vague gesture in the direction of her injured eye.

Sofia couldn't help comparing his attitude with that of the Duke, when he'd come to call. When he'd first seen her face, he hadn't winced and drawn back in horror. On the contrary, he'd reached out, as though wishing to soothe what he perceived was a grievous hurt.

And *he* hadn't cared what gossip might arise from taking a girl with a black eye out for a drive, either.

'No, no,' put in Aunt Agnes hastily. 'Sofia would *love* to go out with you. Some fresh air would do her the world of good. Nobody remarks upon her bruises, you know, Jack. Indeed, there are so many odd-looking people about the place that a girl with a blackened eye causes no gossip at all.'

Jack did not look convinced. In fact, he looked as though the very last thing he wanted to do was take her out, in case people saw him with a girl who was the very furthest thing from being ornamental.

'Don't suppose it is the done thing to take an unmarried girl out in my curricle, anyway,' he said, with what looked like a slight edge of desperation. 'Wouldn't want to damage your reputation.'

'Nonsense!' Aunt Agnes was beginning to look as though she was losing all patience with him. 'She is family, after all. Nobody can possibly wonder at two family members going for a drive together. Besides, this is Burslem Bay, not London. The rules are very much more relaxed here. Why, Sofia went out for a drive with no less a person than the Duke of Theakstone,' she said meaningfully, 'in a vehicle very much like the one I see you have hired and nobody batted an eyelid.'

Sofia watched Jack brace himself before turning to her once more.

'Well, of course, if you *wish* to go out, I should be delighted to tool you through the town and along the seafront.'

Oh, how tempting it was to tell him not to bother. She had no wish to spend another minute in his company, let alone the twenty or thirty such an expedition would take.

But she had a feeling that would be a bit cowardly. She'd been avoiding him long enough. Ever since she'd overheard him mocking her, to his friend, she'd been dreading seeing him face to face. She'd hidden in her room, skipped meals, refused to attend local assemblies or even go to church if she'd known he was in the neighbourhood.

Besides, the first few moments were over. She'd seen him. And survived.

And she *had* been wishing she could go out for a drive. So what if he wasn't the driver she would have preferred to be taking her out? She was fed up with sitting indoors on such a fine day.

'Why, thank you, Jack,' she therefore said. 'I shall just go and fetch my coat and bonnet.' And she tripped out of the room, her face flushing with…well, she wasn't sure what it was. In the past, it would have been a girlish self-awareness. Being in Jack's presence, having his attention fully on her before the incident at the jetty, would have reduced her to a quivering mass of fluttery pleasure. This was not what she was feeling now, though to observers it probably looked remarkably similar.

Snowball, naturally, began spinning the moment she reached for her coat, and trotted down the steps at her heels when Jack preceded her to his curricle.

'Can't have that mutt coming with us,' said Jack, when she reached up to put Snowball on the bench seat. 'Bad enough you looking as though you've been in a prize fight.'

'Oh,' she said, as he deposited Snowball on the pavement very firmly. And then, for the first time since coming to England, chose honesty over trying to please the person she was with. 'Well, never mind. I can see you don't really wish to take me for a drive. I shall just take Snowball for a quick walk along the street and then...'

'What?' Jack's look of astonishment was priceless. He clearly couldn't believe she was attempting to give him the slip.

He glared at Snowball. Glared at her. Clenched his gloved hand on his whip as though wrestling his temper back under control.

'No, of course I want to take you for a drive. Don't be a goose, Sofia. Take the damn cur along if you must. Only don't blame me if people stare, that's all.'

'They didn't stare when the Duke of Theakstone took Snowball up in his curricle last week,' she couldn't resist telling him, even though it wasn't strictly true. Because it had the effect of making Jack grind his teeth. She could actually see his jaw working. And it took him right to the end of the street to master his temper sufficiently to be able to speak to her with any degree of calm.

And even then it wasn't exactly what she'd call a conversation. He simply launched into a series of anecdotes about what he'd been doing over the past few weeks.

'And of course I could have told him how it would end,' he was saying about some idiot with whom he'd been engaged in a lark. 'Up to his knees in horse dung. Ha-ha-ha.'

In the past, she'd have laughed, too, even if she

hadn't thought the anecdote funny. Out of simple pleasure that he was deigning to notice her at all, even if
he did only talk about himself.

Why hadn't she ever noticed how utterly self-centred
he was?

'I say,' he said, when she continued in stony silence
through a series of similar tales. 'You don't seem in
your usual spirits, Sofia.'

No, she was not. She hadn't been since he'd ripped
the veil from her eyes without even knowing.

She took a deep, resentful breath. He hadn't particularly liked what he'd thought were her usual spirits, anyway.

'I have always been quiet,' she pointed out. So quiet,
in fact, that he'd thought her *dull as ditch water.* He'd
told his friend that only the prospect of getting his
hands on her inheritance would make him able to stomach taking her as a wife. That, and the prospect of enjoying other women, *real* women, on the side. 'You
used to say,' she reminded him resentfully, 'that it was
peaceful, being with a female who didn't prattle con-
stantly about dresses and balls, the way your sisters do.'

'Ah, yes, that I did. And it is. Yes. Lord, how my
sisters drive me to distraction with all that feminine
prattle! Only, don't know how it is, but you don't seem
to be quiet in the same way,' he said, glancing at her
uneasily, before clearing his throat.

'Look here, Sofia. Thing is, my mother is very
concerned about you. I thought it was all moonshine,
but now I've seen you…well, perhaps she's right after
all. Perhaps you do need someone to take care of you
a bit more…' He lifted his chin and adopted a long-

suffering expression. 'I don't say your aunt and uncle haven't done their best...'

Oh, no. He was going to make her an offer. She could feel it gathering like an impending thunderstorm. It sounded as though the entire family had been warning him it was high time he came up to scratch. That was why he'd come to Burslem Bay. Why Aunt Agnes had pushed him into taking her out for a drive. Why he'd even put up with Snowball.

'But what I mean to say is, we've known each other a long time now...'

Oh, good grief. What kind of man attempted a marriage proposal while driving a curricle, anyway? She couldn't imagine the Duke doing anything so crass. Nor *any* man who was in earnest. A man who actually liked the woman he was asking to be his wife would give a proposal his complete attention.

Could she tell her aunt that was why she had turned him down? No. It would not do. Aunt Agnes would not believe Sofia could possibly have any valid reason for turning down her beloved nephew. Too much was riding on it. Uncle Ned's sister had married a man with hardly any money to his name and given him not only an heir but a spare as well as a brace of sisters, both of whom had a paltry dowry. And while, theoretically, she could feel sympathy for any female with little allure and no money, she didn't feel sorry enough for them to sacrifice her whole future on their behalf.

Especially since she didn't even like them. And they certainly didn't like her. Jack might have mocked her behind her back, but they'd done it to her face. The first time she'd met them, they'd mimicked her accent with shrieks of laughter and then told her she needn't think they'd let a dirty little foreigner touch any of their dolls. And after that visit, Betty and Celia, the cousins with whom she lived, had followed suit. Before Jack's sisters had been so spiteful, they'd merely been a touch aloof. After that...

She shuddered. They'd left her alone again once she'd learned to creep about quietly, like a little brown mouse, and only weep where nobody could see her.

She glanced at Jack's handsome profile and straightened her drooping posture. She'd done enough cowering and putting up with things so as not to cause trouble. It did not matter how disappointed Aunt Agnes was going to be, she was not going to marry Jack and that was that.

Just as she'd reached that momentous decision, Snowball caught sight of a cat sitting on a branch of a tree, insolently twitching its tail at passers-by. And took exception.

'God dammit,' snapped Jack, when Snowball started barking. 'Can't you get that mutt to be quiet? She's startling the horses!'

'I'm so sorry,' said Sofia insincerely, while Jack hauled at the reins to prevent the horses from bolting the last few feet of the road, straight across the promenade and on to the very beach. And far from giving Snowball the signal to be silent, she merely told her to be quiet. Snowball, sensing that Sofia didn't mean it, threw herself wholeheartedly into the role of protector of innocent curricle passengers from dangerous cats.

'A cat, you know,' Sofia explained, as Snowball turned round and put her front paws on the back of the seat so that she could continue to bark as the cat receded into the distance.

By the time Jack finally got the horses back under control and the curricle bowling along the seafront at a decorous pace, he was fuming. 'I can't believe I permitted you to bring that mongrel with us,' he said. He then proceeded to deliver a series of pithy remarks about dogs of dubious heritage, women with no brains, the temperament of hired horses and people who let dangerous cats roam the public highways. Or words to that effect.

Normally, having someone rant at her in public would have reduced Sofia to tears. But even though she did feel a touch hurt by the things he was saying, another part of her was rejoicing that there was no way even he could propose to her after having given her such a blistering scold.

The thought must have occurred to Jack as well, because all of a sudden he went quiet.

'Anyway, that's…well, you're a very silly girl but… that is, can't expect you to think of horses when you… that is…' He cleared his throat. Thought for a bit. 'This seems like a tolerable little resort. Assemblies, and card parties and so forth going on, so I believe. So, I, um, think I may stay for a week or so. Dare say we shall see quite a bit of each other,' he said, with resignation. 'You'd like to dance with me,' he said patronisingly, 'wouldn't you?'

Once upon a time she'd have been beside herself at the prospect of standing up with Jack. Now, it gave her great pleasure to be able to inform him that her aunt hadn't yet permitted her to attend a single assembly in this seaside town.

'Besides,' she added, 'we will all be going to Theakstone Court the day after tomorrow. Didn't Aunt Agnes tell you?'

'Well, of course she did,' he snapped. His level of resentment confirmed Sofia's suspicion that their aunt had warned him he needed to step up to the mark before she had the chance to have her head turned by the prospect of a coronet and that he would really rather not have been put to so much bother.

'Tell you what, though,' he said, 'by the time you come back, your eye will have healed up nicely. Shan't be ashamed to stand up with you then.'

Sofia gritted her teeth.

'That will give you something to look forward to, while you're at that stuffy old Duke's house, what?'

Something to look forward to? Ooh, the arrogant, insufferable…

'Because I have to say, Sofia, that you are not likely to gain much enjoyment from such a party.'

'Oh?' The word slipped between her teeth like a dagger. 'And why would that be?'

'Out of your depth in such company, I shouldn't wonder,' said Jack, in blithe ignorance of her seething resentment. 'I've been on the town for some time now,' he said pompously, 'and believe me, those *ton*-nish affairs can be deadly. Poisonous tongues, some of that set have. And they will all have known each other from birth. You'll be glad to get away in the end, I dare say. But then, just remember, I will be here, waiting to cheer you up.'

Well, she sniffed. That was what *he* thought.

## Chapter Eight

Oliver turned away from the window for the third time that afternoon and stalked to his study door. This wouldn't do. It was past time he went to the yellow drawing room. He had no business loitering round windows to see if the carriage containing Miss Underwood might, finally, be bowling up the drive.

He'd never regretted inviting her here as much as he did right this minute, as he was striding along the corridors to where the rest of his guests were already eagerly awaiting him. He'd known he'd made a mistake during that last unsatisfactory drive out with her. But it had already been too late. Because of Perceval's efficiency, the invitation had not only gone out, but been received and accepted before he'd returned to Burslem House.

All he could do was regard it as a salutary lesson on the folly of acting on impulse. He really should have stuck to his original plan, rather than making that last-minute and poorly thought-out alteration.

But then that was the effect Miss Underwood had on him. She could overset his carefully arranged plans by the mere act of looking a trifle wistful. Without even knowing she was doing it, that was the worst part!

One of his footmen, whose name eluded him, opened the door of the drawing room and sprang aside only moments before Oliver reached it. The inexperienced footman was still drawing breath to announce him, when Oliver almost cannoned into Lady Margaret Pawson, who'd been looking up at the section of frieze painted just above the lintel.

'Oh, I beg your pardon, Your Grace,' she said, sinking into a deeply apologetic curtsy. Had he been paying more attention, he would not have had to come to such an abrupt halt. 'It is just that this mural is such a fine example of *tromp l'oeil*, I could scarcely drag my gaze from it…' She faltered to a halt, flushed, clasped her hands at her waist and lowered her head.

He realised he was scowling at her. Dammit, it was not her fault she'd caught the brunt of his ill humour. That was all down to one Sofia Underwood.

Nevertheless, he did not care for the way she was shrinking from him, merely because he had frowned in her general direction. If she was that timid, then he couldn't possibly marry her. Her nerves would be in shreds in a matter of weeks. And although he couldn't help looking fierce and speaking abruptly when he was annoyed, he wasn't a brute. He would take no pleasure in making his wife flinch from him, or watch him with wide, anxious eyes to discern his mood, the way his poor stepmother had watched his father.

In spite of that decision, he had no wish to humiliate her by making it obvious. It would not be good *ton* to let her, or, even worse, anyone else, suspect that he'd mentally crossed her off his list.

'Allow me to introduce you to some of the other guests, Lady Margaret,' he said, deliberately gentling his tone as he extended his arm. The hand she laid on his sleeve was still trembling, though. Dammit, was he really such an ogre? Miss Underwood had certainly hinted that she suspected as much. Not that she shrank from him or trembled if he frowned directly at her. No, she flung up her little chin and demanded he explain himself.

Blast the woman, invading his thoughts at the most inopportune moments.

'Are you acquainted with Lord Smedley-Fotherington?' he asked Lady Margaret, pulling himself together as he reached the slender young man's side. Thank goodness he'd taken the precaution of inviting the languid poet for the express purpose of keeping young ladies occupied while he spent time getting to know the other bridal candidates. Since they both had pretensions to being artistic, he hoped they'd have plenty to say to each other. To his satisfaction, Lady Margaret visibly relaxed the moment Smedley-Fotherington bowed over her hand, as though recognising he posed no threat.

Although it was irritating to have mistaken a woman's blushing responses to him in London as merely shyness, at least it was gratifying to see that his method of selecting his future Duchess was already garnering results.

Having foisted Lady Margaret off on to the young fop, he circulated among his other guests, making sure to spend the same amount of time with each family, so that none could claim they were ahead in the Duchess Stakes. Still, he managed to keep half an eye on the door at all times. He wanted to know the exact moment

Miss Underwood arrived, so that there would be no chance of her catching him unawares. He wasn't going to be able to avoid running into her over the course of the week. But he was tolerably sure that after this first meeting was over, he would be able to treat her exactly the same as he would treat all his other guests. With punctilious politeness.

He was not going to let anyone suspect he now believed he'd made a mistake in inviting her here. A man of his rank never betrayed his feelings in public. It was the cardinal rule. He would treat her with the exact same courtesy he would extend to all the other girls who'd come here hoping to be selected for the position of his Duchess.

Although Sofia didn't, did she? Hope to become his Duchess, that was.

Not that he cared. What did the opinion of a mere country miss matter to him? She had *not* hurt him by the way she'd practically shuddered at the prospect of becoming his bride. Nor insulted him with her thinly veiled insults about him being the kind of man who might be concealing all sorts of vices.

In fact, it showed she had more sense than the rest of these debutantes put together, he reflected bitterly, glancing round the room. Men could, and routinely did, conceal their worst flaws from the women they married until it was too late for them to do anything about it. His own mother being a case in point. Not that she had actively sought to become his father's Duchess, by all accounts. It had been her socially and politically ambitious parents who'd arranged the match with his father and they clearly hadn't cared about the third Duke's vices, hidden or otherwise.

Although his father had hidden his true nature pretty well. His reputation, even now, was that of a mentally acute man who had never shirked the slightest of his duties, nor indulged in the corrupt practices that ran so rife in high circles. The only person to openly speak ill of him was his stepmother. And since she was such a flighty, feather-brained creature, nobody paid any heed. The series of scandals and scrapes into which she'd fallen since she'd become a widow hadn't helped her cause, either. People were saying that if her late husband had behaved harshly, she'd undoubtedly provoked him.

It was while his mind was full of his poor stepmother, and what ills she'd had to endure at the hands of his late father, that the door opened and there she was. Sofia.

'Viscount and Lady Norborough, Miss Underwood,' said the footman who was clearly not up to his job. Although he had reminded Oliver that he ought only to think of her as Miss Underwood.

She stood on the threshold looking around the room a little wide-eyed.

She was nervous.

And just like that, his feet were carrying him across the room before he'd given them permission.

'Welcome to Theakstone Court,' he said, ruthlessly forbidding his hand to extend in her direction.

He couldn't stop his heart from hammering in his chest, though. Just at the sight of her.

Which put her ahead of the field once more. For she was the only one of the runners who heated his blood this way; the only one he'd take to his bed with relish, rather than out of a sense of duty to prolong his line; the one who might, if she decided he might suit her, become a far better wife than all those who cared nothing about the man behind the title. Because that was the way she was considering his proposal—as an offer to become his wife, not his Duchess. She'd made that very clear during that last outing.

A strange yearning sensation came over him.

He thrust it aside. He was on the hunt for a woman with the necessary qualifications to become his Duchess.

And come to think of it, if he was going to consider Miss Underwood, then she'd really have to smarten herself up. The colour of her outfit did not suit her. The style was several years out of date. Nor did it fit her about the shoulders. In short, she looked downright provincial, rather than elegant and sophisticated like the other ladies he'd invited here.

The problem was not insurmountable, however. He could swiftly correct that defect in her by hiring an experienced dresser. A dresser who would know how to select clothing that brought out the soft warm brown of her eyes, flatter her creamy complexion, accentuate, rather than disguise, that athletic frame...

'I trust,' he said, wrenching his mind from imagining the body that lay beneath her unflattering, unfashionable gown, to address her uncle, 'you had a pleasant journey?'

'Damn offside leader lost a shoe outside Hebden. Had to root out a blacksmith. Made us damnably late,' said Norborough, reaching out to shake Oliver's hand. 'My lady was all of a twitter,' he said, eyeing his wife with amusement, 'but as I said to her, can't do anything to prevent horses losing their shoes just when it's most inconvenient. Duke knows how it is. He won't mind. Eh?'

'Not at all,' he said, noting the way Miss Underwood's aunt was blushing for her husband's manners. Or, rather, lack thereof.

'And you arrived safely,' he pointed out, 'and in good time to meet my other guests before it is time to change for dinner.'

Miss Underwood shot him a look loaded with resentment which he was at a loss to account for when he took her arm and led her, and therefore her aunt and uncle, to the highest-ranking of his other guests, the Marquess of Sale.

'Lord Sale, allow me to present…'

'Good God, if it ain't Tubby Hetherington,' burst out Viscount Norborough before Oliver had the chance to present him properly. 'Haven't seen you since…when was it?' He stretched out his hand.

Oliver watched with surprise as the usually stiff-rumped Marquess took that hand and allowed Norborough to pump it enthusiastically. 'Torkington's dunking, I seem to recall,' he said, astonishing even his own wife by allowing his lips to melt into the approximation of a smile.

'Torkington, yes. Ha-ha! What became of him, do you know? After they pulled him out of the Isis?'

'Last I heard…' said the Marquess, lowering his voice and leaning in close to Norborough's ear and murmuring something that caused the two men to draw closer still, before wandering off, leaving Oliver alone with a set of four offended females.

'Lady Sale,' he then said, in an attempt to soothe the

feathers ruffled by Lord Norborough, 'may I present Lady Norborough and her niece, Miss Sofia Underwood.'

Perhaps not surprisingly given the way Lord Norborough had just borne her husband off, Lady Sale did no more than accord Lady Norborough a brief nod.

Her daughter, however, he noted with approval, gave Miss Underwood a friendly smile as she dipped a curtsy.

'How lovely to meet you,' said Lady Sarah, dimpling prettily. 'You must find time to come to my room before dinner. All the girls are going to be there.' She waved an elegant hand vaguely about the room, as if to encompass all his younger guests. 'I thought, you know,' she said, turning an earnest face to his, 'it would help Miss Underwood to get to know us all in an informal setting, since she is a stranger to polite society. It must be so hard for her to have to attend an event such as this, without having the benefit of a London Season beforehand.'

She was correct. Why hadn't it occurred to him? Perhaps that accounted for Miss Underwood's peculiar behaviour in the curricle that day. Perhaps it wasn't him that she had an aversion to. Perhaps she just felt ill equipped to mingle with members of the *haut ton*. After all, she'd never so much as been to London, let alone been launched into society.

'Thank you, Lady Sarah,' he said, regarding the Marchioness's daughter with more warmth than he'd been able to summon up for her thus far. 'It was most thoughtful of you to offer to take Miss Underwood under your wing.' For that was what she was clearly doing. 'Most kind.'

And kindness was going to be a trait he must absolutely insist upon in his Duchess. Perhaps the most essential trait.

## *Chapter Nine*

Kind? *Kind!* Lady Sarah was not being kind. She was doing what Jack's sisters used to do when grown-ups were watching—disguising a put-down by delivering it with a smile. Reminding her that she was out of place in this room since she was a *stranger to polite society* and therefore totally unfit to become a duchess.

Not that she needed much reminding. Sofia had never seen, let alone set foot in, such a palatial residence. From the moment their hired carriage had lurched under the massive ornate stone archway that marked the entrance to the grounds of Theakstone Court, she'd felt like a trespasser. The feeling of not being worthy of setting foot on any part of the estate increased the closer they'd driven to the house itself. It put her in mind of the way she'd felt when she'd first seen Nettleton Manor. Surely people who lived in a house as grand as that, with so much land surrounding it, would never let a grubby little orphan across their threshold? Only, the Duke's principal seat was far larger and hidden deep within a much, much bigger estate. The central block alone was about twice as big as her parish church. And then there were wings branching out on either side.

They hadn't drawn up in front of that imposing façade, however. Instead the driver had taken a spur of the drive which took them the entire length of one of the massive wings, before curving into a stone-flagged area on which a sizeable town could have held its weekly market. They'd crossed that, heading for the rear of the main block and finally driven into a glassed-in porch. It had doors at each end, as big as barn doors, so that the entire area could be closed off, with a carriage inside. It meant that when they alighted it felt as if they were already indoors.

The housekeeper, who was standing at the head of a set of three marble steps in front of what Sofia supposed was a back door, gave them all a rather frosty look.

'I am Mrs Manderville,' she'd said with a brief nod of her head. 'You will have to make haste if you wish to have any hope of attending upon His Grace—' and, yes, she had said it with capital letters '—in the yellow drawing room during the hour he has allotted for greeting his guests.' She had then glanced down at Snowball, who was running around making friends with the various staff who were lifting down their luggage, and generally stretching her legs after the long journey. 'Animals are not permitted in the guest rooms,' she'd said sternly. Then beckoned to a liveried footman. 'Take this dog to the kennels.'

The man had picked up Snowball and was carrying her off before Sofia had a chance to explain that her dog was very well trained and would not be any trouble. And Mrs Manderville was marching off into the house with a curt, 'Follow me', anyway.

She led them through a labyrinth of corridors and up several flights of stairs to three sets of adjoining rooms.

'I have had hot water brought up already,' said Mrs Manderville upon opening the first of the doors, into which she indicated Uncle Ned should go. 'To speed things up.'

Sofia spent the whole time she was ripping off her coat and washing off the after-effects of a difficult and dusty journey remembering Snowball's frantic yelping and her ineffectual struggles against the arms of the burly young footman who'd borne her away, then imagining her poor little pet being ripped to shreds by a pack of ferocious animals trained to hunt down smaller creatures. And when she flung open the lid of her trunk, she discovered she had only one gown that she could wear without needing to iron it. Which was, of course, the one she liked least. A pale blue confection that had been Celia's and then altered to fit Sofia when her cousin had purchased all new bride clothes.

She had just scrambled into it and run a comb through her hair, when a knock on the door heralded the return of the housekeeper. Since she hadn't even had time to pour herself a cup of tea she was feeling harassed and upset, as well as out of breath even before the trek through about half a mile of bewildering corridors to a room that was full of people who all seemed to know each other and who all turned to stare when she and her aunt and uncle were announced.

Well, at least she now knew why the housekeeper

had called it the yellow drawing room. Just about everything in it was done up in shades of yellow. Curtains, wall hangings, pottery and even the tunics of the nymphs frolicking round the frieze up near the ceiling. She was just wondering which of the Duke's ancestors could have had such appalling taste, when he had looked her up and down with a sort of sneer and informed her she needed to change for dinner.

So many explanations and complaints had begun jostling for expression that they got tangled in her throat, rendering her completely speechless.

Which was probably just as well, or she'd have given Lady Sarah Whatever-her-name-was a piece of her mind.

Which all went to show that Aunt Agnes was right. The Duke was never going to choose her. She didn't have the style, the poise, or the manners befitting the rank. She'd already been feeling a bit like a cow who'd been fattened up for market, then failed to attract a buyer, after her outing with Jack, because both Uncle Ned and Aunt Agnes had assumed, when she'd returned still not the slightest bit betrothed to him, that it was all her fault. Which it had been, but only because she'd been *deliberately* trying to stave him off. They'd at first been baffled and then annoyed, then started talking the way they always did, about her, as though she wasn't there, in such terms that she'd almost burst into tears. Ironically, that had made them instantly more sympathetic, since they took it as a sign that she was as disappointed about his reluctance to name a date as they were.

They'd stopped badgering her and, she suspected, started badgering Jack instead. Fortunately, before they'd badgered him into coming back and attempting to make a proposal, they'd set off for Theakstone Court, to which property Jack thankfully had no access.

She let out a sigh of relief. Though the place was too big and even the staff too pompous for her tastes, the grounds in which it stood looked delightful. She'd glimpsed a lake on the way up the drive and woods rising up to the crest of the hill. So at least she'd be able to relax for the coming week with no danger of receiving any sort of proposal whatever.

And, since she was never going to measure up, no matter how hard she tried, there was no point in trying to impress the Duke.

While Sofia was contemplating a week of freedom from pressure, Aunt Agnes was attempting to converse with the Marchioness of Sale.

'I had no idea,' she was saying, 'that our husbands knew each other so well.'

'My husband,' said the Marchioness frostily, 'has perforce to mingle with all sorts of persons in the course of his duties.'

Though Aunt Agnes barely reacted, Sofia could tell the snub had found its mark. Far from backing off, however, Aunt Agnes gave the Marchioness a syrupy smile.

'Yes, indeed,' she said, running her eyes over the taller, bony woman from head to toe, 'there is no accounting for the behaviour, nor the tastes, of men in general.'

Before the battle could really get going, the Duke intervened.

'Miss Underwood,' he said, causing both matrons to snap their mouths shut and content themselves with glaring at each other, 'do your rooms meet with your approval?'

'My rooms?'

He drew her to one side.

'Or is it something else about Theakstone Court that you dislike?'

His voice was cold, with an edge to it that made her wonder if somehow she'd offended him.

'My rooms are lovely,' she said. 'As far as I can recall. I was hardly in them for five minutes before we had to come down here.'

'Oh?'

There went that eyebrow again, adding so much more expression to the one syllable he'd uttered.

'I'm sure,' she said soothingly, since he was clearly very proud of his ancestral home, 'there can be nothing about Theakstone Court to dislike.' As long as you didn't dislike yellow.

'And yet you cannot bring yourself to smile,' he said reprovingly.

Smile? Why should she smile? Oh, because he'd deigned to include her among guests that were so far above her that she ought to be down on her knees kissing his hand in gratitude, no doubt. First of all he'd made disparaging remarks about her attire and now he didn't like it because she wasn't grinning like a… like a…well, all the other young ladies in the room, now she came to think of it.

'Is there something, perchance, troubling you?'

His voice had changed. Now, instead of sounding annoyed, he sounded concerned.

Her aunt darted her a warning glance—as if it was necessary. There was no way she was about to refer to all that was going on with Jack. Though there was one worry she could confess.

'I am a bit concerned about Snowball,' she admitted. 'The housekeeper said she had to stay in the kennels, rather than with me.'

'You think she might pine away,' he said scathingly, 'if she cannot be with you every moment?'

'Well, Snowball is an indoor pet,' she retorted. 'She isn't used to being put in a kennel with a lot of other dogs. Especially not dogs that are bred to hunt smaller creatures and…and tear them to pieces.' She couldn't quite keep her lower lip from trembling at the thought, though she hastily caught it between her teeth. Completely out of her control was a hand which, unbidden, flew to rest lightly against his arm.

The Duke's brows drew down into a heavy scowl. He waved an imperious hand to summon a footman. But before the fellow had even reached them, the Duke appeared to change his mind, for he waved him away.

'I shall set your mind at rest,' he said. 'Personally.' And then, without a word of explanation to anyone, he simply started walking towards the door. When she tried to remove her hand from his sleeve, he prevented her from doing so by clamping his hand over it.

She darted a helpless look at her aunt, who was watching their departure wide-eyed. The Marchioness had a flinty look and her daughter a furious one.

*It wasn't my doing,* she wanted to tell them. *I didn't steal him from you all on purpose. I wouldn't! You are welcome to the arrogant so-and-so!*

But before she could even draw breath to begin a much-modified version of that apology, they were out in the corridor and the footman was closing the door behind them.

## Chapter Ten

He couldn't believe she'd done it again—made him act contrary to all his training, all his beliefs. Simply because she was worried about her dog.

All she'd had to do was look up at him, wide-eyed and troubled, to make him feel that he, and he alone, should relieve her of those troubles. So that he, and he alone, would receive her gratitude. With the result that he'd dismissed the footman and abandoned all his other guests.

'I cannot believe you are doing this,' she said rather breathlessly, so uncannily echoing his own thoughts that he stopped dead and whirled round to look at her.

She was several paces behind him, descending one of the stone staircases normally reserved for the use of staff. And she was out of breath.

'My apologies,' he said curtly, for she'd made him so annoyed with himself that he'd been striding along rather fast and had been in danger of leaving her behind. 'I shall slow down.'

He waited until she was on the step above him, putting their faces on a level.

'It isn't *that*,' she said crossly, fluttering a hand to

her mid-section. She was breathing hard. And she smelled of heated woman.

She'd surely slap him if he leaned forward and kissed those invitingly parted lips.

He took a step down, to put a more decorous distance between them.

It put him on a level with her heaving bosom.

'What is it, then?' he snapped, irritated beyond measure by the knowledge that this staircase was deserted and likely to remain so at this time of day. It meant that nobody was likely to catch him if he did yield to the temptation to kiss her. And yielding to temptation was something he would not do. It was the first step on a slippery slope that led...

'How like you not to notice,' she snapped back, cutting across the direction of his thoughts, 'that you have just made me the subject of gossip by hauling me out of the room in front of all those...' She pulled a face. 'Well, I am sure they are all perfectly respectable people, but they will now all be talking about me. About *us*.'

He winced as she scored a direct hit.

But it was her own fault. He'd laid careful plans about how he was going to conduct himself with each and every one of the young ladies who'd be staying at Theakstone Court this week. With rigid propriety. *She* was the one who'd blown his plans sky-high by...by...

By just being herself.

Which made him even more annoyed than ever.

'Whichever woman becomes my Duchess will have to grow accustomed to being the subject of gossip,' he said unfairly, rather than explaining his weakness where she was concerned.

'But I'm not going to be her,' she said with resentment.

'Is that so?'

'Of course it is so.'

'Why, then, did I invite you here?'

'Well, I… I supposed it was a fleeting whim on your part which you regretted almost at once.'

'What makes you say that?' He'd done nothing to give himself away. Had he?

'Well, that last drive… I could see I'd annoyed you by not being…and actually,' she said, descending a step so that they were face to face again, 'I am rather glad to have this opportunity of apologising to you for my mood that day. It was just—' She broke off, chewing on her lower lip, which only made him wonder how soft it was.

His heart beat doubled. His own lips tingled. He forced himself to recall what she'd just said. 'Yes? It was just…?'

'It was my aunt and uncle. Their reaction to the invitation you sent. They…'

'They pushed you into coming here? You really do not wish to marry me?' He got a swooping sensation in his stomach, as though the floor had dropped out from under him and he was plunging into some sort of chasm.

'Oh, no, nothing like that. I mean, I hadn't really thought about it. As I told you that day, I don't really know you well enough to…oh, dear. I'm not explaining this very well. I'm not used to it, you see.'

'Used to what?' Having dukes express an interest in marrying her?

'Explaining myself. I haven't been in the habit of telling anyone what I truly think about anything for so long that I—'

'Is your aunt so harsh with you?'

'Oh, no! Only…it is just that by the time I met her…
Perhaps I should explain that my father was a soldier
who, perhaps unwisely, kept me with him after my
mother died. Because when he died, too, I quickly
learned that small children are a great nuisance to an
army on the move. And although nobody was deliberately cruel, nevertheless, by the time I reached Nettleton
Manor I'd become so wary of grown-ups that, well, it
took me a long, long time to start trusting my own uncle
and aunt. And by then…' She shrugged her shoulders.
'It is different with Snowball. Somehow I can really
open my heart to her. I suppose,' she said, flinging up
her chin, 'you think that is silly.'

'No, not at all.' His own childhood had been a similar sort of desert. He, too, had lost everything, over-
night, and discovered that a child could not necessarily
trust adults to care for them well. And more to the
point, so had Livvy.

'At least you have the dog,' he said, wondering at the
feelings of…something, swirling around and through
them. Through them both, though how he knew that
he could not explain.

Nor did he want to. Feelings were not for examin-
ing and explaining. They were for suppressing and
controlling.

'Come,' he said, holding out his arm. 'Let me take
you down to the kennels, so that you can stop worrying about the welfare of your furry confidante. And
on the way, perhaps you would not mind finishing the
explanation you were going to give me about your behaviour when last we met.'

She placed her hand on his sleeve and they continued the descent of the servants' staircase side by side. But only after she'd shot him a rather resentful look.

'In what way,' he enquired politely, 'have I erred this time?'

'In insisting on a full apology, when I would have thought that a *decent* man would have let me off the hook.'

'But you piqued my curiosity,' he said, pushing open the door at the foot of the stairs, 'by hinting that your aunt and uncle had done something to make you unhappy with me.' They set out along the corridor that went past the kitchens, scattering startled serving maids right and left. 'And I do think you owe me an explanation, if you are taking advantage of my hospitality under false pretences.'

'What? Ooh, you are the most...' She flushed. 'You know full well,' she hissed between clenched teeth as they passed an open door, 'that either accepting or refusing the invitation was not up to me. At all!'

'Are you saying that your aunt has ambitions of seeing you become a duchess?' She wouldn't be the first matchmaking woman attempting to thrust a protégée under his nose. During this past Season, even his own stepmother had attempted something of the sort so that he'd marry a woman loyal to her, rather than him.

Sofia gave a bitter-sounding laugh. 'That is so wide of the mark it would be funny, if it wasn't so...' she sighed. 'The fact is, they are so sure I could never measure up to your high standards that they considered it perfectly safe to come here.'

'Safe? In what way?' The conversation was taking such unexpected twists and turns that he was beginning to feel as bewildered as the kitchen staff looked to see him strolling through their domain with a young lady on his arm.

'Oh, dear. I really ought not to say.'

They'd walked the entire length of the corridor that flanked the kitchens by now. He opened the door, tugged her outside and shut it firmly behind them. The courtyard was bustling with activity, but here, in the porch, nobody would be able to hear anything they said.

'Miss Underwood, you can confide in me, if it would help.'

She looked up at him with longing. He felt as if he was balancing on a knife-edge.

'I suppose,' she said, now looking a touch confused, 'I have already decided you are trustworthy, or I wouldn't have told you about my childhood.'

'I can assure you it will go no further.'

'It had better not,' she muttered. And then took a deep breath, as though preparing to take the plunge. 'The thing is, my aunt and uncle…that is, for a long time now, they have been steering me towards a match with…a person they have chosen.'

'An arranged match? Is that not rather unusual, these days?'

She looked across the courtyard to the wall of the kitchen garden and at once he saw that it was a far better spot for her to unburden herself. He hustled her across the courtyard, opened the door to the kitchen garden and urged her inside.

'Miss Underwood?'

She blinked up at him. 'I think it may be because they don't want my inheritance to pass out of the family. Although to start with I thought it was because they thought I actually wanted to marry—' She pulled herself up short before speaking the name of her intended. 'Only lately,' she said, looking at the butterflies flirting above the rows of cabbages, 'I have started to suspect that they have been deliberately preventing me from meeting anyone else.'

'Hence the lack of court presentation, or a Season in London?'

She nodded. 'They haven't let me out of their sight since the night of the fireworks, if you must know. Your invitation to drive out came as a great shock to them. As did the invitation to attend this…' she wrinkled her nose in distaste '…bride selection process, or whatever it is.'

'It is a chance to get to know you,' he retorted defensively, 'and several other eligible young ladies who have come to my notice, a little better, in less formal surroundings than London can offer.'

'So I suppose you will be taking them all for walks about the place without chaperons,' she said drily, indicating their own isolation.

'Absolutely not,' he said with a shudder, before striding to the gate at the far end of the kitchen gardens. Because any of the others would take advantage of the situation. Shamelessly.

As he opened the gate for her, it struck him that they trusted each other to about the same extent. She would no more compromise him into marriage than he would repeat the confidences she'd shared with him. But before he could point this out, she'd caught sight of the kennel buildings and set off in that direction, leaving him to follow in her wake. She was spurred on, no doubt, by the high-pitched bark of her little dog which even he could recognise above the deeper calls of his hunting hounds.

His kennel man, Barnes, was nowhere to be seen, but he knew his way round the set-up well enough to guess that he'd place Miss Underwood's dog in a pen by itself. Though even she could follow the sound of Snowball's persistent yapping to a small run at the far end, which she did, giving a little cry of joy when she saw her dog above the partition, and then running into the pen and dropping to her knees. Her dog launched herself at her mistress with enthusiasm. Miss Underwood laughed as the dog licked her face.

And he suddenly knew just what the peacock must feel like when the little brown peahen wandered off to peck at grain, in the dirt, rather than take any notice of his magnificent display. He could actually feel his tail feathers shrinking and drooping.

She cared nothing for his title, his lands, or his wealth. All she cared about was this little scrap of fur.

The one to whom she confided her troubles, her hopes, her ambitions.

Although, she had begun to confide in him, too, had she not?

'You know,' he said, strolling closer, determined not to be outshone by a dog, 'I would not have brought you here if I did not think you might be worthy of the title.'

She looked up at him over her shoulder, her lips pursed. 'I mean no disrespect,' she said in a highly disrespectful tone, 'but I'm already attempting to avoid marrying a man who thinks I should be grateful for the honour of being considered.'

Ah. He'd been flaunting his peacocky feathers at her again, instead of using his head.

But then, was it so surprising that he was a little awkward at trying to make a woman look at him for himself, rather than those showy feathers? He wasn't a handsome man. He had only to look in the mirror to assure himself of that fact. Nor a particularly pleasant one to judge from the way Lady Margaret had started flinching whenever he looked her way. Yet he'd had women falling over themselves to attract his notice ever since he'd been old enough to notice women. The other four girls he'd abandoned in the drawing room had probably half-fainted with excitement when they'd received the invitation to come here. He was sure any of them would do just about anything to become his Duchess, even, in the case of Lady Margaret, attempting to conceal the fact that he scared her.

But Miss Underwood, on the other hand…

'Just what exactly do you want from a husband, then, if not the rank and wealth that I have to offer?'

A dreamy look came to her face and then it vanished, as though she'd wiped it away with a handkerchief.

'Well, to start with, I would want a man I could trust.'

Well, she already trusted him, to some extent.

'Someone who would be completely honest with me.'

Honest, yes, he could give her honesty. Could she handle it, though, that was the question?

'Someone who would respect me. And who I could respect, too. But most of all, I…well, never mind.' She hunched her shoulder and turned back to her dog.

He recalled that dreamy look and saw that what she wanted most of all was something he was not prepared, nor equipped, to give.

'You want romance,' he sneered. *'Love.'*

'Well, what is wrong with that?'

'People of my rank do not marry for love. Or not if they have any sense. It always ends in disaster. Love leads men like me to make mésalliances with milkmaids, or actresses,' he said, thinking of Livvy's mother with a pang of regret. It had hurt him to break things off with her, but he'd had to put a halt to things when he'd begun to grow genuinely fond of her. For one thing, his father had still been alive and it had been imperative to stay strong and alert at all times. If he'd started to soften or grow too distracted by a woman... he grimaced as an image from his past seared into his memory. His father with those bloodstains on his shirt-sleeves; bending over him in his bed at night, seizing him by the collar of his nightshirt, asking him whose bastard he was, flinging him to the floor.

He passed a hand across his face, as though he could wipe away that memory, as well as the regrets he still harboured over the way he'd ended things with Ruby. Perhaps, if he hadn't been so abrupt with her...

Miss Underwood stood up, finally, and came to his side. 'Have I said something to upset you?'

'How could you?'

'I don't know. But you looked, for a moment...' She reached out one hand as though to offer comfort. Dammit, but he wanted to take it.

He took a step back. He did not need comfort. He had not needed anything, from anyone, since that nightmarish night his mother had died. He'd only escaped meeting the same fate as her, he was sure, because he'd taken refuge under his bed. And he'd been too small for his father to ferret him out, desperately though he'd tried. Eventually, thwarted of his prey, his father had sat down, placed his hands over his face and sobbed.

The proud aristocrat, fêted in society for being such a paragon of virtue, had sat on the bedroom floor, in his bloodstained shirtsleeves, sobbing like a child, while Oliver had cowered under his bed, praying for deliverance.

It had come the next morning, in the shape of an under-housemaid.

'Your poor mama met with an accident during the night,' she'd said, lifting up the edge of the trailing coverlet. 'Your poor father is prostrate with grief. Did he frighten you? Never mind, here's some bread and honey for your breakfast.' She'd put the plate on the floor, as though he were a dog, and had then set about opening cupboards and pulling out his clothes. 'He's decided the best thing for you is to go and stay with a nice family who will take care of you, until he's got over it.'

She'd made the family sound good. And the bread and honey had looked good. So he'd crawled out far enough to take hold of the food, since he was certain to starve if he stayed under the bed for ever. But he'd kept an eye on the door all the time, lest his father should take it into his head to storm back in again.

But the housemaid had been lying. The family she'd taken him to later that day had not been particularly nice. And during the next nine years, they'd lied to everyone else in that godforsaken little hamlet he'd had to call home, claiming he was the child of a distant member of their own family.

By the time he left, he'd found it safer to assume

that everyone lied as a matter of course. He'd trusted nobody.

And nothing that had happened to him since then had given him any reason to change his opinion. Especially not the way Ruby had, after all her protestations of love, concealed his own child from him.

So why was he suddenly taking everything Miss Underwood said at face value?

'Now that you have seen how unlikely it is that my hounds will eat your dog,' he said, 'perhaps you had better return to your room to change so that you are fit to be seen in Lady Sarah's rooms? Lady Sarah may be very kind, but some of the others would look at you askance if they saw you…' he looked pointedly down at the dirt in which she'd been kneeling '…looking so unkempt.'

She shot him a look that would have made a lesser man flinch, then bent down and made a futile attempt to brush the dirt from her gown. She glared at him when he held out his arm and, even when she took it, she walked all the way back to the house in stony silence.

Objective achieved. He'd resisted the temptation she represented. He'd restored her to a safe distance.

So why didn't he feel content?

## Chapter Eleven

Sofia wasn't all that surprised when the Duke snapped his fingers at the first footman they encountered when they reached the house and ordered him to escort her back to her room.

What on earth had she been about, revealing the size of her inheritance? It was the equivalent of flaunting her wares. It certainly hadn't been the muddy paw prints on her gown that had made him look at her with such disdain. He hadn't looked at her like that when she'd first knelt down, or when Snowball had been frisking about and covering her face with doggy kisses. She might as well have hung a placard round her neck proclaiming *Slightly tarnished heiress on offer.*

He'd never respect her now.

'Oh,' she groaned, leaning back against the door to her rooms the moment she was inside. And then kicking it with her heel. For, apart from anything else, she was going to have to change her gown *again.* And there was nothing in her trunk that she…

Hold on a minute. Where was her trunk? She'd left it standing at the foot of her bed when she'd gone down to that bilious drawing room, the lid open, and the contents exploding out of it in all directions. But she couldn't see it now, even though she could see her bed through the open bedroom door.

Puzzled, she pushed herself off the outer door to her rooms, crossed her sitting room and went into the bedchamber. She saw the trunk at once. It was standing on end in a small space between the wardrobe and the window. And inside the wardrobe, she discovered when she yanked open its door, were all her clothes, either hanging from pegs, or neatly folded on the shelves.

Well. That housekeeper might be a bit of a dragon, but she was definitely efficient. And it could only have been one of the Duke's staff who'd unpacked for her. The one maid they'd brought with them from Nettleton Manor, Marguerite, considered herself her aunt's personal maid and would never deign to unpack for Sofia, let alone help her to dress for dinner.

Still, at least it meant that Sofia was well able to wriggle out of her soiled gown and into the beautifully ironed topaz silk she normally wore for dinner, completely unaided.

All that she needed then was somebody to show her the way to Lady Sarah's rooms. And yet again, she discovered the Duke's household was run so efficiently that she'd scarcely rung the bell to summon one before an impeccably dressed and bewigged footman appeared at her door.

As she followed his stately progress through the house, she started to wish she had a more modish gown. Even the portraits on the walls looked more fashionably dressed than she was. And some of them were centuries old. Wearing hand-me-downs had never bothered her much before. But then, she'd never had to walk into a room full of titled girls who were all competing for the Duke's favour and who would therefore all no doubt be dressed to the nines.

Just as she was wondering if she could make some excuse for returning to her own room, the footman stopped, and knocked on a set of double doors.

A maid wearing an apron and starched cap opened it and ran a disdainful eye the length of Sofia's figure.

'Miss Underwood,' said the footman firmly. 'She is expected.'

The maid's haughty stare paused at the side of Sofia's face, which was a hotchpotch of purple and green, and gave a disdainful sniff, but she did stand back to let her in.

Sofia stepped into a sitting room that was at least twice the size of hers. And which had tall windows overlooking the front drive and the sweep of the immaculate green lawns flanking it. She realised several things in swift succession. Her own rooms, from what she'd glimpsed out of her windows while dashing past, overlooked the courtyard across which coaches rattled up to the house. And they were at least one floor higher up, not to mention at the far end of one of the wings, nowhere near the main part of the house.

The Duke had done the equivalent of sticking her in the attics.

While she was standing stock-still, taking in the magnificence of the rooms contrasted with what she now saw was the simplicity of her own, Lady Sarah came gliding across the velvety carpet, both hands outstretched as if in welcome.

'Dear Miss Underwood,' she cooed. 'We have all

been on tenterhooks, waiting for you to make your appearance.'

The comment made Sofia glance at the clock standing on the marble mantelshelf and noted that it was indeed several minutes behind the time she ought to have attended. And also that she could have stored her trunk and half her belongings in Lady Sarah's fireplace. Three other young ladies were already sitting on various chairs scattered throughout the room, staring at her with unabashed curiosity.

'But of course, you were with His Grace,' said Lady Sarah with a suggestive little smile. 'Naturally, you could not bear to tear yourself away.' She tittered, then added, 'Though I can see that you made all speed with your toilette to make up for it.'

Sofia's hand instinctively went to her hair to straighten it, before smoothing over her skirts. The maid had already made her feel self-conscious about her black eye. Though even if her skin had been unblemished, and she taken hours and hours over her toilette, she would never have measured up to all the lace and pearls and pedigree on display in this room.

'Now, dear Miss Underwood,' said Lady Sarah, linking her arm through Sofia's. 'I shall make you known to everyone. After all, that is why we are all gathered here, is it not?'

One of the other young ladies, who had silvery blond hair and a rather sharp nose, made a noise that expressed her disagreement in a way that Aunt Agnes would have described as extremely vulgar.

'You must take no notice of Lady Elizabeth's ill manners,' said Lady Sarah haughtily. 'The rest of us are very glad to make your acquaintance.'

'I have nothing against meeting this country miss,' said Lady Elizabeth, setting down her teacup with a snap. 'What I dislike is you using her as a pretext for gathering us all here.'

'Why,' said Lady Sarah, laying one hand upon her bosom in a rather theatrical manner, 'whatever are you implying?'

Lady Elizabeth got to her feet. 'Since you have not the wit to understand without me saying it plainly, it is this.' She advanced upon them with eyes flashing militantly. 'You have no right to act as though you are the hostess in this house.'

'I am doing no such thing!'

Sofia had managed to slide her hand out of Lady Sarah's grasp when she'd pressed her own to her bosom. And now she took a step to one side, for good measure.

'Yes, you are. Taking this poor girl up and making her believe you have her interests at heart...'

'But I do! Only think how uncomfortable it must be for her, knowing nobody in society, when we are all such good friends...'

'Friends? We may have attended the same functions during the Season and we may be on nodding terms. But by no stretch of the imagination would I ever describe us as *friends*.'

'Oh!' Lady Sarah recoiled, with a tragic little wail.

'Have no fear, I shall not stay to spoil your little party,' sneered Lady Elizabeth. She then turned to Sofia. 'Nothing against you. We may grow to like each other, we may not. But a word of warning. Do not be taken in by this...' she shot Lady Sarah a look of loathing '...person.'

So saying, she strode to the door, opened it herself and marched off.

'Oh,' cried Lady Sarah again, tottering to a sofa and sinking on to the cushions next to a girl of fragile mien. The fragile girl took her hand and patted it.

'There, there,' she said soothingly. 'Pay no heed to Lady Elizabeth. We all know what a good-natured, kind person you are. Don't we?' She turned rather protuberant, pale eyes to the other girl in the room. Who mumbled something that might have been assent through a mouth full of cake.

'I don't know what I can have done to incur Lady Elizabeth's enmity,' said Lady Sarah to the room at large. 'I just hoped that we could all embark upon this house party in a spirit of…fairness. I mean, it would be dreadful, positively dreadful, if we permitted our desire to win His Grace's favour to develop into the kind of rivalry that must surely give him a disgust of us all. Also, we must not forget, one of us is going to be a duchess, in due course, and will become a very, very powerful lady. It would not do to make of that person a bitter enemy.'

The other girls nodded and murmured that Lady Sarah was very wise.

But Sofia couldn't help wondering if they'd noticed that when she'd spoken of the future Duchess, Lady Sarah had made little gestures with her hands that hinted she believed she would be that person. Had they heard the subtle threat implicit in the warning not to incur the wrath of the future Duchess?

Or was Sofia just being fanciful?

But then why had Lady Elizabeth taken such umbrage if Lady Sarah were not playing some kind of game with them all?

Besides, Lady Sarah had already given Sofia a couple of set-downs, cunningly disguised under a mantle of kindness. So perhaps Lady Elizabeth was a bit more intelligent than these two girls. She certainly looked it.

'Oh, but I am forgetting my manners. Dear Miss Underwood,' said Lady Sarah, stretching out a pale, slender, pearl-braceleted arm in her direction. 'Please, do come near, so that I may make you known to my...' she smiled mistily in turn at the girls who remained '...dear, dear friends.'

Sofia saw no point in rocking Lady Sarah's boat. So she stepped forward and made her curtsy to the room in general.

'Now this,' said Lady Sarah, patting the hand of the girl with the pale, protuberant eyes, 'is Lady Margaret Pawson. Her father is the Earl of Trimley.'

'Pleased to make your acquaintance,' said Lady Margaret with a distinct lack of sincerity.

'I am Lady Beatrice,' said the other girl, striding up to her and shaking her hand in a rather mannish fashion. 'My father is an earl, too, but don't let that weigh with you. I don't think His Grace is going to choose his bride according to rank.'

'Whatever,' said Lady Sarah rather sharply, 'makes you think that?'

'Well, otherwise, why would he have invited a nobody,' said Lady Beatrice, rolling her head in Sofia's direction. 'No offence,' she added, to Sofia.

'I am sure that Miss Underwood,' said Lady Sarah, 'is not a nobody. His Grace would never wed a nobody. Just because *we* know nothing of her...'

'Oh, yes, you must tell us all about yourself,' put in Lady Margaret. 'We are positively dying of curiosity.'

'Yes, who are your people?' said Lady Sarah. 'My father clearly knew yours when they were up at Oxford, but that is neither here nor there. All sorts of people go there, Mama says.'

'Oh, that wasn't my father you saw earlier on,' said Sofia. 'That is my Uncle Ned. He married my father's sister and they took me in when Papa died.'

'So you are not the daughter of a mere viscount?'

Sofia refused to react to that provocation. Ladies, so Aunt Agnes was always telling her, never displayed emotion in public. They remained polite and calm at all times. And so, very politely, Sofia smiled at Lady Sarah.

'Oh, dear me, no,' she said. And then, for some reason that escaped her, instead of explaining that actually she was the granddaughter of an earl, found herself saying, 'My father had no title whatsoever. Except what the army gave him, which was Captain at the time of his death.' And then, to round it all off, added, slightly inaccurately, 'And my mother was the daughter of a Portuguese wine merchant.'

There was a collective gasp.

'Then…how do you come to know His Grace?'

'We met during a fireworks display at Burslem Bay,' she said, also slightly inaccurately. But then, since you couldn't slap someone you'd only just met, the only thing left for a lady to do was to shock them.

'Fireworks? How very unconventional,' said Lady Sarah, with a puzzled air. 'Most unlike His Grace.'

'Perhaps he wanted another female to make up the numbers,' said Lady Margaret, eyeing her up and down.

'That would account for it,' Sofia agreed cheerfully.

'I don't know,' put in Lady Beatrice with a frown. 'There's no accounting for what a man will look for in a wife. So Mama says.'

'Well,' said Lady Sarah, as if gathering her strength. 'You must have some tea. Your nerves must be positively shattered by the dreadful display of, well, I can only describe it as shrewishness, from Lady Elizabeth.' She waved a regal hand at the maid who'd been hovering in the background. 'Though one must make allowances, I suppose, since she has recently lost her father. Who left the entire family in an...' she raised one eyebrow '...embarrassing state.'

The maid, meanwhile, had gone to a sturdy sideboard upon which a teapot, cups, saucers and so on, were set and was pouring Sofia a cup.

Sofia went to a chair directly opposite the sofa occupied by the Ladies Sarah and Margaret, accepted her cup of tea and took a meditative sip. If Lady Sarah could call Lady Elizabeth a shrew behind her back and spread gossip about what sounded like financial difficulties, there was no telling what she might say about Sofia, either.

In spite of all her protestations, Lady Sarah had no intention of being anyone's friend. And only a fool would believe she ever could be.

'Shouldn't wonder,' suddenly blurted Lady Beatrice, who'd been staring intently at Sofia all the while, 'if His Grace has had one of those what-do-you-call-its? A *coup de foudre*. Because you are far prettier than the rest of us.'

'Only if you care for dark looks,' Lady Sarah objected. 'And a certain whiff of the prize ring.'

'Well, his last two fancy pieces were dark-haired,' the fragile-looking Lady Margaret pointed out, ignoring the jibe about Sofia's black eye. 'So he obviously does.'

Sofia's tea went down the wrong way and for several minutes she could do nothing but cough and wipe at her streaming eyes, while the other ladies fell into a twitter about Lady Beatrice's uncouth manners, which ended only when that lady, also, stormed out of the room.

'Oh, dear, and I did so want us all to be friends,' sighed Lady Sarah in the direction of the slammed door.

'Bea cannot help it, you know,' said Lady Margaret. 'She is always speaking before she thinks it through. And she's always sorry after. She will apologise once she's got over her chagrin about having said something so unladylike, you just see if she doesn't.'

Ironically though, Lady Margaret wasn't showing any symptoms of acknowledging she'd been just as unladylike in mentioning the Duke's preference for dark-haired paramours.

'Dear Meg,' said Lady Sarah, pityingly, 'always so ready to think the best of everyone.'

'And anyway, it isn't likely, is it,' Lady Margaret persisted, 'that someone as high in the instep as His Grace would make his choice out of any consideration but rank and fortune? Not when he is in such a hurry.'

'A hurry?' Lady Sarah's eyes narrowed. 'Whatever do you mean?'

'Oh, well…,' Lady Margaret's face flushed. 'I am not supposed to repeat this, only, Mama says it is on account of his stepmother's latest…' she lowered her voice '…indiscretion.'

'His stepmother? What,' said Lady Sarah, 'has she to do with it?'

'Well,' said Lady Margaret, leaning forward, her eyes gleaming with pleasure at being the bearer of some gossip Lady Sarah had not yet heard, 'you must know about that guardsman she took up with. The one who was young enough to be her son. And how she and His Grace came to cuffs over the affair.'

'Yes, yes, everyone knows *that*,' snapped Lady Sarah.

'Well, the latest on dit, according to Mama, is that he's determined to put a stop to her scandalising London on such a regular basis by forcing her to return to Theakstone Court. And that is why he's suddenly become so determined to find a bride this Season. It is his way of prising his stepmother out of his town house. Because when he takes a bride there, then naturally *she* will be the mistress of the house and his stepmother, and all the servants who have remained loyal to her, will *have* to decamp to the dower house.'

'Oh? Well, then I am truly grateful to her for being so scandalous,' said Lady Sarah with a cat-like smile.

No. It couldn't be true. He wouldn't just get married to spite and thwart his own stepmother. Would he?

Except…it did account for the way he'd assembled a clutch of candidates with the intention of making one of them an offer by the week's end.

Her heart plummeted. Once again she'd let a man pull the wool over her eyes. He'd made her think he was decent, forthright, and…and…

She set her teacup down on a convenient side table and got to her feet. 'Would you excuse me, Lady Sarah?

Only I have spilled some tea on my gown and will have to sponge it off if I have a hope of looking respectable by dinner time.'

'Oh, of course,' said Lady Sarah, oozing false sympathy. 'I completely understand. It must be perfectly horrid to have so few gowns that you need to clean one rather than simply changing into another.'

She made a little signal to the maid, who went to open the door. 'It was so lovely to meet you and have this little chat. I do hope you will come and take tea with me again some time.'

'Thank you so much,' Sofia replied with a polite smile, knowing full well that her hostess didn't mean a word of it. She'd discovered all she'd wanted to know and was now dismissing her. There would be no invitation to take tea again.

And even if there were, Sofia would turn it down flat.

## Chapter Twelve

Sofia opened her wardrobe door and frowned at the selection of gowns hanging there. Not one of them could hold a candle to anything she'd seen the other girls wearing. Except for her ball gown, but if she wore that tonight, what would she wear for the last night of the house party, for which she'd planned to keep it?

Her gaze snagged on the sombre bronze twill of her Sunday best. It had long sleeves and a modest, square neckline that would make her look a bit Quakerish if she wore it to dinner, but at least it was one of the few she'd chosen and had made up from new. So, she'd feel like herself.

And she would also, she hoped, send out the message that she was *not* going to compete for the Duke's hand. Because what kind of girl *would* fight for the right to join forces with a man who was getting married primarily to spite his stepmother?

The sober Sunday dress it was then. Setting her lips into a determined line, she pulled off the third soiled gown of the day and dragged on her fourth fresh one.

There. She regarded her reflection in the mirror

with a critical eye. So much for Lady Beatrice's fanciful notion that the Duke had taken one look at her and fallen wildly in love. Men did not fall in love with girls like her at first sight. She was too plain and dull and boring.

Although, she hadn't been behaving in a boring fashion when he'd first seen her, had she? Nor had she been exactly dull during their subsequent meetings. She studied the oval of her face, the curves of her figure beneath her gown, the sheen of her newly brushed hair...

And ground to a halt at the bruising round her eye.

Which prompted her to recall precisely how she'd escaped being dull when she'd been out with the Duke. She'd handed him her dog and more or less accused him of having hidden vices and finally suggested Snowball might meet with a ghastly fate in his kennels.

Which squashed the silly, hopeful flutter flat. It was far more likely that he had invited her along to make up the numbers, as Lady Margaret had suggested. There was probably some other damsel who should have come, who'd had to cry off at the last moment.

Or something of that nature.

And anyway, she didn't care what his motives for inviting her here might be. She had no ambition to become a duchess. And no intention of marrying any man who could use the institution of marriage to further such shabby ends.

So it was with a rather defiant smile on her lips that Sofia left her rooms.

Which petered out the moment she reached the door

to her aunt's suite and realised that she ought to knock and go down to dinner with her aunt and uncle, if he was about.

Only, if Aunt Agnes saw her in this gown she might insist Sofia went back to her room and get changed again. And then she'd have to reveal the fates that had befallen all the other gowns that were suitable for wearing in company.

Just as she was wondering how she could prevent Aunt Agnes from stifling her little rebellion before it had even got going, she spotted a large footman, loitering at the end of the corridor.

'Excuse me!' She waved to attract his attention, then scurried right up to him.

'Yes, Miss Underwood,' he said, surprising her by knowing who she was. 'How may I help you?'

It was the same young man who'd escorted her to Lady Sarah's rooms, she realised. And, now she came to think of it, from the kennels to her own rooms before that.

'I was hoping you could help me find my way to the dining room,' she said.

'You mean the Rubens room, miss. That is where everyone will be foregathering.' He stepped forward and pointed out a staircase, leading down from the corridor to their right. 'Go down one flight and you will find one of my colleagues, who will point you in the right direction from there.'

'Thank you,' she said with a smile. 'Just like a treasure hunt.'

He looked puzzled.

'You know,' she said. 'You get your first clue, which leads you to the location of the next, until finally you come to the place where the treasure is hidden. Or, in this case, my dinner.'

'I never thought of it like that before,' he said, his wooden features splitting into a grin. 'But what with this place being so big and in the past some people wandering off along the wrong corridors, His Grace was determined there was to be none of that, this week.' His cheeks turned red. 'That is…'

She giggled. And then, because he'd been the friendliest member of staff she'd come across in Theakstone Court, she asked him his name.

'My name?' He could not have looked more startled if she'd pulled out a pistol and asked him to hand over his valuables. 'Well, it's Peter. But I don't see why…' He pulled himself up, clearly remembering that it was his job to serve His Grace's guests, not question them.

Which reminded her she ought not to be standing here chatting, either, but making her way to the next hurdle she had to overcome.

Dinner.

'Good evening, Peter,' she said brightly and made her way to the next sentinel. She didn't embarrass any of the other footmen by stopping to chat with them and thus reached the large room where everyone was gathering for dinner in less than fifteen minutes. But then, none of them were so young, or so friendly. In fact, they'd grown ever more stately and more intimidating the closer she'd drawn to the immense salon in which all the other guests appeared to have already arrived. Peter, she deduced, as she stood in the doorway gazing in mild revulsion at the pictures of writhing limbs festooning all the walls, must be a very junior footman, to be standing sentinel on a corridor that housed such a lowly, insignificant set of guests as her family. It struck her even more forcibly how very out of place she was here, amidst a veritable sea of silks and satins and diamonds and feathers.

Though she need not have worried that her aunt would have forced her to change out of her deliberately drab dress. If Sofia had knocked dutifully on her door, Aunt Agnes wouldn't have answered. Because she was already here, hanging on Uncle Ned's arm. Uncle Ned, who was at the centre of a cluster of men who, to judge from their average age, just had to be the fathers of all the hopeful brides. And he *was* at the centre. Never mind the fact he was *a mere viscount*, he was keeping them all rapt with some anecdote, at the end of which every single one of them gave an appreciative chuckle.

The rest of the Duke's guests were ranged about the room in groups of two or three, apart from one young man who could only be described as posing by a window. He'd raised one arm and was leaning on it as he gazed out into the park, his long, fair curls tumbling over his forehead.

It was just as Sofia was smiling in amusement at the impression the rather beautiful young man was at such pains to create that Aunt Agnes spotted her—first the smile froze on her face and then she went rigid.

Finally she detached herself from Uncle Ned's arm and bore down upon Sofia with eyes flashing in a way that warned Sofia she was about to pay for her moment of rebellion.

Sofia braced herself.

'Where have you been? I looked for you when all the other young ladies came down from tea—'

'Not all of them, surely?' The Ladies Elizabeth and Beatrice had both left Lady Sarah's rooms before she had.

'That's beside the point,' said Aunt Agnes, a little taken aback by Sofia's uncharacteristic interruption. 'The point is,' she continued, firmly taking charge of the conversation once more, 'that gown. What on earth possessed you to change into that…monstrosity?'

'It's a very lovely gown…'

'For church! Only an imbecile would think it suitable for dinner in this sort of company…'

All of a sudden, out of nowhere it seemed, the Duke was there.

'I am sure,' he said to Aunt Agnes in a tone of mild reproof, 'Miss Underwood has a perfectly logical explanation for coming to dinner dressed as she is.'

Sofia sucked in a breath as she fought to decide which emotion was uppermost. On the one hand, she was grateful to him for coming so swiftly to her defence. On the other, he knew full well why she'd had to change her gown. At least on the first occasion. He'd practically ordered her to do it.

'The blue silk,' she said to her aunt, as calmly as she could, 'got muddy when I went to the kennels…' Aunt Agnes pursed her lips and shook her head.

'And then I spilled tea down the topaz which I changed into. This,' said Sofia, gesturing to her serviceable skirt, 'was the best I had left.'

Aunt Agnes was just taking a breath to say something Sofia was certain she wasn't going to like, when the Duke intervened.

'Does Miss Underwood not have a personal maid to see to her clothes?'

'Well, no,' said Aunt Agnes. 'But…'

He drew down his brows in such a way that her retort petered out. He didn't need to say, out loud, that if Sofia didn't have a maid of her own then it was surely down to her aunt to ensure she came down to dinner suitably attired, rather than berating her when it was too late to do anything about it.

Sofia promptly forgot she didn't like the way he was going about getting a wife, nor his motives for doing so, because it had been so sweet of him to stick up for her like that. Or at least, his eyebrows had done so.

Could you love a man's eyebrows even while disapproving of his character?

Not that his intervention would do Sofia much good in the long run. She rather suspected that from now on Aunt Agnes would be keeping an eagle eye on her, to make sure she didn't create a similar situation.

Which put paid to her rebellion, minor though it was.

'At least there was no chance of me getting lost,' she said, hoping to divert the conversation away from her gown and to stop Aunt Agnes and the Duke of Theakstone from standing there glaring at each other all night. 'You have so many footmen, posted at strategic locations, ready to point the way.'

His gaze swung round to her and softened. 'It is more efficient to do that than to allow my guests to think they will run my staff ragged by ringing for a personal escort. And also,' he said, with just the suggestion of a twinkle in his eyes, 'they can keep watch, to make sure nobody pilfers the valuables.'

'Has that ever happened?'

'Not recently,' he said solemnly.

Was that…his idea of making a jest? Well, when she grinned at him, he dipped his head in acknowledgement, so it must have been.

And then with a half-smile playing about his lips, he beckoned to a plump and bespectacled young man who had been watching the interplay keenly.

'Allow me to present your dinner partner for tonight, Miss Underwood,' he said.

There was no reason for her to feel such a piercing sense of disappointment. Of course she wouldn't be sitting next to him tonight. She was far too unimportant.

'Perceval,' the Duke explained, 'is my personal secretary.'

Well, of course he was. He was the only male in the room, unattached or otherwise, dressed plainly enough to match her, garbed as she was.

There was hardly time to curtsy to Perceval and say what was necessary before a man who could be nothing other than the butler flung open a set of double doors at the far end of the room and announced that dinner was served.

Since this was a ducal household, everyone waited for him to lead the way, which he did, but only after offering his arm to Lady Sarah. It shouldn't have made her grind her teeth, but it was just that as everyone else followed in strict order of precedence it meant that Sofia and Mr Perceval brought up the rear. And because they were last in line, they were probably the only ones to detect the rather triumphant smile Lady Sarah flashed in the direction of Lady Elizabeth as the Duke sat her at the head of the table, next to him.

'Do not be disheartened,' said Mr Perceval as he seated Sofia.

Sofia started and looked up at him in alarm. What had she done to give herself away?

'His Grace,' continued Mr Perceval smoothly, 'will be selecting a different young lady to be his dining companion each night.'

'In order of precedence?'

'Naturally,' he said, taking his seat beside her. 'It has come to my attention,' he said as he took his napkin and folded it across his lap, 'that for various reasons you have not been made known to everyone here. So, during the course of this meal, I am at your disposal to answer any questions you may have about His Grace's other guests.'

'Thank you,' she said. And then thought about the tone of his voice. And the wording he'd just used, which had been, she suspected, deliberately vague about whether he was acting under his own initiative, or under the Duke's orders.

Not that it mattered. Whoever had thought of it, she was grateful.

'I met all the young ladies at tea in Lady Sarah's rooms,' she said, 'but I don't know anything about anyone else at this table, apart from my own aunt and uncle.'

'And His Grace, of course.'

She supposed a man had to be a bit, well, pedantic, to rise to the position of personal secretary to a duke. So, keeping her polite smile in place, she simply said, 'That still leaves an awful lot of people for you to tell me about.'

'Not really,' he said repressively. 'This is rather an intimate gathering, in comparison with what we are used to at Theakstone Court.'

Intimate? She looked at the twenty or so people sitting round a table on which you could have held a ball, if it wasn't for the profusion of epergnes spilling flowers and fruit and such, creating obstacles at regular intervals.

'Really?'

'Oh, yes. Apart from the parents, or in your case, the guardians, of His Grace's potential brides, there are only a handful of single gentlemen, carefully selected from His Grace's friends and neighbours, to act as escorts to the young ladies when His Grace is otherwise engaged.'

'Otherwise engaged...?'

'His Grace is a very busy man. He cannot possibly dance attendance on young females,' he said with a hint of a sneer, 'all day long.'

'Absolutely not.'

From that point on, she found she had to do very little besides agree with whatever Mr Perceval said, every now and again. He was very, very fond of the sound of his own voice. However, since he was explaining who everyone was, and in what relation they stood to His Grace, she didn't see the point in trying to stop him.

So, while she consumed the most sumptuous meal she'd ever eaten, she learned that Lady Elizabeth's father had also been a marquess, but that the title and estates had all gone to a distant cousin, since he'd had no sons. Which must have been horrid for Lady Elizabeth and her mother. It was hardly surprising she was a bit touchy, particularly since it looked to her as if Lady Sarah was taking every opportunity to goad her into losing her temper.

The man who'd accompanied Lady Elizabeth's mother in to dine was actually His Grace's personal physician, Mr Perceval explained. He also informed her that the Ladies Margaret and Beatrice had earls for fathers; that the young man with the fair curls, who'd been posing by the window, was a viscount, as well as being a poet. Which explained a lot.

Another young man she hadn't noticed earlier, who was now sitting virtually opposite her, had such a thick, black moustache that it looked as though a small animal was perched on his upper lip. He was a captain in the guards.

And finally, the rather intense and very quiet young man seated on her other side was a most promising student of the sciences, a plain Mr Septimus Brown.

She did wonder why the young man who'd been with His Grace—as she was now starting to think of him, *in capitals*—at the fireworks was not here to-night, but swiftly thought better of asking. Although Mr Perceval had said she could ask any questions she liked, she could tell that he much preferred doling out information in his own way. He was probably married already, she guessed, trailing her spoon through a frothy syllabub and wondering if she could risk eating any more.

The answer was taken out of her hands when Lady Sarah's mother got to her feet.

'Ladies,' she said. Regally. Which was the signal for all the ladies present to withdraw and leave the men to their port, whether they wanted any more syllabub or not.

From the look Lady Elizabeth shot at Lady Sarah's back as she linked arms with her mother and preceded everyone from the room, it was a good job the dinner knives hadn't been sharpened.

Or there would be one less contender for the position of Duchess of Theakstone.

# Chapter Thirteen

Since all the other girls were pairing up with their mothers, Sofia made for her aunt's side. They walked, in strained silence, at the end of the trail of ladies heading for the drawing room.

By the time they arrived, Lady Sarah was already standing by the pianoforte, shuffling through the sheets of music. Lady Margaret joined her and they put their heads together. The other girls and their respective mothers were selecting sofas upon which to sit. And there were plenty of them, dotted about one of the smallest, and least overpowering, rooms Sofia had seen so far.

Aunt Agnes had chosen a sofa which had a view over a terrace leading to some formal gardens, which also happened to be the furthest away from Lady Sale. They had just sat down when Lady Margaret came over.

'Lady Sarah says that we ought all to take a turn tonight, showing His Grace what we can do,' she said, gesturing towards the piano. 'And that in the interests of fairness, we should help each other show to the best advantage. So, would you prefer to sing or play?'

'Oh…er…'

'Sofia sings far better than she plays,' said Aunt Agnes before she had a chance to say something more truthful. 'Perhaps, if someone were to play for her…'

'She should definitely perform with Lady Bea, then,' said Lady Margaret, smiling in a way that made Sofia feel rather wary. 'She would be the first to admit that she has a voice like a bullfrog.' She tittered and then went over to the sofa upon which Lady Beatrice was sitting, to inform that damsel, in a rather carrying voice for one so wispy-looking, that she would not have to sing tonight, since Miss Underwood apparently had a voice like a veritable angel, but lacked the skill to accompany herself.

'What a cat,' muttered Aunt Agnes as Lady Beatrice's shoulders slumped.

Lady Elizabeth picked up her fan and began to wave it before her face rather swiftly, shooting dagger glances between Lady Sarah and Lady Margaret. But neither lady was foolish enough to attempt to tell her what, or with whom, *she* ought to perform that evening.

Lady Beatrice's mother dug an elbow into her side and flicked her fan in Sofia's direction. The girl heaved herself to her feet and crossed the expanse of carpet to Sofia's side.

'I hear you need me to play for you,' she said gloomily.

'You don't have to if you don't wish to,' said Sofia.

Lady Beatrice shrugged. 'Might as well. At least then nobody will expect me to sing. Come on, let's go and look at what music there is.'

After receiving a nod of permission from Aunt

Agnes, Sofia followed Lady Beatrice to the piano, where Lady Sarah was still standing.

'I have found just the thing for you two,' she said, holding out some sheet music. 'A lovely little ballad, which I am sure even you will be able to cope with.' She gave Lady Beatrice a patronising smile and handed it over. 'I am only sorry that I do not know your range, Miss Underwood. I *do* hope you do not find this too taxing,' she finished on a syrupy smile, before sitting down on the piano stool into which she'd thrust all the remaining sheet music and beginning to caress the keys.

Sofia was beginning to see exactly what Lady Elizabeth meant about her queening it over everyone else. She found herself wishing she could somehow flout her.

She glanced over Lady Beatrice's shoulder at the music. 'Where the Bee Sucks'… Oh, dear. How on earth was she going to manage the tricky arpeggio section? She would need a ladder to reach the upper end of it.

'I suppose,' Lady Beatrice said miserably, 'it could have been worse.'

'At least it suits my taste,' Sofia said, trying to find something pleasant to say, rather than giving in to the urge to say what she really thought about Lady Sarah's domineering ways and Lady Margaret's spite, since that would be sinking to their level. 'In that I'd much rather be outside on a bank amidst the cowslips than in a drawing room singing about it.'

Lady Beatrice started and raised her brows. 'Me, too,' she said. 'On horseback, that is.' She lowered her voice. 'I know that Lady Sarah thinks she's helping us…awkward ones, in the drawing room, but truly, I am not going to show to advantage anywhere but on horseback. Do you ride?'

'I used to have a pony,' Sofia said wistfully, recalling the lively little beast on which she'd gone everywhere when her papa had been alive. 'But when I…' she'd been about to say, *When I went to live with my uncle and aunt*, only she didn't know Lady Beatrice well enough to know if it would be safe to confide in her. And so she altered it to, 'When I got older, there never seemed to be a suitable mount for me.'

'That's a shame. I wish I'd brought more than just my Forked Lightning with me. I have a lovely old mare…well, she used to be lovely, she's a bit worn down now, but just the sort of thing for an inexperienced rider, like you. Only, Papa said I wasn't to fill His Grace's stables up with my cattle. Not the thing.'

'No, quite.'

She then went on to describe the various rides she hoped to take while she was staying at Theakstone Court, because there were some lovely gallops, she'd heard, once you got away from the formal bit of parkland. Sofia was sure that Lady Beatrice could have gone on talking about her horses indefinitely had she not been interrupted mid-flow by the arrival of the gentlemen. They gathered in a knot at the door, respectfully lowering their voices so as not to detract from the rather lovely lilting air Lady Sarah was currently playing.

When she finished the tune and the gentlemen broke into a round of polite applause, Lady Sarah lifted her head. 'Oh, the gentlemen are here,' she said with apparent surprise. As though she'd been lost in the music.

'Now, dear Lady Margaret, you must take your turn,' she said, ceding the piano graciously, 'so that His Grace may see what a talented performer you are.'

And then, instead of returning to her mother's sofa, the brazen creature went straight across to the Duke, placed her hand on his arm, and said something in a voice too low for anyone else to catch, since the married men were now making their way to the seats on which their wives were sitting and the single ones were sort of fanning out, leaving him alone by the door.

But whatever she'd said hadn't pleased him. For his scowl darkened to positively thunderous proportions.

Which was a *terrible* shame.

'I do hope you enjoy the programme tonight.' Lady Sarah simpered up at Oliver. 'Not that we have had much time to prepare, but I did just make sure that all of us have something to contribute.'

It was a fortunate thing that his expression, according to those who were close enough to him to speak frankly, so very often resolved into a scowl, since he rather thought he must be scowling at this very minute. Only this time it was with genuine annoyance.

For one thing, what kind of girl approached her host, a man she knew was casting his eye over her with a view to making her an offer, rather than returning, modestly, to her own mother's side? What kind of girl puffed herself up by claiming she had organised his other guests into some kind of order, come to that?

A girl who wanted the title and didn't care what she had to do to get it, he answered himself. But then, he'd known Lady Sarah was ambitious before he'd invited her here. So he had no business criticising her for running true to form.

'Thank you,' he therefore managed to bite out. And then, because he could not let her think she could manipulate him so easily as she had done the young ladies in this room, he added, 'And now, perhaps we should stay quiet, so that we might better appreciate Lady Margaret's performance.' It was as near as he could come to telling her to hold her tongue, without appearing rude.

The trouble was, once he'd decreed they should pay attention to Lady Margaret's rendition of a ballad about a shepherdess mourning her lost love, he could not very well escort her to her mother's sofa, with the result that she remained standing at his side throughout the entire dismal dirge.

When it ended, everyone else burst into spontaneous applause. One or two of the gentlemen were even dabbing at their eyes with their handkerchiefs.

'Dear Lady Margaret is so talented, is she not?' Lady Sarah cooed. 'So talented, she could perform on a stage.'

Well, well. Even though, on the surface, Lady Sarah had been paying Lady Margaret a compliment, in hinting that she could turn professional she was bringing to his attention the fact that her performance had been a touch…

And it wasn't the first time he'd heard her bring another female down under the guise of pretending to be kind. She'd made Sofia damned uncomfortable the moment she'd set foot in his home by drawing attention to the fact that she didn't know anyone, had never been presented in society and was clearly out of her depth.

He'd invited her here because in London she'd always seemed so capable that he'd been sure she would easily cope with his demanding schedule. And take the management of his daughter in her stride.

But he couldn't expose Livvy to this sort of management. While pretending to be kind to his daughter, she might well inject similarly subtle barbs into her speech.

'Indeed,' said Oliver. 'Lady Margaret, do, please, play for us again. If the other young ladies do not mind?' He looked round the room at the other bridal hopefuls. And for some reason his gaze snagged on Sofia, who was standing next to Lady Beatrice.

'No, absolutely not, Your Grace,' said Lady Beatrice on behalf of them both. 'For my part, I could listen to Lady Margaret play all night.'

Lady Beatrice was a nice girl. He'd always thought so. It was just a pity she was so lacking in social graces. And that, given the chance, she'd spend her whole life on horseback. She didn't seem all that bright either and, though that would definitely prove a stumbling block to her ever becoming a duchess of whom he could be proud, at least she didn't have the brains to carry out the kind of subtle warfare in which Lady Sarah was currently engaged. Anyway, he wasn't taking the plunge into matrimonial waters primarily to get himself a duchess. First and foremost he was seeking a mother for Livvy.

'Oh, no, no, that will not do,' put in Lady Sarah, just as he was taking a breath to express his own opinion about having Lady Margaret play all evening. Which sealed her fate. She might think she was demonstrating how capable she would be as his hostess, but how could she possibly think he'd tolerate a woman speaking for him?

'We must all,' continued Lady Sarah, oblivious to the fact she'd just disqualified herself on several counts, 'do our part, you know.'

'Indeed,' he said again, placing his hand over hers, so that he could urge her into motion. 'Allow me to return you to your seat, so that you may listen to Lady Margaret perform her next item, in comfort.'

Having got rid of her, he took up a station by the fireplace. Which was as far from her sofa as he could justifiably go during the time it took Lady Margaret to rearrange the music upon the stand.

The second ballad Lady Margaret inflicted upon his guests was just as dismal as the first and infinitely more irritating. The way she was attempting to pluck at everyone's heartstrings convinced him he'd made the right choice in discounting her. For not only would she find him a deuced uncomfortable husband, he really didn't think he could stomach having to admit, in public, that she was the woman he'd chosen to marry.

Which left him a choice of three. Upon whom he could concentrate his attention over the rest of the week.

'Lady Elizabeth,' he said, once the polite applause for Lady Margaret's efforts had dribbled to a halt. 'Would you care to play for us this evening?'

'With pleasure, Your Grace,' she said, eyes flashing with some emotion he could not identify—though it became clear when she stalked to the piano in the manner of a tiger lashing its tail. And then proceeded to give a rollicking and rather risqué performance of a song about Irishmen, which was on the verge of being unfit for polite society.

It certainly cut through the rather maudlin atmosphere that Lady Margaret had left hanging over the room. Like mustard, she brought some tartness to a bland event.

Most of his male guests certainly found it highly amusing, though her mother looked about ready to sink through the floor. Lady Elizabeth was clearly a bit of a handful. She certainly had a temper but he could hardly blame her for reacting to the way Lady Sarah had been attempting to dominate the evening, given that she was equally well born though not, nowadays, as wealthy. Besides, it was the spirited way she'd weathered the scandal surrounding her father's death that had made him consider her. She was strong enough to hold her head high in public no matter what gossips said of her, or her family. *She* wouldn't care what anyone said about him insisting that she raise his illegitimate daughter as her own. She would defy them all...providing, of course, that she believed she was doing the right thing. That was what he needed to learn about her this week. Would she be willing to support him in the somewhat unusual stand he was taking over his daughter?

As he was mulling over Lady Elizabeth's potential, a pale-faced Lady Beatrice took a seat on the piano stool. Miss Underwood went to stand at her shoulder.

Lady Beatrice flexed her fingers and looked at the music as though it was a dose of bitter medicine.

Miss Underwood glanced at Lady Beatrice's hands, which appeared to be shaking, and then turned to the audience, with a rueful smile.

'We have only one piece for you tonight,' she said, brightly. 'Since neither of us can hope to match the lovely playing you have already heard, we beg your clemency for our joint, humble contribution to this evening's programme.'

Lady Beatrice took a deep breath, then attacked the piano with far more determination than skill. She picked her way slowly through the more complicated sections of the introduction, then sped up again when she'd got through them. How on earth was Miss Underwood going to be able to sing alongside that?

From the look on her face, she was thinking exactly the same thing. The lyrics did come out rather haltingly at first, as she attempted to keep to the same pace as Lady Beatrice was setting. But after a truly agonising arpeggio she began to relax into the performance. In fact, she looked as though she was enjoying herself. As though…yes, by heaven, the minx was trying not to burst out laughing. And actually, the next time they reached the arpeggio, she did make it sound just like musical laughter.

When they'd finished, while the audience was applauding in a way which implied relief that the assault upon their ears had finished, she bent down and whispered something into her accompanist's ear that removed the anguished expression from the poor girl's face.

He had no idea what she could have said to bring such instant comfort to a girl who'd just been humiliated through the medium of music, but whatever it was, it had been kind. Genuinely kind, restoring the poor, gauche girl's confidence. And kindness was a rare quality to find in a woman. Most girls, put in a similar position, would have been furious, might even have lashed out at the way Lady Beatrice's inept playing had made her look slightly ridiculous.

Miss Underwood was a gem.

He wanted to take her pretty face between his hands and kiss her. In front of everyone. So much that he made himself turn away and stalk instead to the sofa upon which Lady Beatrice had just collapsed in an untidy heap.

'Lady Beatrice,' he said. 'I believe you have brought your favourite mount with you, with a view to exploring my estates, while you are here.'

'Oh—ah, yes, Your Grace, I have...' she said, straightening up guiltily.

'Then tomorrow morning, I would count it an honour if you would permit me to accompany you on your ride.' Away from a drawing room, she would feel more relaxed and he'd be able to see her as she could be, to find out whether he might be able to grow used to her ways. 'I believe you are in the habit of going out early?'

'Well, yes, I am, but...' Her mother, Lady Comerford, dug her elbow into her ribs.

'What she means, Your Grace, is that she would be delighted to have your company.'

'And that of Captain Beamish, of course,' he put in smoothly, lest her mother suspect he was going to do something as foolish as take the girl out of sight of the Court unchaperoned.

'And her groom,' said Lady Comerford tartly, informing him that she was not the kind of woman who was so ambitious to see her daughter married to a duke that she'd sink to those kinds of depths.

'Good,' he said, with genuine approval. And felt

that this was a mother-in-law with whom he might be able to get along as well, if he actually did offer for her daughter's hand. 'I shall look forward to it.'

Lady Beatrice flushed with pleasure, as though he'd just paid her an extravagant compliment.

And Miss Underwood, he noticed with surprise, was smiling at him as though he'd just done something of which she heartily approved.

Which ought not to matter.

Only somehow, it did.

## Chapter Fourteen

Well, they'd muddled through fairly well, all things considered, Sofia decided. Lady Beatrice had played almost all the right notes, if not at a steady tempo. And she'd managed to weave the words into more or less the correct bits of tune. It was only during the arpeggio sections that they'd parted company altogether, which had given her an almost irresistible urge to giggle.

It had been the set of Lady Beatrice's shoulders that had stopped her. The poor girl was clearly mortified, or bracing herself for some sort of rebuke. So that by the time they reached the end, which they somehow did at virtually the same time, all Sofia could think of was consoling her poor pianist.

'I am sorry that I didn't keep time very well,' she said. 'I am not used to performing in public, let alone with so many exalted people watching me, most of whom would love to see me trip up.'

'Oh, yes, it's perfectly frightful, isn't it? Performing in public when you have so little skill. I mean,' she added hastily, 'me, not you. You have a lovely voice.

I'm,' she said, looking down at her hands, which she snatched back from the piano, 'all thumbs.'

'Well, at least after this they will think twice before asking either of us to perform again. We can rest easy.'

'Yes, there is that,' said Lady Beatrice thoughtfully. 'Or we can say that we wish to leave the ones who shine in this sort of setting to dazzle him... I mean... er...everyone.'

'Yes, and we can shine in our own sphere.'

Lady Beatrice brightened considerably. She brightened even further when the Duke asked her, in front of everyone, to go riding with him the next morning.

And Sofia was pleased for her. She really was.

But that was the last bright spot in the evening. So she was really, really glad when the arrival of the tea tray meant she could legitimately ask Aunt Agnes if she might retire for the night.

'Of course,' said Aunt Agnes. 'You aren't used to sitting up playing cards until all hours, are you? Not in your state of health.'

She'd then startled Sofia by patting her cheek, before trotting over to the card tables where Uncle Ned was loudly proclaiming he didn't want anyone but his wife to partner him at whist.

It didn't take Sofia long to undress and get into bed. Getting to sleep was another matter. For one thing, she missed Snowball, who usually slept across the foot of her bed. For another, she'd had such an eventful day that she could not still her mind. Her thoughts kept dashing hither and thither. From the ridiculous amount of times she'd had to change her clothes, to the appallingly sly behaviour of the ladies which reminded her so much of Jack's sisters; which led her naturally enough to Jack himself, or rather, what she was going to do with her life now she wasn't going to become his wife.

She'd finally started to drift off when she heard her aunt and uncle return to their rooms. At least, she could hear Aunt Agnes giggling, all the way along the corridor. Even after they shut their bedroom doors, she could still hear her positively shrieking with laughter at something Uncle Ned was saying...if it was what he was *saying* that was making her laugh so.

She had to turn over and put her head under the pillow and, after that, it took her ages to settle again. And then she jerked awake to the sound of somebody pacing back and forth, right above her head. She could only assume one of the servants had the toothache or something. And though she was very sorry for whoever it was, pacing back and forth in the dead of night, she also heartily wished she had a broom handy so she could bang it on the ceiling.

By the time it began to grow light, Sofia felt as if she hadn't slept a wink all night. Still, as she threw off her bedclothes, she reminded herself that not long after she'd gone to live at Nettleton Manor she'd found that early morning was the best time to get outside for a walk. If she ever felt like crying, first thing in the morning was the one time she could do it without anyone seeing her and thinking she was ungrateful even though they'd given her a roof over her head. Also, once she was outside she could claim—since she didn't have a watch—that she'd lost track of time, thereby managing to stay away from her aunt and uncle and, most importantly, all her sleek, complacent cousins, for most of the day if the weather was clement.

And today, she decided after taking a look out of her bedroom window, was going to be perfectly glorious. She could only see a few tiny clouds of the purest white drifting lazily across the sky.

She washed and dressed swiftly, in her most comfortable, and therefore in her aunt's eyes, most disreputable, walking dress—although she did not really think her aunt would be out of bed early enough to come in and try to prevent her going down to the kennels and collecting Snowball. Not after the amount of wine it sounded as though she'd consumed the night before, from all that giggling. But Sofia wasn't taking any chances. Pausing only to snatch up a chip straw bonnet, which was perfectly serviceable when walking a dog, she slipped out of her room.

She wasn't entirely sure she could remember the exact way down to the door by which she'd come in from the kennels, but she could certainly keep heading in that general direction by going down every staircase she encountered and stopping every so often to peer out of one of the windows to make sure she hadn't accidentally turned around.

Eventually, she reached corridors which were flagged with stone, rather than being carpeted and heard the sound of pots and pans clattering up ahead.

She paused at a gallery of windows on one side of the narrow corridor which looked not to the outside, but into the busy kitchens, wondering if she dared nip in and snatch up a heel of a loaf to take out with her. That would mean she need not come back in for some time.

But then, if she didn't put in an appearance at breakfast, and decently attired to boot, Aunt Agnes might start keeping such a close eye on her she'd never have the chance to nip out like this again. It was better, she decided, to snatch an hour or two of freedom, then behave for the rest of the day with perfect propriety. It was, after all, the tactic she'd adopted soon after going to live with her aunt and uncle, so that they'd come to believe she was meek and biddable.

*Dull.*

She trudged across the courtyard, head down, hating the need to behave in a way that was foreign to her nature. She'd only started doing so because Aunt Agnes had kept on telling her she was in England now and had to behave accordingly, had to put the past—which she'd often said with a shudder—behind her. Then, when her cousins had begun teasing and mocking her, she'd become convinced she wasn't good enough just as she was.

She yanked open the door to the walled kitchen garden. She hadn't been good enough for Jack even though she had worked so hard to prove she was naturally meek and biddable.

Oh, if only she was old enough to come into her own money, so she could live exactly as she pleased!

Until then…

A frenzied yapping broke into her train of thought. Snowball had obviously caught wind of her. She hastened her steps, crossing the kitchen garden in no time at all and emerging into the area that led to the kennels.

By this time, all the other hounds had started baying as well so that, as she reached Snowball's enclosure, the din was deafening.

She dropped to her knees, relishing the way Snowball smothered her face with doggy kisses.

'Come on, Snowball,' she said, getting to her feet. 'Time to take our walk.'

Snowball understood her perfectly to judge from the way she spun round and round, her whole body wagging along with her tail.

Sofia had not really formed any idea of which direction she wanted to walk, but fortunately Snowball knew exactly where *she* wanted to go. Nose down, she headed straight for a stand of trees that stood at the crest of a nearby rise. She'd probably been snuffing up scents coming from that direction all night.

How simple life was for a dog. Smell something interesting and run off in pursuit of it.

She shook her head, smiling ruefully at herself. Fancy being envious of a dog!

She could perhaps learn something from Snowball's attitude. She could stop wishing things were different and start enjoying what she had: the stillness of the early morning; the freedom of being outside without anyone to make her do anything she didn't want; breathing the dew-scented grass and the more vigorous scent of the trees when she drew closer; listening to the sound of birdsong; Snowball yapping furiously as though she'd run some hapless creature to ground. And...a child's laughter?

Surely not. It was far too early for children to be out here, so far from any houses.

She hurried deeper into the woods, following the sound of Snowball's barking, and found her bouncing on the spot at the foot of a very gnarled old oak tree. She was trying and repeatedly failing to reach a pair of legs which were dangling from one of the lower branches. The sight of her dog twisting and turning when she jumped up and down like that had always made Sofia want to laugh and was clearly amusing the child who had climbed the oak tree, too.

'Good morning,' said Sofia, drawing near. 'I hope my dog didn't scare you up that tree?' It wasn't likely, since she'd heard the child laughing, but it was as well to make sure. 'She just wants to play, you know. It is perfectly safe for you to come down. She won't bite.' And then, to show the child how well trained Snowball was, she said in a firm voice, 'Down, Snowball', making the appropriate hand signal at the same time.

Snowball dropped to the ground, her front paws stretched out ahead, though she never took her eyes from the child's legs. A little girl's legs, Sofia now noted, from the froth of skirts about the knees.

'I ain't afraid of no dog,' said a scornful voice.

'Oh, you were already up the tree, were you?'

There was a pause. 'No...' said the girl, as though reluctant to tell an untruth.

'Then there is no reason not to come down, if you'd like to play with my dog. I'm sure she'd love to play with you.'

There was another pause. 'I'd better not. I'm not supposed to bother fine ladies like you.'

Sofia supposed this must be the daughter of one of the estate workers, then, given the run of the grounds on the condition that she kept out of the way of any of the Duke's titled guests.

'I'm no fine lady,' said Sofia, suddenly glad of her black eye. 'Do fine ladies go outside with bruising like this on their faces? And you certainly wouldn't be bothering me if you came down from your tree. After all, I invited you to come and play with my dog, didn't I?'

'That won't make no odds,' said the resentful little voice. 'She'd still say as if it was my fault, if she catches me.'

'Who would?'

'Mrs Starchypants. My governess.'

'You have a governess?' Then she couldn't be the daughter of a servant. 'My, then you must be a fine young lady yourself.'

'Well, I ain't! I'm the Duke's Disgrace, that's what I am,' said the little girl, finally leaning down to glare at Sofia from the screen of leaves behind which she'd been concealing the upper half of her body.

Sofia almost gasped, for the little face that was glaring down at her had the same ferocious brows, the same beak of a nose and the same snapping dark eyes as the Duke. She could not be anything but his daughter. But he wasn't married, which meant...

Her stomach lurched. How cruel of someone to tell such a little girl that she was the Duke's Disgrace! If there was any disgrace, it was in making a child feel guilty of the sins her parents had committed. As she knew only too well. For hadn't she hidden out in the woods whenever she'd needed to escape? So that she could weep where there was nobody to see? And this child had been weeping. There were clean tracks down each grubby cheek to prove it.

Oh, but she would love to give the Duke a piece of her mind. How could he make his own child feel she had to climb up a tree to avoid being seen by his 'fine' guests? And that had to have been what he'd done, for just as she heard the sound of approaching hoofbeats the little girl gave a scared little sob, reared back and tucked up her feet so that she was completely hidden from the ground.

Her actions made Sofia so angry that when she whirled round to face the party of riders approaching along the bridle path, she actually clenched her fists.

## Chapter Fifteen

Just as Oliver had suspected, the moment Lady Beatrice set foot in his stables, her eyes lit up and all her awkwardness melted away.

'Splendid set-up,' she'd said to him approvingly. 'Not a better one in the country, I'd warrant.' And then she'd eyed him speculatively for a moment or two, before mounting up. As though, for the first time, she was seriously considering him as a husband.

He'd suspected for some time that it was her mother who had designs on his title, rather than her, but now he'd finally managed to prise her away from the woman, it had become crystal clear.

He didn't think she'd decline his proposal, should he make one. Not now she'd seen his stables. But he suspected that if he did marry her, she'd spend the majority of her time out here, rather than indoors where he truly needed a woman.

That suspicion solidified not long after their party set out. Captain Beamish, who was only supposed to be there to lend propriety to the outing, remarked she had a splendid seat. She returned the compliment.

And then they fell into a conversation about various mounts they'd owned, or borrowed, which led on to an exchange of horse-related anecdotes. Presently, they began enjoying each other's company so much that neither of them noticed when he drew ahead, to give them the liberty to ride side by side.

He was just reflecting that he'd have more appeal for Lady Beatrice if he only had another set of legs, a mane and a tail, when he spotted Miss Underwood, standing beneath a tree. And apparently holding an earnest conversation with it.

After advancing a little closer, a smile playing about his lips, he noted a pair of little legs dangling from one of the lower branches which Miss Underwood had been looking up at. Legs which whisked out of view at the same time as Miss Underwood whirled round, stepped forward and clenched her fists.

His nascent smile withered and died.

'Good morning, Miss Underwood,' he said, keeping his eyes fixed firmly on her face, so as not to betray the fact that he'd seen Livvy as well, for she obviously did not want to be seen. At least she was well concealed before Lady Beatrice, and Captain Beamish drew up alongside.

'Good morning, Miss Underwood,' said Lady Beatrice, while Captain Beamish touched his crop to his hat in salute. 'You are up early.'

'Yes. I wanted to exercise my dog before…before the day's activities crowded in.'

'And are you,' Oliver asked her politely, 'enjoying exploring my grounds?'

She clenched and unclenched her fists, glancing

at Captain Beamish, and Lady Beatrice. She turned back to him with a frustrated expression on her face, as though there was something she wished to say to him in private.

Well, if she'd discovered the existence of his daughter, he wasn't surprised.

She was the first of his potential brides to see Livvy. And now that she had, he'd be very interested to see what she made of her. Very interested indeed.

'Yes, of course,' she said with a rather strained smile.

'Then this afternoon…oh…' he turned, as though casually, to his companions '…please, do not let me keep you. I just have a couple of things I need to arrange with Miss Underwood.'

Captain Beamish grinned at him conspiratorially. 'Of course, Duke. Come on, Lady B. Race you up to the monument.'

'Monument? What monument?'

'You'll see it, through my dust,' he said, clapping his heels to his chestnut's flank.

With a whinny of laughter, Lady Beatrice set off in hot pursuit with her groom following behind.

'And now, Miss Underwood,' he said, turning to Sofia, 'you may tell me what you are doing, standing here under this tree.'

'What do you think I'm doing?' she said, lifting her chin. 'There is no law against standing still for a few moments, admiring the…the vista,' she said, waving her arms in the direction of a thick tangle of hawthorns, 'is there?'

She had not, as he'd half-expected, been waiting until there was nobody to hear before giving him her opinion of his morals.

She was, instead, shielding his daughter from exposure.

Even from him.

His heart leapt.

He'd known from the first moment he clapped eyes on her that Sofia might be just what Livvy needed. He'd selected the other candidates because he'd believed that each of them was capable of defending his daughter from the world's censure, in one way or another. But Sofia was the only one who might genuinely understand her, given what she'd been through in her own childhood. Who might come to truly care for her. Perhaps even love her.

He glanced up at the tree, noting the way some of the leaves were shaking, even though there was no breeze to stir them. His daughter didn't want him to know she was there. And Sofia was standing buff.

The question was, did she know that Livvy was his daughter and not just some random child who was playing where she ought not to be? Would her stance alter, once he told her the truth? People, particularly well-bred ladies, could be very unforgiving towards those who were born on the wrong side of the blanket. It was why he'd selected each of his bridal candidates with such care. Each one of them either patronised charities that cared for children, or took an interest in the underprivileged in some other way.

The sooner he made his confession, the better. Only, not here, not now, not when Livvy's little ears would hear every word and might get hurt by them.

'As I was saying earlier, I should like to spend some time with you this afternoon,' he said. 'I shall send someone to fetch you at two o'clock. Be ready,' he said, and by glancing up just once more at the quivering branch, then giving Sofia a direct look, informing her that he knew exactly who was up that tree, he set off at a steady canter.

'I think it's safe for you to come down now,' said Sofia, once the sound of hoofbeats had faded into the distance.

The little girl's face appeared among the leaves. 'Are you going to make me go back?'

'Well, you...' She pulled herself up short. She'd been about to say she couldn't very well stay out all day, but then remembered she'd done exactly that herself on many occasions. 'Don't you want your breakfast?' she asked, instead. 'I know that I am hungry.'

The girl pushed her tumbling black curls behind her ears. 'I am hungry, yes. But...' Her face fell.

'Are you in trouble of some kind? Are you afraid you will be punished for coming out here on your own?'

The girl nodded. 'And for letting you see me. Out of sight and out of mind, I'm supposed to be.'

'Even from your... I mean, the Duke?'

She nodded vigorously. 'If he knew I'd been out here, when I'm supposed to stay up in the schoolroom when respectable folk come here, Mrs Starchypants would give me what for.'

'That's dreadful!' What kind of man had his own child...?

But then she reflected how much stricter children were treated in English society than she'd been used to with her own father. Though he'd never so much as raised his voice to her, she could see that his gentle, caring form of parenting hadn't really prepared her for life in England. Also, some of the 'respectable' folk here this week were, to be truthful, not the kind of people to whom she would want a vulnerable child exposed.

Besides, he hadn't hauled his daughter down from the tree and threatened her with all sorts of dire retribution, even though he'd clearly known she was up there.

So perhaps he was being protective, rather than as harsh as this little girl believed. Although…

At that point, Snowball's patience must have run out, because she jumped up and barked.

'I do think you might come down now,' said Sofia. It would be safer if she was there to oversee the descent for the tree was big and the girl small. 'Snowball wants to play with you,' she added. 'See?' As if to back her up, Snowball began bouncing up and down, letting out a series of plaintive barks.

'Can she do any tricks?' the child asked wistfully. 'Mama did a play once where there was a dog who did all sorts of tricks.'

'Well, she can walk on her hind legs and lie down and stay silent,' said Sofia. And promptly gave a demonstration of all that Snowball could do.

The little girl's face brightened. And then, allaying all Sofia's concerns about the danger of falling from the tree, she scrambled down with the agility of a little monkey.

Snowball was in heaven. And, from the looks of her, so was the little girl. Sofia watched as the pair romped round each other in an impromptu game of chase to which only they knew the rules. However, she did manage to subtly shepherd the game steadily in the direction of the house. When they finally reached the edge of the woods and the child noticed where they were, she looked up at Sofia with a frown.

'Are you going to snitch?'

'No,' said Sofia, remembering the word from the time in her childhood when she'd been allowed to play with an entire regiment's brood of disreputable offspring. And then, when the suspicion did not clear from the child's face, she added, 'How can I, when I don't even know your name?'

The girl considered that point. 'I told you, I'm the Duke's Disgrace. Everyone would know who you meant, if you said that.'

'Well, I refuse to call you any such thing,' she said with irritation. 'Fancy blaming a child for something that wasn't her fault!'

'You don't think I'm a disgrace, then?'

'Absolutely not. The very idea!'

'I been naughty, though, running off when Mrs Starchypants weren't looking.'

'Well, I can't blame you for wishing to come and play outside on such a lovely morning. And, besides, Snowball likes you. And she, you know, is a very good judge of character.'

The girl dropped down on to her knees and gave Snowball a hug. 'I like Snowball, too. Can I play with her again?' She turned a hopeful look up.

'I only wish you could. But Snowball is not allowed in the house. I have to return her to the kennels.'

The little girl's face closed up in resignation, as though she was familiar with disappointment.

Sofia's heart went out to her. 'I know I am not as much fun as Snowball, but perhaps I could come up

to your nursery some time and play with you instead?'
It would certainly beat spending time with the candidates for the Duke's hand in marriage.

But the little girl's eyes widened in alarm. 'You mustn't! You mustn't come up to the nursery, or they'll know for sure I spoke to you.'

Good lord, but what kind of household treated a child with such severity? Aunt Agnes might have been strict, but Sofia had never once felt afraid of her, not in this way. She *had* been afraid of disappointing her, but that was another matter.

'Very well. I wouldn't want to get you into trouble.'

The girl chewed on her lower lip. 'I could come to your room, though, when nobody else is there. If…if you wouldn't mind…'

'Of course I wouldn't mind. But do you know how to find my room? I'm afraid I can't exactly tell you where it is, except that it's on the third floor.'

'Oh, I know where it is. I know where all the ladies have been put, and their mothers and fathers. And their servants. I know all the rooms in Theakstone Court and all the back stairs, and all the secret passages.'

'There are secret passages? How thrilling.'

'Well, not *'zactly* secret. Coz the servants use them. But the guests don't know.'

Ah. She meant the service corridors that staff used to move about the place, so that noble guests like Lady Sarah and her parents never had to encounter a maid carting a slop pail down to the midden.

'You may come to my room whenever you wish,' said Sofia. 'As long as it won't get you into trouble.'

'Oh, I'm always in trouble, whether I try to be good

or not. So,' she said lifting her chin, 'mostly I don't bother trying to be good any more. What's the point?'

Sofia eyed her with respect. Instead of tying herself in knots to try to win approval from the people who'd given her a home, she was being magnificently defiant.

'I wish I had been as brave as you, when I was your age.' She wished she was as brave right now. Why on earth didn't she just tell her aunt and uncle she had no intention of marrying Jack? And that, though she had no fixed plans for her future, they most certainly did not feature handing over her money to someone who was going to treat her like a…a…well, with absolutely no respect. Or kindness.

But the little girl was not looking brave and determined any longer. She'd caught sight of something beyond Sofia. When Sofia turned to see what it might be, she saw a brace of footmen carrying all sorts of equipment, trailing behind Lady Elizabeth, who was carrying a bow.

'They're all out of bed,' wailed the little girl. 'There'll be no dodging them now.'

'Is there no other way back into the house? Other than going across that lawn?'

The little girl frowned. 'A couple of ways. But I'm just as likely to get caught on any of them now. I didn't notice it was getting so late.' She looked over her shoulder at the relative safety offered by the woods. But if she went back there, she'd miss not only breakfast, but possibly lunch, as well. And though Sofia had done much the same at Nettleton Manor, she'd been at least twice this child's age. And she'd known how to forage.

'If I create a diversion, do you think you could sneak past them?'

'What's a diversion?'

'It's something that will make everyone look one way, so they won't notice one small child somewhere else.'

'Oh.'

'Snowball and I will make everyone look at us. She can steal Lady Elizabeth's arrows, or knock the target over, or jump up at one of the footmen. And while they are all running around trying to make her behave, you can get back indoors safely.'

'Oh.' The little girl looked at her for a moment and then smiled. 'I like you,' she said. 'You're almost as nice as an actress. Even if you are a lady.'

Which was, Sofia gathered, the highest praise the child could bestow.

## Chapter Sixteen

Smedley-Fotherington and Lady Margaret were already in the long gallery when Oliver got there. And what with her tremulous airs and his foppish manner of tossing his curls from his forehead every two minutes, it felt like an eternity before Miss Underwood finally arrived.

'Here you are at last,' he said, striding to greet her and only just barely managing to stop himself holding out his hands and seizing both of hers.

'Am I late? I thought we were all meeting at two o'clock.' Her anxious gaze darted past him to where the other two were standing beneath the portrait of his great-great-grandfather, mounted on the horse he'd ridden at the Battle of Naseby.

'You are punctual,' said Oliver. And then, leaning in, murmured, 'The others arrived early. Presumably to impress me with their love of art.'

'Or something.'

He could not tell what she might mean by that cryptic remark, so he ignored it. He pulled the map he'd drawn her earlier from his sleeve and pressed it into her hand.

'Don't read this until the tour is over,' he warned her. 'And don't let anyone see it.'

She blinked just once before sliding the folded note up her own sleeve. For a moment he wasn't sure whether to admire the quick way she'd caught on to the need for discretion, or to worry that she was so adept at entering into conspiracies. He put both reactions from his mind firmly and, without making any comment, took her arm and drew her into the gallery.

'These,' he said in a normal tone of voice, waving his free arm at the pictures hanging the entire length of the gallery, 'are my forebears. For the most part.'

'Yes, we have already noted the portrait of King Charles,' simpered Lady Margaret. 'Godfrey Kneller, is it not?'

'*After* Godfrey Kneller,' he corrected her smoothly, while Sofia looked bewildered. She clearly had no idea who Godfrey Kneller was. And why should she?

'A copy,' he explained, 'commissioned to show enthusiasm for the restoration of the monarchy and to demonstrate support for the restored monarch.'

'His Grace's family,' Lady Margaret said to Sofia, in a rather patronising voice, 'rose to pre-eminence during that time. Most of the house dates from that period.'

'The present house,' he corrected her. 'There have been Norringtons living in these parts since the time of the Conquest.'

'It is a very good copy,' Lady Margaret persisted. 'We were just commenting on the brushwork, were we not? But what do you make of this painting, Miss Underwood?'

Sofia cocked her head to one side. 'I think he looks very bored, considering he is sitting on a wildly rear-ing horse,' she said. 'It makes me wonder what he's thinking about.'

Lady Margaret curled her lip.

'Sitting for a portrait is a tedious business,' said Oliver. 'You may note a similar expression on the faces of many of the people here. Take the children in this picture, for example,' he said, drawing them along the gallery to the reason he'd arranged to bring her here. 'It is of my father, as a child, and his sisters.'

'By,' said Lady Margaret, 'Gainsborough?'

Well, Lady Margaret might be showing off her vastly superior knowledge of art, but Sofia, to judge from the way she stiffened upon catching sight of an eight-year-old Aunt Mary, had seen exactly what he'd wished her to see.

'So…they are your aunts? Those little girls,' said Sofia.

'Yes. The family likeness is uncanny, is it not?'

'Unmistakable, I should have said.'

'Indeed. You will notice those particular brows, and the nose, crop up again and again throughout the generations on display here. In the females of the line.'

'Not the men?'

'Not as often, for some reason.' He paused, choosing his next words with care. 'You will notice that my father, when he was a boy…that is, it is generally held that he favoured his mother's family.'

'But the girls…'

'Yes. The girls in my family do tend to have dark eyes, straight brows and that very prominent nose.'

'How unfortunate,' put in Lady Margaret, with a titter.

'Why would you say that?' Oliver had almost forgotten the dratted woman was there, for a moment, so intent had he been on gauging Miss Underwood's reaction to the sight of the infant Aunt Mary, who was the image of Livvy.

'Only, that feminine beauty is…that is, people think… I mean, *some* people think…females are more attractive if they have less, er, dramatic features.' She faltered and fell silent, finally discerning that she'd irritated him. Which irritated him even more.

She didn't even have the courage of her convictions.

'I dare say,' he said coldly, indicating the portrait hanging to the right of his Aunt Mary's, 'you find these children far more attractive, then, aesthetically speaking, Lady Margaret?'

A flush gilded Lady Margaret's cheeks as the four of them inspected the three blonde, angelic-looking creatures gathered about the skirts of a strikingly beautiful woman in rather wispy robes.

'Who are they?' Sofia finally asked, cutting through the strained, tense silence. She alone needed to ask the question, since she was the only one who did not know.

'These are the children of my father's second marriage. And,' he added, 'their mother.'

She looked at his stepmother. Looked at him. 'Your stepmother,' she said in a voice that sounded…off, like a wineglass that didn't ring like a bell when tapped, because there was a crack in it.

'Correct,' he said. And then, because he wondered what was going on behind those dark, hardening eyes, he asked her, 'What do you make of this portrait?'

Out of the corner of his eye, he saw Lady Margaret preen. She probably thought Sofia was about to make a colossal fool of herself, since she knew so little about painters that she hadn't even recognised the name of the one who'd done the copy of King Charles.

'The little boy looks as if he's about to run off and get into mischief,' she said thoughtfully, her gaze fixed on the smile tugging at one corner of that little pink mouth.

'He still does,' said Oliver.

Lady Margaret tittered. Again.

He could never live with that kind of laughter.

'The Marquess of Devizes,' she said, 'is notorious for his escapades.'

Had the foolish girl no idea how badly she was offending him? Was she so intent on scoring points over Miss Underwood, by flaunting her superior knowledge of his family, as well as art, that she'd completely lost all reason? Or did she think that by insulting that side of his family, she was demonstrating some kind of loyalty to him?

Not that he cared. With every minute that passed, she was confirming his decision to strike her from his list had been the correct one. For his own sake, as well as hers.

'What do you make of the girls, Miss Underwood?' he said, ignoring Lady Margaret's tactless remark about his rakish half-brother. 'Since your prophecy regarding my half-brother's character was so accurate.'

'Well…' She studied them for a moment or two.

He'd always thought the painter had tried to make them look as though they were little copies of their mother, though he hadn't quite succeeded.

'They both look rather…' she paused '…well, as though they are looking down their little noses at the man who is painting them.'

Lady Margaret clucked her tongue in disapproval. But then both his sisters were now married to powerful, influential men. Only his scapegrace brother, apparently, was safe to criticise.

But Oliver felt his mouth pulling into a smile. 'You have it in a nutshell. They do, both, still look down their little noses at the rest of the world.'

'What a pity,' she said, taking a step back as though she wanted to take in the whole family a bit better. 'When their mother looks as though she's a rather nice person.'

Which she was. 'Say, rather, that she is an amiable goose.'

She gave him a strange look. 'It sounds as though you feel sorry for her,' she said.

'As do most people who meet her,' he replied. Himself included. 'Very pretty, of course. Which is why my father married her.' His stomach churning at the mess his father had left behind him, he urged the whole group along to the next picture. At which Miss Underwood frowned.

'I take it,' he said to her, 'this picture does not meet with your approval?'

'Oh, no, it isn't that,' she said. 'It is just that I was thinking the next one would be one of you. I mean, these are your nearest relatives, are they not? And there is a painting of your father's second family. So I assumed...'

'It is never a good idea to assume anything about my family,' he said witheringly.

'I beg pardon. I didn't mean to offend you. I just wondered...that is...'

'What Miss Underwood means, I am sure,' put in

Lady Margaret smoothly, 'is that we were hoping to have sight of a portrait of you, as a child.'

'Then you are doomed to disappointment,' he said. 'For there are none.'

'None? How…? I mean…'

'I was sent away the day after my mother died,' he said. 'My father did not invite me to return here, to Theakstone Court, until I was twelve.'

'How *tragic*,' put in Lady Margaret in a thrilled voice. 'The poor man must have been so distraught he could not bear to be reminded of his first wife by the sight of her son.'

Well, that was the story Oliver's father had put about. The one everyone still believed.

'That's awful,' said Miss Underwood. 'It must have been like losing both of your parents at a stroke. How old were you?'

'I was not four years old, so I hardly remember it,' he lied. That night was seared into his memory with terrifying clarity. 'However, I do have a very clear recollection of the foster family upon whom I was thrust, which has given me a very firm resolve never,' he said, looking her directly in the eyes, 'to see any child suffer the same fate. Not if I can help it.'

Miss Underwood stared right back at him, her chin lifted in a challenging way. But what was she challenging? His determination to flout convention by bringing his illegitimate daughter to live at his principal seat? Or something else entirely? He could not tell. And he had to know.

But he could not ask her outright. Not here, in front of Lady Margaret and the foppish poet. Not anywhere else in the house, by daylight, when they risked being overheard by anyone who might care to stroll past.

Which was why he'd arranged the meeting later on, out in the grounds where nobody would be strolling.

But it would be hours before they could be alone to discuss the matter freely. That was, if she kept the assignation he'd proposed in the note she'd tucked up her sleeve.

Lady Margaret shot him a confused look. 'So, do you plan to open an orphanage of some sort? That is most commendable,' she then gushed, 'given your own history...'

'I think Miss Underwood understands me upon this point,' he said, cutting through. And then, because he was impatient to hear her views and could not wait until midnight, he risked asking her, 'Since you lost your own parents at a young age, tell me, do you think it is better to pay strangers to look after an orphan child of noble birth? Or to send her to live with her nearest relations?'

'Ah,' she said. And thought for a bit before continuing. He liked that she was choosing her words carefully; that she didn't just blurt out the first thing that popped into her head. 'I think it depends, very much, upon the relations in the case. And the strangers. I mean, some people naturally like children and some don't. Even if they are closely related, that doesn't make them good guardians.'

'Whatever can you mean?' said Lady Margaret.

But Oliver could guess. Bringing her here, because he could not bear to think of her with strangers, had not won him any points, necessarily. He needed to prove that he was the best option for Livvy.

Which he would take damn good care to do, tonight.

Sofia laid her hairbrush down on the dressing table and turned her head from side to side.

Neat as a pin. She might be the most simply dressed female at table, but at least tonight she wouldn't look as if she'd dragged on her last clean gown and rushed down to dinner without pausing to look in the mirror. Although there was no doing anything with the bruises, which were more green than purple, today.

She gathered up her reticule and was making her way to the door when it opened and Aunt Agnes came in.

Sofia flushed and lifted her chin.

'No, no, I haven't come to find fault,' said Aunt Agnes, shutting the door. 'I was just checking to make sure Marguerite had managed to get the tea stain out of your topaz silk so you could wear it tonight. Very strong views, she has, about what I pay her to do and serving anyone but myself is one of the...but never mind that.' She clasped her hands together, as though she felt ill at ease. 'If I had known, when we set off from Nettleton Manor, that we would end up staying in a ducal household, and with such fellow guests, I would have made sure you had more pretty gowns.'

An apology? From Aunt Agnes? If she weren't afraid of creasing her gown, Sofia would have collapsed on the nearest chair.

'There simply wasn't time,' Aunt Agnes continued, in that same, definitely apologetic, tone. 'Besides, your Uncle Ned is so firm about not dipping into your capital.'

So firm, that they'd sometimes struggled to support her while in the midst of launching their own daughters into society, on what she suspected was a very modest income. It had meant wearing an awful lot of gowns that had been passed from Betty to Celia before reaching her.

'My family accused me of marrying down when I chose Ned, but say what they will about him—' and Uncle Barty said plenty '—they will never be able to say we took you in so that we could feather our own nest. And you've never really wanted for anything, have you?'

Only yesterday she'd mourned the lack of a pony. Only, how would it have looked if Uncle Ned had bought her one, when he hadn't been able to provide mounts for his own daughters?

'No, no, I haven't,' conceded Sofia meekly. For she'd always been so grateful for being allowed to stay with the family, in spite of all the difficulties her arrival had caused them, that she'd never liked to ask for things she knew they could ill afford.

'So, there is no justification for the Dowager Lady Tewkesbury,' said Aunt Agnes, her voice rising a little indignantly, 'to accuse me—us—of being poor guardians?'

'What? I mean, no, of course not, Aunt Agnes.' They had been strict, very strict with her. At least, Aunt Agnes had been, especially at first when she'd been so determined to eradicate the vulgarity and hoydenish manners she'd apparently picked up when 'following the drum'.

'Then you have not been complaining, loudly, about our treatment of you?'

'No! Who…? I mean…' But then her mind flew back to the speculative expression on Lady Margaret's face, earlier, when she'd been trying to let the Duke know that she didn't think he was doing all that well with his daughter if she felt she had to hide up a tree when he rode into view, without mentioning her by name. Could it have sounded as though she was complaining about her own family circumstances? And could Lady Margaret then have repeated that information to her mother?

Very probably.

But she couldn't explain much to Aunt Agnes without revealing the existence of the Duke's daughter, which she didn't feel right about doing, not without asking him first if she might.

Nevertheless, she did owe Aunt Agnes some sort of explanation.

'We were speaking of the Duke's own upbringing earlier,' she therefore said. 'I think Lady Margaret took some remarks I made about his foster family and twisted them to…to…well, I cannot think why she would have done such a thing.'

'Well, I can,' said Aunt Agnes, managing to sound both cross and relieved at the same time. 'To sow discord. The cat. But we shall show her,' she said with a militant light in her eyes, 'show them *all* that they have not succeeded. We will go down to dinner arm in arm to show them we are the best of friends in spite of all their efforts. And what is more, that we don't give a fig for any of 'em!'

Her stance reminded Sofia of the way she'd dealt

with all those people who'd prophesied she'd have her hands full with any child of Captain Underwood's, and reminded her of the reason she'd worked so hard to ensure her aunt would never regret taking her in.

And so she didn't hesitate to do exactly as she was told.

## Chapter Seventeen

Sofia's heart was thudding as she sped along the corridor by the kitchens. From the moment she'd unfurled the note the Duke had given her and read his very precise directions to a structure called the Italian Summer House, along with the time he wished to meet her there, she hadn't been able to help thinking that if she heard that any of the other bridal candidates were planning on sneaking out after dark to meet him, she'd assume they were up to no good. And she was sure that it was not at all wise of her to be scurrying down deserted corridors and stumbling about moonlit gardens, either. But there was absolutely no other way she could speak to him about his little girl without someone else overhearing. Not given the number of eagle-eyed chaperons watching every girl's movements, zealously ensuring none of them could steal a march on any of the others by indulging in a private tête-à-tête.

Even Sofia. Even though nobody really thought she stood any hope of ever becoming a duchess. Least of all Sofia herself.

Her decision to risk her reputation, by doing as he'd

asked, had put her all of a fidget, the whole evening. Occasionally she'd been distracted by the way the ladies circled each other with backs arched and claws extended. And seeing Uncle Ned drawing the men to him with his good nature and down-to-earth attitude, the way tavern keepers drew thirsty farmhands at the end of a day's haymaking, had been enlightening. But, fascinating though it was to observe everyone else, she couldn't stop thinking about the upcoming rendezvous.

In the end, even though curiosity had stifled circumspection, Sofia didn't want to risk having her reputation ruined by giving the appearance she was rushing out to some secluded spot at the fringes of the formal gardens for an assignation, which meant that rather than following the Duke's directions faithfully, she made a detour to the kennels to collect Snowball. If by any chance somebody did happen to see her, then she could tell them she couldn't sleep and was taking her dog for a walk. They'd think she was touched in the upper works, but that was better than being branded a hussy.

Snowball was so delighted to be let out of canine prison that she made hardly any objection to exploring formal shrubberies and flower beds, rather than the woods which were full of rabbits and other game.

It was rather difficult to make out the map by moonlight, but eventually Sofia reached a curving length of tightly clipped yew, about twice her height, behind which she hoped she'd find the Italian Summer House.

When she rounded the end of the hedge, she saw a structure resembling a miniature temple, gleaming white in the moonlight. It sat on an island of grass in a sea of gravel. Between the columns, which resembled rather depressed-looking women in flowing draperies, were several heavily shuttered windows and a stout wooden door. It all combined to make the place look rather funereal.

Nevertheless, since she'd come this far, she might as well just step inside. And if it was too dark and dank and gloomy, she could come straight back out again and wait for the Duke in the porch area.

Only, the moment she pushed open the door and stepped inside, he materialised from out of the shadows, making her jump. Snowball let out one warning bark and took up a protective stance in front of her.

'I beg your pardon,' said the Duke. 'I did not mean to startle you.'

'No, no, not at all,' she said, pressing her hand to her heart, which was thumping wildly. 'It was just that it was so dark, I did not think anyone was here.'

'I did not wish to draw attention to ourselves by leaving a lantern lit. I do not mind the dark, you see. But if you are nervous…'

'Not at all. I don't mind the dark, either.' Snowball, hearing the two humans speaking to each other in friendly tones, sat down, her tail thumping gently on the floor. 'And I totally agree that we would not wish anyone to know what we are up to. I mean,' she corrected herself hastily, 'not that we are doing anything wrong. Well, not all that wrong, but…'

It was strange, but even though she could not see more than his outline, she could tell that he was smiling.

'You understand that I do not want to appear to favour any of my…female guests, by openly spending more time with one, than another.'

'Yes.' They were competitive enough as it was, without him giving any of them an excuse to think they were in the lead.

'But I needed to speak to you, in complete privacy, regarding Olivia.'

'Olivia?'

'The little girl you met in the woods this morning. The one who hid up a tree rather than speak to me. The one you shielded from any possible repercussions from her avoiding her lessons.'

'Olivia,' she echoed. Named after him. She'd seen his name, Oliver, printed on the invitation Uncle Ned had tossed on the breakfast table. If anything had been required to confirm her suspicions about her parentage, that name did it. 'I don't think she was hiding from *you*, specifically. In fact,' she said, deciding she might as well tell him the truth, 'I know she wasn't. Because she told me that your guests are not supposed to know of her existence.'

'Not yet,' he said. 'I do not want her exposed to unkindness.'

'Then you ought not to have let people refer to her as the Duke's Disgrace,' she snapped.

'The...what?' He sounded shocked.

'The Duke's Disgrace. That's what she said she was. And that she was not supposed to talk to *respectable* people.'

The Duke made a low growling noise. 'She is not a disgrace. The disgrace, if there was any, was her mother's.'

'Oh, so now you are blaming the woman you... you...well, I suppose you are going to say it was her fault she bore your child!'

'On the contrary, it took two of us to conceive my daughter. Her fault was in concealing the child from me. If I had known about her from the first...' He moved away from Sofia and paced back and forth a couple of times. 'I only learned of Livvy's existence a few months ago, when one of...her mother's colleagues brought her to my London house. Left her on my doorstep, like an unwanted package,' he said in a tone of outrage. 'Said there was no money left and that it was my responsibility to provide for her no matter what her mother's wishes had been.'

He stopped talking but, head bowed, continued pacing back and forth as though wrestling with extreme emotion. Sofia had certainly detected both outrage and hurt in what he'd told her this far. Even though she couldn't see his face very clearly, both emotions were pouring off him in waves.

Since it looked as though it might take him some time to regain sufficient control to be able to speak of his daughter in the cool, practical manner he liked to show the world, she looked round for somewhere to sit down. Beneath one of the window embrasures was what appeared to be a small sofa. She made for it and since she didn't want the Duke to accidentally tread on Snowball in the dark, she snapped her fingers, making the dog come and curl up at her feet.

'I do not intend to provide you with the details of the relationship I had with Livvy's mother,' he bit out. 'You are an innocent and should not...'

'Excuse me, but I know a great deal more about the kinds of relationships men have with ladies, outside marriage, than you might think. After my mother died, my father had a whole string of them. Living with us.'

'Like a harem?' He sounded shocked. So shocked that he stopped pacing and stood staring at her. She could just make out his features by the moonlight that was peeking in through some tiny, triangular openings high up near the roof, now that her eyes were growing used to the gloom.

'What? No!' She thought back over what she'd said. 'He didn't have them all living with us at once. One at a time.'

'Still,' he said. And then began pacing again, as though he was more comfortable doing that than looking at her directly while making his confession.

'Livvy's mother died only a few months ago. And apparently her dying request was that her colleagues should look after her daughter, which they did to start with, while touring the provinces.'

'Ah, that explains it.'

'Explains what?' He sounded affronted.

'Oh, just something Livvy said about actresses. It sounded very odd, at the time, but now I can see that it was because she has nothing but the highest regard for them.'

'Regard? For creatures who couldn't wait to wash their hands of her, the minute their troupe returned to London? Not that I mind for my own sake, but it... confused her. They appear to have treated her like a little pet while she was with them. So to deposit her with a man who was a total stranger to her...well, you can imagine what effect that had.'

She didn't need to imagine it. She knew almost exactly what it felt like, having gone through a similar experience herself. Maria had put on such a great show of doting on her that both she and her papa had trusted her completely. But the moment her papa had died Maria had shown her true colours. After that betrayal Sofia had found it hard to trust anyone. For a very long time.

He stood still, his head bowed. 'I find it hard to forgive her mother. What was she thinking?'

'Well, I don't suppose she was thinking of dying and leaving her daughter at all.'

He made a strange, choking laugh. 'No. She never did strike me as being the sort of woman who planned anything. Impulsive. Generous. That was Ruby.' He suddenly stood up straighter, as though pulling himself together. 'But it is not of her that I wish to speak with you. I wanted to know whether you had deduced that Livvy is my natural daughter and, if so...'

'Of course I did. The fact that she described herself as the Duke's Disgrace made it pretty obvious,' she said drily. 'Even if she were not so very like you in looks.'

'To which I drew your attention this afternoon, in the portrait gallery.'

'Which confirmed what I'd already suspected.'

'You are not shocked? Or...disapproving?'

'The only thing of which I disapprove is that someone should make her feel not good enough to mix with what she terms respectable people.' She'd lived with that feeling herself, so knew how crushing it could be.

'For which you blame me.'

'Well, you are her father. You are the one who is hiding her away...'

'For her own protection. You have no idea how unkind people can be to children...'

'Oh, can't I?' Then she bit down on her lower lip.

'That is, a child who has lost her mother is unlikely to be happy, even if the people who take her in do their very, very best.' Which Uncle Ned and Aunt Agnes had done. It wasn't their fault she'd been so unhappy with them to start with. She'd been mourning her father and reeling from the aftermath of losing his protection. Now that she was older, and less suspicious of everyone's motives, she could see that they had their reasons for the way they'd acted. Reasons which she would not have understood at all had they tried to explain them to her when she'd first gone to live with them.

But he suddenly strode forward and stood right in front of her, so that she had to crane her neck to look up at him. 'That is why I hoped you would understand and sympathise with Livvy. You know exactly what it is like to be removed from your natural sphere and be thrust into a world for which you are not prepared.'

'Yes, but…'

'Livvy needs you. Someone like you, to replace the mother she lost. I cannot do it alone. I… I have no notion of what a small child needs. Let alone one who appears to have had such a close bond with her own mother.'

'But…'

'I touched upon my own childhood this afternoon, did I not? I couldn't say much in front of the others, but I don't want Livvy to endure what I did. The moment I saw her, standing on my hearthrug, her eyes half full of fear, and half defiance, I knew exactly how she felt. It was the way I felt when one of the housemaids dropped me off in the house of my new foster parents. And there was Perceval, telling me I ought to send Livvy to the same sort of place. But how could

I farm her out to people who would only take care of her because I paid them to? My instinct was to sweep her up and bring her here, and…' He stopped. 'Well, at that point I ran out of ideas. I did hire a governess and a nurse and a maid, but…' He raised both hands to his head briefly before flinging them wide. 'None of them are making up for her losing her mother. Instead of growing used to her new life, every day she seems to become increasingly unhappy.'

Sofia wasn't surprised, if some of the staff were telling Livvy that she was a disgrace who wasn't fit to speak to so-called respectable people.

'So I decided I would marry and bring some female here to live with us, a woman who would know how to care for a lonely, orphaned little girl. A woman who wouldn't despise Livvy because I hadn't been married to her mother.'

'Oh, I see,' she said. So *that* was why he'd suddenly started looking seriously for a wife, after so many years of appearing unattainable. Nothing to do with a feud with his stepmother at all. It was for Livvy.

'But…how will you know she doesn't? I mean…oh, dear.' Was she going to have to tell him about Maria? Though she'd never told anyone else, she couldn't stand back and let another little girl go through what she had, because that girl's father had been taken in by a pretty face and a caressing manner. 'No, no, Oliver,' she stood up so she could put her point across, face to face. 'You cannot trust the welfare of your daughter to anyone else. Not even a wife. Any woman could deceive you into thinking she would be kind, in order to gain the title of Duchess.'

'But she needs a mother.'

'No, she doesn't. I never had one—at least, I don't remember her—and my father was…well, actually, he did make a lot of mistakes. But I never doubted he loved me and was doing his best for me. Even if many people thought it wasn't a very good best.'

The Duke made a strange sound, like a choked laugh. She supposed it was on account of the very ungrammatical way she'd expressed herself.

'I do need to find a duchess, though.'

'Well, I'm sure you will, one day. But surely that is a separate issue from doing what's best for Livvy?'

'No, it isn't.' He whirled away and started pacing again. 'It's all bound up together. My Duchess will be the woman who, eventually, will launch Livvy into society. She needs to show her how to stand up for herself. Needs to teach her how to defend herself from the malicious gossip that the circumstances surrounding her birth are bound to cause.'

'That's all very well. But what about you?'

'Me?' He stopped pacing. 'What do you mean?'

'I mean, what do you want from marriage?'

'I have just told you. I want a woman who will be a mother to Livvy and a duchess upon whom I can depend.' He turned and started pacing again. 'I hope that my Duchess will share my political views and support me in my aims.'

'And those are?'

He paused, as though choosing his words carefully before starting to pace again. 'Because of my childhood I have seen how the underprivileged have to live. The means they must employ simply to put food on the table. And now I am one of the wealthiest men in England. I want to… I need to have a duchess at my side who will agree that something needs to be done to address the current imbalance. In a measured, lawful manner, naturally. We don't want our country flung into the kind of turmoil they experienced in France. Therefore, those of us who have the power to make changes need to do so before desperate men take the law into their own hands.'

Golly. She would never have guessed, from his haughty, forbidding manner that he could feel so passionate about reform. 'Golly,' she said out loud.

'What do you mean by that?' He came to a dead halt and looked at her intently.

She shook her head. 'Oliver, you clearly have very noble ambitions. But…what about love? Oh…' she put out her hand before he could give her a set-down '…I know you mistrust the emotion, but without it…' She took a step in his direction. 'If your wife cannot love you, she will be neither a good mother, nor a good duchess. If you must marry, you should find a woman who will love Livvy because she loves you. And who will support your work for the same reason. And more than that…' She took a deep breath, the way she would if she was going to dive into the lower lake, since she knew she was likely to get an equally chilling reception. 'You deserve to be loved. And don't say it's not true. *Everyone* deserves to be loved.'

'You…' He swallowed. 'You take my breath away. I never thought…'

And then suddenly he was right in front of her. 'Thank you,' he said huskily.

The next thing she knew, he'd put his arms round her waist and was kissing her. She was so surprised that she gasped. At which point, he deepened the kiss.

And even though she was amazed he was doing this, even though a part of her knew it was wrong to be kissing a man, in the dark, in a secluded part of the estate, it felt so amazing that she made no protest whatsoever. In fact, after grabbing hold of his waist to steady herself against the onslaught of his mouth, she slid her arms round to his back, just to have something solid to hang on to, since her head was spinning and the bones seemed to have dissolved out of her legs.

Her first kiss. Oh, it was lovely. Much, much nicer than she'd ever thought a kiss could be. It filled her whole being with a sort of fizzy joy. It made her want to run and dance, and wriggle closer to him, all at once.

Which she must not do. It was all very well basking in all that masculine admiration, for a moment or two. But it wouldn't do to let this amazing man keep on kissing her for very long. Or he would think she was no better than she ought to be.

So she slid her hands to his chest and gently pushed against it, while, very regretfully, tilting her head to one side.

'Oliver,' she whispered, the moment she'd managed to untangle her lips from his. 'We mustn't...'

He stiffened. 'No, you are right. Someone is coming.'

And then she noticed shadows dancing crazily upon the ceiling and walls. And the unmistakable sound of footsteps crunching across gravel.

'Quick,' he growled and tugged her behind the sofa, pushing her down on to the floor.

'Snowball,' she hissed. 'Here, girl.' The dog wriggled right under the sofa and lay down with her head on her paws as though delighted to be playing a new game which involved her mistress diving behind furniture with a duke.

But Sofia was trembling and her heart was pounding. And not because she was afraid of being discovered in the summer house at dead of night. Or not altogether. No, she was fairly sure that it had more to do with the fact that the Duke had his arm round her waist and was breathing hotly down her ear, and in the confined space behind the sofa, they were plastered so closely together they could have been carved from one piece of wood.

And it felt absolutely amazing, being held so closely by a man who was so hard all over. And yet so warm. And gentle, somehow, in the way he was holding her. As though he was shielding her, rather than restraining her.

Heavens. Perhaps she really *was* no better than she ought to be.

## Chapter Eighteen

She couldn't see who it was, from behind the sofa. But whoever it was set their lantern down with a grating sound and then began to pace back and forth, just as the Duke had done earlier. She hoped it was because they were waiting for someone, rather than just pacing for the sake of it, or they could be here all night. And, pleasurable though it was to be held in a pair of such strong and protective arms, the floor was awfully hard and cold.

To her relief, not long later, light flickered across the ceiling again and another person entered the summer house.

'Darling,' said the first person. A man. 'I thought you were never going to come.'

There was a muffled noise of clothing swishing, deep breathing, and rather sloppy sounds as though someone was sucking on a juicy orange.

They were kissing! Oh. Had *they* made the same sounds when they'd been kissing? Ugh, surely not. The Duke hadn't slobbered. His mouth had been firm and warm and determined. Just like him. Nothing sloppy about him.

'It was harder to get away than I'd thought,' said the second person, in a voice that sounded rather like Lady Elizabeth, only rather more breathy. 'Next time I shall have to doctor Connie's drink with laudanum to get her to go to sleep earlier. Though it wasn't just her,' she added resentfully, sounding much more like herself. 'The place is crawling with footmen. Don't Theakstone's staff ever go to bed?'

'It is hopeless, anyway,' said the man. 'Your family is never going to allow me to marry you.'

'Never mind, darling. Once I am married, I will have far more freedom.'

'No,' the man groaned. 'You must not marry anyone else, I couldn't bear it.'

'Well, I'm not going to elope with you. I have to think of my family. They need me to marry a wealthy man. Besides, eloping with me would destroy your prospects. It would be a disaster all round.'

The man groaned again. Sofia envied him the freedom to do so. She was by now almost sure that the floor on which she was lying was marble. It was definitely the coldest, hardest substance she'd ever stretched out upon for this length of time.

'You are going to have to be practical, my love,' said Lady Elizabeth. 'The Duke is not a sentimental man. He isn't going to care what I do once I've given him an heir, which is why I agreed to come here, don't forget. Theakstone will be perfect for me. I mean, for us.'

Not surprisingly, the Duke in question stiffened and made a sort of growling noise, low in his throat.

'What was that?' It sounded like the man had dashed to the door. 'I think someone is coming. We will have to hide.'

Oh, no! There wasn't room for all four of them be-hind the sofa. Not that anyone would be doing any more hiding, actually, if the man with Lady Elizabeth did attempt to dive behind the sofa, since he'd land on the very man he would least wish to meet.

'I didn't hear anything,' said Lady Elizabeth. 'It was probably just a fox, or an owl, or something.'

'Yes, yes, it is my nerves,' said the man shakily. 'The thought of deceiving His Grace, when he has been such a generous benefactor of late...'

'Well, just carry on thinking of him as a generous benefactor, Septimus. Only, in future he is going to be generous with his wife, rather than his funds.'

The Duke was now breathing rather deeply through his nostrils.

'I don't know,' said the man Sofia now knew was the scientist she'd always thought looked troubled. And now she knew why.

'I must get back before I am missed,' said Lady Elizabeth before the scientist could give his guilty con-science free rein. 'Kiss me, one last time,' she com-manded in a husky voice.

To Sofia's disgust, there came the same rustly, gaspy, slushy noises she'd heard before. Only this time, she could picture the intense young man and Lady Eliza-beth devouring each other, even while they were hop-ing she might still marry the Duke. Which made Sofia shudder.

The Duke was still breathing heavily. She could actually feel his outrage mounting the longer the kiss went on.

It felt like an age before the other couple broke

apart, gathered up their lanterns, stumbled out of the summer house and shut the door behind them.

'My goodness,' said Sofia, after raising her head above the sofa back, to make sure they'd really gone.

'Goodness has nothing to do with it,' growled the Duke, getting to his feet and brushing down his clothing.

'No. I can see that from your point of view...'

'From anyone's point of view!'

'No, but they are clearly very much in love.'

'Love!' He spat out the word as though it was a lump of gristle. 'That's the sort of behaviour your much-vaunted love gives rise to! They are plotting to cuckold me. Before I've even proposed to the baggage!' He strode to the door and flung it open. She could see his broad-shouldered outline silvered by moonlight in the doorway. She got up and rubbed ruefully at her sore hip.

'I cannot believe she would agree to marry you when she's clearly in love with another man,' she said, walking over to join him. 'What a pity he could not be wealthier. Or her family not depending on her so much.'

'What?' He whirled round to glare at her.

'Well, only consider. If they could just marry each other, then neither of them would even consider going to such desperate lengths.'

'Hmmph.' He glared in the direction the other couple must have gone. 'I suppose, in a way, I can see your point.'

'You mean, you can see you ought only to marry a woman who loves you?'

'I can see,' he growled, 'that Lady Elizabeth certainly should not marry any man but Brown. Look,' he said, taking her by the arm, 'you had better get back to the house as well, before anyone else takes it into their heads to take a moonlight stroll. It appears there is no telling who next may turn up in the one place I thought was sure to give us some privacy. Lady Margaret and Perceval, I shouldn't wonder.'

'Oh. Is she in love with him, then? I thought she had more in common with that poetical chap.'

'It was a figure of speech,' he said irritably. 'I have no idea what she may be plotting. Or him, for that matter. Go on,' he said, planting a swift kiss on her forehead. 'Back to the Court with you. We will speak further tomorrow.'

And with that he thrust her out of the door, shutting it behind her. Fortunately, Snowball had stayed close to her skirts the whole time and was on the same side of the door as she was, so she had company on the long walk back to the house.

It was heart-wrenching to have to abandon her when they reached the kennels. Snowball whined and hung her head in dejection when she realised what was happening. 'I know, I know, it must be horrid,' she said, caressing the dog's head. And vowed to bring a treat for her pet the next day to make up for being locked away like a criminal.

So the next morning she went in to breakfast before taking Snowball for her walk, planning to sneak a couple of sausages into her reticule.

'Good morning, Miss Underwood,' said Oliver, from the head of the table. 'You are late to breakfast this morning. Did you not sleep well?'

Sleep? How had he expected her to sleep after the

discoveries she'd made in the summer house? Not only about his real motives for wishing to marry, but also the shocking plans Lady Elizabeth was making with her secret lover.

Not to mention the fact that every time she had closed her eyes she felt Oliver's arms round her and his lips upon hers. Her spine tingled just the way it had done when he'd breathed down her ear. It had made her feel restless and hot. Flinging off the covers hadn't helped. Nor had getting out of bed and opening the window. The tepid breeze that had sighed over her body had not been able to erase the feel of his hands. In fact, it had felt almost like a caress—so much like a caress that she'd had to pull the sheets back up over her.

Which had made her too hot.

'Not terribly well, no,' she replied, making for the buffet. 'It was so hot,' she added, helping herself to a plate of cooked food…and slipping a sausage into her reticule.

'It is likely to remain hot for the next few days,' said Oliver, eyeing her keenly as she made her way to a vacant seat about halfway along the table. 'Which is why I have organised a picnic for us all, down by the lake, for later today.'

'How thoughtful of you, Your Grace,' cooed Lady Sarah. 'Being by the water always feels so refreshing.'

It would be even more refreshing if they could actually swim in it, Sofia reflected as she turned over her teacup. Not that it was likely.

'Are there trees close by, for shade?' asked Lady Elizabeth. 'I should not wish to risk ruining my complexion.'

Sofia could not help shooting her a startled glance.

How could she care so much about her complexion and so little for her marriage vows? She couldn't have a *scrap* of integrity. Why, she looked as fresh as a daisy this morning. No signs that she'd been up late last night meeting her secret lover. Or lying in bed tossing and turning, remembering what it had felt like to have his hands all over her person.

Sofia took a gulp of the tea a footman had just poured her, to hide the fact she was flushing with guilt. For what right had she to criticise Lady Elizabeth when she was no better herself? At least Lady Elizabeth was in love with her solemn scientist. She had no such excuse for kissing Oliver. Or letting him kiss her, to be more accurate.

'Not only are there trees for shade…' Oliver was telling the breakfasting guests, in a very masculine voice.

She set her teacup down with a snap. How could his voice be anything but masculine? He was a man.

A man who'd held her pressed along every inch of his solid body while they'd been hiding behind the sofa…

'There are also boats which you may take out on to the water. Or rather,' he continued, 'you may employ some gentleman to row you out on the water.'

Would he remove his jacket and roll up his shirt-sleeves if he were to row her across the water? He must have fine, sinewy forearms to judge from last night. Probably, with his colouring, covered in a lot of black hair…

Her mouth ran dry. She had another cup of tea, but it made no difference.

As she glanced across the table at the scientist, who

looked even more gloomy than usual this morning, she caught him yawning. And promptly had to stifle a yawn of her own.

'If you will excuse me,' she said, getting to her feet.

'Leaving the table so soon, Miss Underwood?' Oliver gave her an amused look.

'Yes. I have not yet taken Snowball for her walk.' Hopefully, a brisk walk through the grounds would clear her head. Even though it was well past the freshest, dewiest part of the morning.

He nodded, his eyes flicking briefly, and with amusement, to her reticule.

Oh, he must have seen her filch the sausage from the sideboard. How…how mortifying! Her face aflame, she walked to the door, conscious of that lazily amused gaze boring into her spine. As surely as she'd felt his breath on the back of her neck when they'd been clasped in that close embrace behind the sofa.

She wiped her hand across her forehead, which was clammy. Oh, lord, but it was hot already, today. Hopefully it would be cooler in the woods, where she was planning to take Snowball. But as for a picnic down by the lake, later…that was going to be extremely uncomfortable.

In more ways than one.

## *Chapter Nineteen*

It hadn't been any cooler in the woods. The only effect Sofia's walk had on her was to make her feel gritty, as well as tired. She trailed up the stairs to her room, looking forward to having a wash and changing into a fresh gown.

Her heart sank, therefore, when the first thing she saw upon entering her room was her aunt, and her aunt's maid Marguerite, apparently intent on exhuming every item of clothing from the wardrobe and scattering it across the room.

'Sofia, you clever girl!' Aunt Agnes clasped her hands at her breast, a broad smile on her face.

'Clever? In what way?'

'In landing a marriage proposal from His Grace.' She clapped her hands this time.

'A marriage proposal?' Was the room spinning, or was it just her brain?

'Yes. His Grace summoned your uncle to his study right after breakfast to inform him of his decision.'

'Oh, did he?' His *decision*? *His?*

She felt as if she'd been ambushed. She'd told him

exactly what she thought about his ideas about marriage. She'd told him to find a wife who loved him.

How could he trample all over her opinions like this? Had he no respect for them? For her?

And what about Aunt Agnes? How could she be looking so pleased? What of her plans to marry Sofia to Jack?

'Surely Uncle Ned did not give his consent?'

'Well, he was a bit reluctant and tried explaining that you had an understanding with your cousin, but His Grace overrode him. Said that a definite proposal trumped a mere understanding.'

'But...surely...'

'Oh, don't worry about your Uncle Ned. I shall soon make him see the advantages to all of us of you becoming a duchess. You will be in a position to do something for Betty and Celia, and their children which, I must say, I shouldn't think Jack would ever have permitted. Oh, I can hardly believe it.' Her eyes shone. '*My* niece, a duchess. In spite of my family prophesying no good would come of me marrying down. That'll show 'em! And Lady Sale, too. If you only knew the way she's been looking down her nose at me and assuring me that the matter was as good as settled. She told me that the only reason any other girl was invited here was so that His Grace's intention of marrying her precious daughter should not be too obvious. Hah!'

'Wait...wait...' Sofia finally put her finger on what had disturbed her so much about what Oliver had said to her uncle. 'You said he said that a definite proposal trumped a mere understanding?'

'Yes. He did. He means to marry you, Sofia. You!'

'But he hasn't proposed.'

'Well, naturally, he would have wished to speak to your uncle first,' said Aunt Agnes, with a dismissive wave of her hand. 'But now he has gained consent to the match, he means to make you a formal offer. In fact, he asked that you go to him in his study, the moment you returned from your walk. That's why I'm picking something out for you. You will always remember what you were wearing the day a duke proposed to you, you know. Now, let me see. Oh, how I wish you had something a bit more…'

She bustled back to the wardrobe leaving Sofia standing, stunned, in the doorway. But only for a moment. While Aunt Agnes and Marguerite had their heads together, she turned and left the room.

There was no point in getting changed. Not to give the Duke a piece of her mind. Besides, they wouldn't find anything *more*, as her aunt had put it, no matter how long they rummaged through her wardrobe.

She'd reached the end of the corridor before realising she had no idea where, in this vast, sprawling building, the Duke's study actually was.

Fortunately, as Lady Elizabeth had said the night before, the place was infested with footmen, whose sole task it was to direct bewildered guests to their intended destination. Even more fortunately, it was the friendly footman, Peter, whom she encountered first. And rather than merely pointing her in the right direction, he offered to escort her personally to Oliver's domain.

There, they encountered another footman, a far more senior one to judge by the supercilious expression on his face.

'His Grace is occupied at the moment, miss,' he said with a slight sneer. 'And had he wished to speak with you, he would have sent for you.'

'Well, he did,' she retorted. 'That is, he told my uncle, who told my aunt that he did.'

'Indeed?' The man clearly did not believe her. Did he really spend his days refusing to admit importunate girls to his employer's private rooms?

Well, she was not going to be turned away by this… flunkey! She crossed to the side of the corridor directly opposite the door to the study, leaned against the wall and crossed her arms over her chest.

'I will wait until he's finished whatever it is he's doing, and then you may ask him yourself if he wants to speak to me,' she informed the snooty footman.

'I will go and fetch you a chair,' said Peter sympathetically.

She was just about to thank him when the door opened and Lady Elizabeth's scientist emerged, white-faced and trembling. He stumbled away, a dazed look on his face. It hardly surprised her. Oliver had never looked, to her, like a man who took plots against him lying down. She had no idea what form his retribution would take. She only knew she wouldn't be in Septimus Brown's shoes, not for all the tea in China.

It made her pause. This was not going to be a good time to confront him.

On the other hand, he might as well get all his quarrels over with in one fell swoop.

She stepped forward.

The footman held up his hand, went into the room and shut the door in her face.

He emerged a few seconds later, his expression

wooden. 'You may go straight in,' he said, holding the door open for her. It was all Sofia could do not to poke her tongue out at him on the way past.

Oliver, who was sitting at his desk, rose to his feet and came around it, his hands outstretched in greeting, a smile softening his usually harsh features.

'How dare you,' she cried, forestalling him, 'tell my uncle that I would marry you?'

He came to a dead halt, lowering his arms and his eyebrows. 'Because last night you spoke of loving me...'

'What?' He thought she'd been making a declaration?

Oh! No wonder he'd kissed her.

But then, almost straight away, he'd said love was for fools.

How...humiliating.

'I never said I wanted to marry you,' she shot back at him in self-defence.

'You make a habit of kissing men to whom you are not betrothed, do you?' He planted his fists on his hips. 'I certainly would not have kissed you, had I not believed you had just agreed to become my wife.'

'You never said a word about marriage! You just... pounced!'

'I said a great deal about marriage.' His frown deepened. 'That is, I explained why I needed to marry. I laid out the kind of woman I needed to be a mother to Livvy. You countered with your own version of what kind of marriage you wanted. And then you let me kiss you.'

She went over the conversation they'd had immediately before he kissed her. To be honest, that kiss had been so explosive it had pretty much blown everything else out of her head. And even later it had been all she'd been able to think about…the feel of him holding her close, behind the sofa.

She wiped a hand across her forehead.

'No. I mean, yes, I did, but you…you were speaking in a general way. About your plans to find some woman. A woman who would know how to protect Livvy from malicious gossip and take a stand with you in your bids for reform. Neither of which I can do. Of course I didn't think you meant me!'

Though it certainly explained why he'd kissed her. She had been a bit bewildered, briefly, before she'd caught fire. And then, of course they'd been interrupted by the arrival of Septimus Brown and there hadn't been time for him to enlighten her as to why he'd so suddenly and unexpectedly thrown propriety out of the window.

'So all that talk of love was a lie then, was it?'

For a moment she thought she saw pain flash across his face, though he swiftly closed it off.

'No,' she said, appalled that somehow she'd made this haughty, insular man reach out for something that wasn't there. 'I wasn't lying. You do deserve to find love. Just…'

'Just not with you?'

'Well, no, because…' She took a deep breath. 'Because I deserve to be loved, too. And you recoil from the mere mention of the word.'

His brows drew down. 'I am never going to allow any woman to reduce me to the state where I lose the ability to behave rationally, no.'

'And I am not going to settle for a man who only

wants me to be a mother to his child and an asset to his political ambitions.'

'Settle? A girl does not *settle* for a duke.' He looked so affronted that Sofia saw red.

'No, she schemes and plots and pushes other girls out of the way for the honour of receiving your title, doesn't she? At least, that is the behaviour you seem to think is your due.'

'I think no such thing,' he said, his nostrils flaring in distaste. 'Such behaviour revolts me. Which is why, over the last couple of days, I came to see that you would make me a better wife than any of the titled ladies I had been considering before. That opinion only strengthened when I saw you defending Livvy and was confirmed when you addressed me as Oliver, and let me kiss you.'

Sofia's head was swimming. 'I never thought...' She *had* used his given name, hadn't she? In the dark intimacy of the summer house, she'd forgotten every single etiquette lesson Aunt Agnes had ever given and crossed one of those invisible lines that shored up English society. She guessed this had, in turn, made him think he could do the same.

'That is... I suppose it *is* a great honour, you choosing me to be your wife, but...'

He closed the distance between them, took her by the elbow and led her to a chair. 'Sit down, Miss Underwood. Let me pour you a drink.'

Not only did he pour her a glass of water, but once she had it in her hand he went and flung open the windows—not that it made any improvement. The air outside was even hotter than that in his study.

He looked so stern, so disapproving. Her face flared

even hotter. Could he now be thinking she'd behaved as badly as Lady Elizabeth?

'I don't make a *habit* of kissing men,' she said, returning to the point he'd made earlier. 'In fact, nobody has ever kissed me before, so I did not know how to… that is, what I was supposed to do.' She stared into her glass, miserably realising that what she should have done was slap his face.

Only, she'd been enjoying it too much.

'You did not appear to dislike it,' he pointed out ruthlessly.

'No, well, I didn't. Dislike it, I mean.' She hadn't thought it possible to blush any harder, but the moment the admission spilled from her mouth that was exactly what she did. To the very tips of her toes.

'That,' said the Duke, 'is a good start.'

'Is it?' She gazed up at him and caught, briefly, an extremely predatory look in his eyes before he banked it down.

'It means that you will not find my attentions, as a husband, repellent.'

'No. What?' He still wanted to marry her? Even after all she'd just said? 'But you can't possibly want to marry *me*. I've just told you, I'm not fit for the role of Duchess. You want someone who can be a political asset to you…'

'Being a duchess is not as important to me as what you can do for Livvy.'

'But I can't launch her into society. I have no idea how to go on myself.'

'I will introduce you into society and you will soon learn how to go on. And in the meantime, I know I can trust you never to hurt her.'

'No, I couldn't, but... I will fail you in other ways. My mother was Portuguese. And a Catholic. People will say...'

'That you are an exotic beauty, if they don't wish to offend me.'

She gaped at him. A beauty? Exotic? 'But... I...' She was running out of objections. And it was hard to think of anything other than the look in his eyes when he'd said she was a beauty. 'I have no idea how to run a place this size...'

'I have an excellent housekeeper and well-trained staff.'

She cringed, remembering the way that woman, and various others of his retinue, had looked down their noses at her.

'You would be able to rely on them to keep on running things smoothly.'

Oh, yes. They'd be only too happy to keep her firmly in her place.

'You have not,' he said, 'mentioned the match I believe your uncle wished you to make. To the man you told me only wanted you for your fortune. I am surely better for you than him?'

She grimaced. 'That is not saying very much. I idolised him for years, thinking he liked me. And then I overheard him one day, mocking me. Overheard his plans for how he would treat me once we were married...' She couldn't help shuddering in revulsion at the memory of how cold and shocked she'd felt, huddled under that jetty, listening to Jack ripping her whole future to shreds.

'I, at least, have no designs on your money. You may spend it as you wish.'

'Thank you,' she said listlessly. For it wasn't really about money, anyway.

'You could do a great deal of good with it,' he persisted, as though holding out a shiny toy to a recalcitrant toddler. 'Remember Mrs Pagett?'

'The...the burnt woman, from the fireworks display?'

'Yes. I know you wanted to do something for her and fretted because you were not permitted even to visit her. She is not going to be able to find work easily, not now that her face is so scarred. Even were I to set her up in some trade, she would find it hard to find customers. But if you, as my Duchess, were to patronise her—dress shop, or hat shop, or whatever she has the skill to work at—her future would be assured.'

'Yes...' She turned the glass around in her fingers. 'I can see that I could do a lot of good, if I were to marry you. Only...' She looked up at him. Really looked at him. He seemed decent. He cared about poor Mrs Pagett and his little girl, certainly. And he could kiss so amazingly well that her toes were curling in her slippers just from looking at his mouth.

She lowered her gaze and wondered if she really could entrust her whole future to a man she'd known a matter of weeks.

The trouble was, she'd been let down too many times already by men she'd trusted. First her father, by dying, and then his family, who'd taken her in, but then done their utmost to change her into somebody she could never be. And then Jack, who'd led her on, only to destroy her hope, bruise her heart and make her feel like such a fool.

'This would be the rest of my life,' she said.

'And mine.'

'But we hardly know each other.'

'I know you have a compassionate heart and that you are too well bred to fling yourself at me the way so many women have done. And that if you were to marry me, I would not feel as if I were shackling myself to a grasping, deceitful harpy, which has been my fear for some time.'

'I... I need time to think about this. I never dreamed...'

'That is another thing I like about you. You have no vanity.' He took the now-empty glass from her hand and set it on his desk. When he turned back to her, his face was a haughty mask.

'I will give you the time to think my proposal over, then. The house party does not come to an end for another three days. You will inform me of your decision before then.'

Three days? How on earth was she to make a decision that would affect her whole future in three days? What could possibly help her make up her mind? In three days? Why, she'd known Jack for twice that number of years. And been totally wrong about him. If she hadn't overheard him joking with his friend, she would still have no idea how he really saw her.

Oliver *sounded* sincere. When he looked at her, she could believe he meant every word he said.

But then, she'd believed in Jack, too.

## Chapter Twenty

'You did what?' Aunt Agnes eyed Sofia with incredulity. 'But you would have been a duchess,' she cried in bewilderment, waving Marguerite out of the room.

Sofia braced herself.

'I suppose…' Aunt Agnes paused, appearing to struggle with herself. 'That is, I can see that your attachment to Jack is even stronger than I suspected. Well,' she said, crestfallen, 'at least your Uncle Ned can boast that you didn't have your head turned by the prospect of a coronet.'

What? No! Jack had nothing to do with her turning down Oliver's proposal. Or not directly. But that was what her whole family was going to think if she didn't speak up. But while she was still plucking up the courage to confess what she'd heard Jack saying about her, Aunt Agnes spoke again.

'I suppose it hardly matters what you wear for the picnic now,' she said gloomily, casting the froth of muslin she'd been holding over the back of a chair. 'As long as it is clean,' she finished saying, casting a withering glance over the outfit Sofia had worn both to walk Snowball through the woods and to turn down Oliver's proposal. She then strode from the room with her back ramrod straight, as though determined not to show how disappointed she was that all her dreams of a glittering future as aunt to the Duchess of Theakstone had just come crashing down.

Sofia stared at the door for a good few minutes after Aunt Agnes had shut it behind her. She would give almost anything not to disappoint her aunt. But what was worse was that anyone might think she was so infatuated with Jack she'd even throw over a duke. That possibility was so appalling she had half a mind to go straight back down to his study and tell him she'd thought it over and decided to marry him after all, just to prove it wasn't true.

Only, that really wasn't a good enough reason for marrying anyone. Especially a man who deserved so much more. If she did decide to marry him, she wasn't going to do it just to thumb her nose at anyone. No matter how tempting it was.

She eyed with misgivings the flimsy muslin gown that Marguerite had produced from somewhere. It was the most impractical thing to wear to a picnic. She always came back from picnics covered in grass stains. Nevertheless, Aunt Agnes had intended her to wear it. And so, Sofia decided, to make it up to her for her disappointment at not presiding over a match with a duke, she would put it on. It had the advantage of being more likely to keep her cool than anything else she had in her wardrobe.

And, she discovered later, when she reached the rear of the house where all the ladies were gathering to wait for the carriages which would take them the short distance to the lake, at least she fit right in. On the surface, that was, since everyone else was wearing white—insubstantial creations that looked too delicate to wear in a drawing room, never mind a field.

But none of them greeted her. Or even appeared to notice she and her aunt had arrived. She lifted her chin. They all knew her family had arrived in a hired post-chaise. They all knew she had no means of getting down to the lake, but none of them looked the least bit inclined to offer them a lift.

Sofia and Aunt Agnes hung back when the carriages came into view, the men of the party riding beside them on horseback. But the footman standing up behind the first carriage to arrive, an open carriage with a ducal crest on the door, was Peter. And he was grinning at her as he jumped down, opened the door, let down the steps and then beckoned them to get in.

'This,' said Aunt Agnes from the side of her mouth as she stalked regally to the carriage, 'has made my day. Do you see the look on Lady Sale's face?' She opened her parasol with a flourish as soon as she'd taken her seat. 'That dreadful woman thinks she ought to go first, because she is the highest-ranking lady. But her carriage is now second to ours.'

Oh, good grief. What did it matter whose carriage went first? Was that all these people cared about? Position? And rank and wealth?'

'Sofia, put up your parasol,' said her aunt the moment they drew out of the porch. 'You are squinting in the sun. And your complexion is bad enough as it is, what with you romping about all over the place with that ridiculous little dog of yours whenever you think I'm not watching you.'

But there was hardly any sting in her voice and Sofia discovered why as she was obediently raising her own parasol.

'His Grace clearly has not given up all hope if he has set you above all the other ladies, like this,' said Aunt Agnes with a smile.

'Set me above them? What do you mean?'

'He's put you at the head of the procession, you goose. What do you think it means?'

It meant he wasn't the kind of man who gave up at the first hurdle. Or sulked when it looked as if he wasn't going to get his own way.

The carriage went over a bump and it occurred to Sofia that it could just as easily mean that he hadn't been anywhere near as hurt as he'd looked, that his feelings were not engaged in the slightest.

She twirled her parasol thoughtfully. Hadn't he made it crystal clear that his motives for asking her to marry him were of a practical nature? He wanted someone to replace Livvy's mother.

And though he'd only mentioned it obliquely, some-body to provide him with a legitimate heir, too.

Her stomach flipped as she relived that kiss and the moments behind the sofa when he'd held her so closely—which were the sorts of activities they'd do more of, in order to get that heir. Though hopefully not behind a sofa.

She looked at the scenery through which they were driving with new eyes. Theakstone Court would certainly be a lovely place to live. Snowball loved the beech plantation already and, if only she could have the charge of Livvy, she could make it a wonderful playground for the little girl. To start with, she'd build her a tree house...

But to do any of that, first she'd have to marry Oliver.

And would that be such a hardship? She didn't actively dislike him. On the contrary...

She thought of all the times she'd compared some aspect of his behaviour with that of Jack, or Uncle Ned; the times he'd come to her defence when someone had been trying to undermine her.

And the way he'd made her feel when he'd kissed her. If that was anything to go by, she'd certainly enjoy the physical side of the union.

Come to that, he couldn't have kissed her like that if he didn't find her attractive, could he?

If only he wasn't so determined not to love her. If only he would ride beside her carriage and act like a proper suitor, instead of staying right at the back of the cavalcade with Captain Beamish and...oh... Uncle Ned. Was that significant?

She forced her gaze away from the Duke, even though he did look particularly splendid on horseback, and gazed in the direction of the lake. She couldn't help smiling. There were so many chairs and tables set out under pavilions along the shoreline that it looked more like a town fair than a picnic. Or perhaps an army bivouac, with the picket line for the horses strung out under the shade of some elms. Although, an army bivouac wouldn't have an area to park all the carriages as well—or not carriages like these. Nor would there be liveried grooms helping the ladies from their carriages and pouring out glasses of iced punch. Nor would the army make use of any of the frivolous little boats drawn up on the shore, just as the Duke had promised, should anyone wish to go out on the water.

Uncle Ned made straight for the nearest refreshment tent the moment he dismounted from the fine grey he'd obviously selected from the Duke's stables. The Duke followed close behind. As soon as the ladies descended from their carriages, they started drifting in the same direction.

Lady Sarah, being in the second carriage to arrive and being more ambitious than the others, reached Oliver first.

'How delightful all this looks, Your Grace,' she cooed. 'I cannot wait to take a turn in one of those charming little boats,' she said, fluttering her eyelashes up at him.

'Of course,' he said, beckoning the nearest footman. 'Take Lady Sarah out on to the lake, would you, Simmons?'

As the footman dipped his head in acknowledgement, Sofia caught a momentary look of acute annoyance on Lady Sarah's face. She stifled it swiftly, however, and by the time Oliver was looking down at her again she'd summoned up a syrupy smile.

'Of course you may not abandon your other guests so soon after arriving,' she said, as though sympathising with the onerous nature of his duties.

Sofia spun away before anyone could catch her laughing…though not so quickly that she didn't see Lady Elizabeth stepping into the vacant slot beside him.

Oh, dear. It was going to be like that, was it? Well, she had no wish to stand there watching the other girls all making fools of themselves as they fought to win his approval, without knowing he'd already proposed to her. She'd walk away from the city of tents and go down to the water's edge. Maybe there would be a breeze down there.

For the first time since meeting her rivals, Sofia felt a pang of sympathy for them. But it had passed before she'd reached the lake because at least they all knew what they wanted out of life. They wanted to be duchesses, have lots of money and the right to go first. None of which mattered to Sofia in the least.

She strolled along the sandy shoreline in the direction of a jetty which projected several feet into the water. As their shrill voices faded, and the soothing sounds of lapping waves took their place, she asked herself what she did want, if she didn't want rank or money or the right to go first?

Well, to be honest, she did want money. Her own money, that was. Which Oliver said he would give her.

She stepped up on to the first plank of the jetty and couldn't help thinking of the day she'd hidden beneath a very similar structure and overheard Jack's plans for her future. At least Oliver respected her. He must do, to say he could entrust his own daughter to her, mustn't he?

And he was genuinely attracted to her, or he couldn't have kissed her the way he had. Or spoken of it the way he had. Nor had she imagined the heat smouldering in his eyes when he'd mentioned getting an heir. He wouldn't simply be *doing his duty*, the way Jack had been bracing himself to do.

Golly, but it was hot today. She strolled along to the end of the jetty and gazed out over the water, her lips firming in annoyance as she thought of all those women Jack had planned to take to his bed, women he would enjoy being with, once he'd got her safely with child.

Would Oliver have other…amusements, if she married him? He hadn't said he planned to be a faithful husband and he was clearly active in that regard or he'd never have fathered Livvy.

It made her feel a bit queasy to think of him with other women, in that way. Upset, if she was perfectly honest. In a different way to when she'd imagined Jack with other women. It was Jack's rejection of her that had wounded her. He'd made her feel as though she wasn't good enough, which had brought back all the insecurities she'd felt upon first arriving at Nettleton Manor. It wasn't the same as this possessive, visceral feeling she had imagining the Duke breaking their marriage vows. If she ever discovered he was playing her false, she wouldn't hide in her room feeling sorry for herself, too embarrassed by his betrayal to be able to face anyone else. On the contrary, she would track him down and…and, well she wasn't totally sure what, but there was definitely a pair of scissors in her hand as she marched into that imaginary, faceless, adulteress's boudoir.

She had to unclench her fists. And then wondered if, perhaps, if the thought of him being unfaithful was so upsetting, she ought not to marry him.

What, and give him licence to…to frolic with whatever woman took his fancy?

Insupportable!

Oh, dear. It looked as though she was going to have to settle for whatever he had to offer her, rather than strain for something she wasn't even sure she could describe. It wasn't as if she was ever likely to meet a man she'd like more than she liked the Duke. And, oh, the way he kissed! She flushed at the thought of it and promptly delved into her reticule for a fan. Nobody would think it odd for her to ply it before her overheated face, not on such a day. But, oh, how she wished she could sit on the edge of the jetty and dangle her feet in the water. But that would mean removing her shoes and stockings. In public. Which would shock not only Aunt Agnes, but also every other lady present.

She sighed. The clear green water of the lake looked so cool and inviting. If she'd been at Nettleton Manor on such a day, she'd have made the excuse of taking Snowball for a walk, made straight for her favourite pond, stripped down to her chemise and dived right in.

Which sort of answered her question about what she wanted from life. She wanted the freedom to swim when it was as hot as this, that was what! She was just smiling wryly at how little it would take to make her happy, if husbands didn't enter the equation, when she registered the sound of footsteps tapping along the jetty behind her. Reluctantly she turned to see Lady Margaret marching her way, a militant light in her eyes. As though she was spoiling for a fight.

Instinctively, Sofia took a step backwards. If there was one thing she hated, it was confrontation with another person, which made her reaction to the thought of how she'd behave should Oliver ever stray all the more startling.

'I know you cannot help it,' said Lady Margaret, 'being brought up by that vulgar woman who calls herself your aunt, so I have come to tell you that it is not at all the thing to come apart by yourself like this.'

'Oh?' She edged back, as Lady Margaret thrust her face forward angrily.

'And what is more, we don't like the way you have taken sides with Lady Elizabeth.'

*We?* 'Sides?'

'Don't give me that innocent look. We saw you, out of the window, yesterday. You and that dog of yours, fawning round Lady Elizabeth. Pretending you were as keen on archery as she. Making a total fool of yourself!'

Ah. Yes, well, she had made a bit of a fool of herself, it was true, but it had only been to draw attention away from Livvy. And it had clearly worked. While Lady Elizabeth had been concentrating on showing her how to hold a bow and the footmen had been running to retrieve stray arrows before Snowball bore them off into the shrubbery, Livvy had managed to sneak from pillar to fountain to shrub, and finally to the gatepost of the kitchen yard entirely unnoticed.

'I suppose you think His Grace is going to offer for her.'

'No, I don't think that,' Sofia said with a smile. In fact, she knew he wouldn't, not after what he'd seen her getting up to in the summer house.

'Then what are you laughing at?'

'I am not laughing,' she protested, although the more she thought about Lady Margaret's ridiculous assumptions, the funnier she found it.

'I see,' she said, drawing herself up to her full height. 'You are mocking me, for being true to Lady

Sarah. For coming to say to you what the others are all thinking.'

'No, indeed, I…'

'Well, I have had just about enough of it. The way you watch us all with that supercilious little smile on your face, as though you think you are better than us, when you are a nobody. Do you hear me?' She thrust her face into Sofia's with such aggression she had to take a step back. 'Nobody!' She went to poke her in the chest, for emphasis, just as Sofia took another step back.

Only there was nothing behind her but air. She'd been inching back during Lady Margaret's tirade and had finally reached the end of the jetty.

The result was inevitable. With flailing arms, Sofia went off the end of the jetty, right into the water.

Her first reaction was to laugh. She'd been wishing she could take a swim and now here she was, in the water, after all.

Her second was to turn over and dive as deeply as she could possibly go, which she did, after surfacing briefly to take a deep breath. Because, now that she was in the water, she intended to make the most of it. If she could swim a few yards away from the jetty while she was underwater, then, once she surfaced again, she could take her time making her way back to shore. It wouldn't be the same as having a leisurely swim, unhampered by clothing, but it would still be sufficient to cool her down.

And she might as well be hanged for a sheep as a lamb. Even though she hadn't gone into the water on purpose, she was bound to get the blame for *causing a scene*. The Lady Margarets of this world always blamed someone else at times like this and invariably got away with it.

But who cared, when the water was so deliciously cool and refreshing?

## *Chapter Twenty-One*

Even though Oliver made a point of mingling with all his other guests, he was always aware of exactly where Sofia was and strangely sensitive to the expressions that flitted across her face.

He could see she was thinking deeply. Hopefully about his offer. Although with Sofia he could never be sure that he was at the forefront of her mind. Nor could he think of a single thing that might sway her opinion in his favour, even if it was his proposal that was putting that thoughtful expression on her face. He'd offered her everything: his name, his title, the freedom to spend her money however she wished, as long as she would agree to be a mother to Livvy.

And all she would say was that she would think about it.

Dammit, he hadn't felt this helpless since the day that housemaid had swept him up and into the coach, and dropped him off at the house of the people she said were his new parents.

He was abrupt to the point of rudeness to the girls who kept approaching him and fluttering their silly eyelashes up at him, because he didn't want any of them any longer. He only wanted Sofia. But they wouldn't take the hint. They hovered round him like so many pesky flies that he wished he could swat away.

While she…she was strolling along the jetty, looking out over the lake, a wistful expression growing stronger as though…yes, he could see it. There was *something* she wanted.

If he could only persuade her to tell him what it was, he would swear to give it to her. And then maybe she'd agree to be his wife. And mother to Livvy, too, of course. Yes, being Livvy's mother was the most important thing.

He would ask her. Right now. He turned to give his empty tankard to the nearest footman, but when he turned back in the direction of the jetty, he saw Lady Margaret already marching along it, as though she was as intent on speaking to Sofia as he was. Though not, to judge from her brisk step and the tilt of her chin, from friendly motives.

Yet it still came as a shock when, after a brief altercation, Lady Margaret pushed Sofia off the end of the jetty.

The massive splash as she flopped backwards into the water caused everyone else to turn and stare, but he'd already started running for the jetty.

Sofia bobbed to the surface briefly, gasping for air, but then sank beneath the foam caused by her initial fall. And then, ominously, her bonnet floated to the surface.

A cold hand fisted in his stomach. She couldn't drown. Not now. Not in his lake. He tore off his jacket as he ran, casting it aside as he reached the wooden planking of the jetty. He ran to the end, where Lady Margaret was standing with her hands to her mouth, staring in horror at the bubbles breaking the surface where Sofia had gone in, and roughly shoved her aside.

'Oh, oh,' she wailed. 'I think I am going to swoon...'

'Get back to shore and do it there,' he growled as he sat down to rip off his boots. 'I don't want any more women falling into the lake today.'

He stood up so that he could search for any trace of Sofia through the cloudy green water, his heart thudding so hard it made him feel a bit sick. The thought of her coming to harm, of possibly losing her life altogether was so appalling he wanted to roar in defiance. He'd only just found her. Fate couldn't be so cruel as to take her from him so soon! He needed more time with her. Years. The rest of his life. Even if she couldn't love him—and what woman could—he would have made sure she'd never regret taking a chance on him.

There! A trail of bubbles. He dived in, aiming in that direction. Once beneath the surface he could see a white mass which had to be Sofia's gown, just where he'd hoped to find her. It took him only a few determined kicks to reach her and get his arms round her waist.

A couple more to bring them both to the surface.

'Don't be afraid,' he said, as she struggled against his hold. 'You're safe now, I've got you.' *I've got you. I've got you.* He wanted to weep with the sheer relief of having her in his arms, breathing air. If he had his way he'd never let her go again.

'I'm not afraid, you great...bully,' she hissed.

'Bully?' Why could she not simply be grateful, like any other woman would? Why did she always have to make everything so difficult? 'I just saved you from drowning, you ungrateful baggage.'

'No, you didn't. I wasn't drowning.' This time, when she struggled, he let her wriggle out of his arms. And she trod water—with marked proficiency, he noted—while glaring at him, her hair straggling all down her face.

'I was just swimming underwater,' she said. 'I would have come in all by myself in my own good time if you hadn't come along and...'

'Well, pardon me for being worried. For rushing to your aid.' From the corner of his eye he could see the rest of his guests gathering by the shore, while a couple of the footmen were launching one of the boats. For two pins he'd swim off and leave her here. Leave her for the footmen to haul out of the water and into their boat...

Only, the thought of any other man, even a servant, putting his hands on her was out of the question.

'Which you still need,' he continued coldly.

'No, I don't. I'm perfectly capable of swimming to shore.'

'Where you will face the censure of every person there. Every person you scared with your outrageous prank.'

'It was not a prank! I...'

'Decided to take a swim and make a spectacle of yourself.'

'That's not true. And it's not fair.'

'It is true.' Though it might well not be fair. Lady Margaret had pushed her. So she hadn't gone into the water of her own volition.

Staying in it, however…that *had* been totally reprehensible.

'Everyone is staring,' he said. 'Your aunt looks as though she is about to faint.'

'What?' She stopped glaring at him, briefly, to look wildly in the direction of the shore. At last, she had started to think about someone other than herself.

'And if she finds out you were not in any difficulty, I should think she will want to wring your pretty neck. Just as I do.'

She bit down on her lower lip.

'So this is what will happen,' he said, firmly. 'I shall help you to shore, where you will act upon the verge of swooning. I will then carry you to your carriage and I will despatch you, and your aunt, back to the house, where she may wreak whatever vengeance she wishes upon your stubborn, wilful, rebellious head!'

She glared at him, but did not struggle again when he got hold of her by the shoulders, flipped over on to his back and began towing her to shore.

She didn't struggle when, the moment he could touch the bottom, he stood up and waded the rest of the way, with her cradled in his arms. She didn't put her arms about his neck, though, not her. But she did turn her face into his shoulder when the other guests began crowding round, and wound the fingers of one hand into his sodden shirt. Fingers that were trembling.

As he strode across the grass to where the carriages were all drawn up under the trees, he was sorely tempted to fabricate some reason which made it essential he carried her in his arms all the way to the house because he found he was strangely reluctant to let her go. She'd infuriated him, scared him, but the way her little fingers were clutching at his shirt made him want to prove that he was able to keep her safe in his arms for…for ever.

If she would let him.

It was all he could do not to drop a kiss on her forehead after he'd placed her gently on the seat.

The groom, who'd seen him coming, was hastily hitching up the horses, which he'd been watering further along the lake, away from the guests. This gave Oliver the excuse to linger, his arms braced over her, while he studied the shamed expression on her face.

But not for long. First of all, a footman came running up with his jacket. Rather than attempting to put it back on over his sodden shirt he draped it round Sofia's shoulders.

And then her aunt and uncle reached them.

'She is not hurt,' he said, turning around as they pushed their way into the carriage. 'Only a bit…' Chastened, he wanted to say. By the way he'd shouted at her.

'You must send for a doctor,' said her aunt, cutting through his statement in a way he would not have forgiven, in most circumstances. 'She is only just recovering from an inflammation of the lungs and heaven knows what a dunking in that filthy pond water will do to her. If she should have a relapse…' The woman seized one of Sofia's hands and began chafing it. Which made Sofia, at last, show some sign of remorse.

'Of course I will send my physician to her,' said Oliver, rather more abruptly than he should have done. But then he was annoyed that he hadn't thought of it himself. 'In the meantime, I will send a footman to alert the housekeeper you are on your way and will need hot water for a bath. I shall do everything possible to ensure Miss Underwood's comfort,' he said, straightening up and beckoning the footman who'd come running with his jacket. On horseback, the lad would reach the house well before the carriage. Especially since he could cut across the paddock, rather than having to stick to the carriageways.

Sofia turned her hand over and gripped Aunt Agnes's. If anything could prove her aunt was truly fond of her, the way she'd just ordered a duke to fetch a doctor had done it.

'He seems fond of you, that I will concede,' said Uncle Ned bracingly, after the carriage carrying them had been rolling along for a while and neither of the females had recovered enough to make any sort of conversation. 'The look on his face as he dived in to rescue you...' He looked Sofia up and down and sighed. 'Can't deny I'm disappointed to think you will be going so far from us. I hoped that marrying Jack would mean we could keep a bit of an eye on you, what with your own parents being gone.'

What? Did he really mean that?

Had it only been Jack himself who was more interested in her money than in her?

She wanted to say something along the lines of them being able to visit whenever they wished. Only, did Oliver still wish to marry her? The things he'd said made her suspect not.

Uncle Ned handed her his handkerchief.

'I'm sorry,' she said, dabbing at the tears she hadn't realised were welling from her eyes.

'You couldn't help falling into the water, I suppose.

Loose plank, or something, was it? Caught the hem of your gown?'

'No, I...' She paused. She didn't want to stir up any more trouble than she'd already caused by her thoughtless wish to indulge in a swim. Which she was bound to do if she pointed out that she'd only fallen in because she'd been backing away from Lady Margaret. 'It is about... Jack that I'm sorry.' It was time to tell them. And she felt she could, now, knowing that they'd only promoted the match in an attempt to protect her. 'Because, you see, no matter what else happens, I could never marry him.'

'What?' Her aunt and uncle both looked at her as though she'd grown two heads.

'But you are so fond of him,' said Uncle Ned with a perplexed frown. 'Whenever he visited, you would follow him around like a little puppy. Which was why I thought of it in the first place, why I spoke to my sister about a match. I thought it would spare you having to fend off all the rogues who'd come sniffing after your fortune if we took you to London for a Season.'

Oh. He'd thought he was doing her a good turn. It wasn't his fault Jack had been exactly the sort of rogue he'd been trying to save her from.

'I... I *was* fond of him.'

When they both frowned, she suddenly baulked at the prospect of confessing what she'd overheard him saying. Not only would it be humiliating to repeat the horrid things he'd said, but she'd have to admit she'd been swimming on that day, too. And they'd never let her out of their sight again...if she did go back to live at Nettleton Manor, that was.

And what was more, it might cause a rift between the two families.

'That is, I *am* fond of him, of course…'

'Oh, I see,' Aunt Agnes broke in when she hesitated. 'In the way a girl thinks of a brother.'

'Um…'

'Well, naturally a girl cannot marry someone she thinks of in that light.'

'Um,' she said again, but they both looked so relieved and then Uncle Ned leaned over and patted her knee.

'Glad you explained that,' he said. 'Thought I'd bungled it. Bungle just about everything, according to most people.'

'That's not true, Ned,' said Aunt Agnes. 'There's not another man would have supported my decision to bring Sofia up as one of our own, the way you have done.'

'Did nothing, really,' he blustered.

'Oh, yes you did. Never raised a single objection, even though you knew there was bound to be talk about the way my brother…'

'Pooh,' he said scornfully. 'Didn't we cause our own scandal when you married me in the face of all that opposition from your family? What did your brother do that was so very different? Eh?'

'Ned, you are the best of men,' said Aunt Agnes, giving his hand a squeeze.

'Well, well, glad you think so old girl,' he said, squeezing back. 'And what of you, Sofia?' he said, startling her by asking her opinion. 'No hard feelings over me getting it so wrong about Jack, eh?'

'None at all.'

'So I can wish you well of your Duke with a clear conscience, then?'

Ah. Well, that was another matter entirely.

By making the most of her time in the water rather than striking out for the shore straight away, she'd worried everyone. And someone who put her own wishes first wasn't the kind of woman he'd want to be a mother to Livvy.

The carriage swept into the courtyard, and, as Sofia looked up at the massive edifice over which she might have presided, had she not been so silly, her stomach turned over.

What if he didn't wait until the end of the house party to hear her answer to his proposal? What if, instead, he selected one of the others? Someone more sensible? And better behaved?

'Sofia, Sofia!' Aunt Agnes was peering at her intently. 'What is it? You have gone so pale.'

She felt pale all of a sudden. Pale and hollowed out. How could she have been stupid enough to insist Oliver wait for her answer? All she'd achieved was to give him the chance to come to his senses and realise, like practically everyone else already had, that she was just not cut out to be a duchess.

# Chapter Twenty-Two

By the time Peter tracked down Dr Cochrane, Sofia had taken a warm bath and, at her aunt's urging, put on nightclothes and got into bed.

After giving her a brief examination, and listening to the history of her winter ailments, the doctor was happy to agree with Aunt Agnes that it was essential she stay warm and rest in bed until everyone was satisfied she was not going to take another chill from her wetting.

In spite of believing it was a totally unnecessary precaution, Sofia did not argue. Being sent to bed felt like a completely reasonable punishment for frightening everyone and arguing with Oliver, and finally, allowing her aunt and uncle to believe an untruth about Jack. Even if she had only done so to spare their feelings. Because she really didn't regard Jack in a sisterly fashion.

Unless sisters absolutely loathed their brothers as a matter of course.

However, she soon found that it wasn't much of a punishment at all. First of all, a friendly, smiley little maid came to her room with all sorts of interesting books from Oliver's library. And then, at dinner time, instead of having to go downstairs and face anyone, the same maid brought up a tray laden with a tempting array of dishes. And, later, dessert and tea.

Which all had Sofia writhing with guilt. And not only about what had happened today. Her aunt and uncle might not have known how to deal with her grief when she'd first gone to live with them, but in their own way they appeared to have become fond of her. And after today's conversation on the way back from the lake she had a better understanding of the way they'd treated her. To be perfectly honest, the way her father had lived had not been very respectable. Looking back, she could see that all the lectures about impropriety and the importance of making a good impression on people had stemmed from a wish to undo the evil to which they believed he had exposed her. And her aunt's insistence that she never do anything that anyone might interpret as loose behaviour must have been because rumours of her father's irregular relationships with the ladies he'd brought in to look after her had been running rife. She could see now how careful they'd been to demonstrate that even though she had been exposed to a certain type of sin in her youth, it had not rubbed off on her—which she'd interpreted as them being stiflingly strict.

And Uncle Ned wasn't as uninterested in her as she'd thought, either. Now she came to think of it, he'd had as little to do with Betty and Celia's upbringing as hers. He really did believe it was Aunt Agnes's role to raise the girls.

Everything they'd done had been from a determination to do their best. She just knew it. It certainly explained the way they suddenly seemed to have done such a complete about-face regarding Jack's suit since Oliver had started showing an interest. After all, the Duke certainly wasn't a fortune hunter. And he was so high on the social scale that her own slightly scandalous background meant little to him. He could have married his actress, had the fancy taken him, and nobody could have done anything about it.

Not that it had any bearing on the matter. She lifted her plait up off the back of her neck as she heaved a doleful sigh. Instead of growing cooler as darkness fell, the air was becoming so sultry it felt as if it was pressing down on the roof of Theakstone Court. And, by the sound of the footsteps pacing back and forth in the room above hers, robbing at least one of the other inmates of sleep.

So, the next morning, when Aunt Agnes came in to ask how she was feeling, just as the smiley housemaid was bringing in her breakfast tray, she couldn't help telling the truth.

'I feel wretched.'

Aunt Agnes didn't ask her to explain in what way she felt wretched, she just placed a hand on her forehead, saying, 'You do seem a trifle warm.'

Well, that wasn't surprising considering she'd hauled the blankets over her legs the moment her door had opened. And the temperature outside was already as hot as anything she could remember experiencing as a girl, in far more southerly climes.

'You had best stay in bed until the doctor has seen you again,' said Aunt Agnes decisively, before leaving her to go down for her own breakfast.

The moment she'd gone, Sofia pushed the tray aside and got out of bed. She went to the window and flung up the sash. Some air did trickle into the room, but it wasn't any cooler than what was already inside. She leaned on the windowsill and gazed yearningly in the direction of the beech wood, the treetops of which she could just make out above the opposite wing of the Court. There would be some shade there. And more of a breeze, up on that rise—but she couldn't leave this room.

It was a fitting punishment for her, only she wished Snowball didn't have to suffer, too.

Would anyone think of taking her dog for a walk? The kennel man exercised the hounds daily, but she didn't think he'd allow Snowball to run with them.

It didn't seem fair for Snowball to suffer because of her own misbehaviour. She chewed on a bit of loose skin beside her thumbnail. Could she ask Peter to take Snowball for a walk? Or would he not be allowed to shirk his other duties? Would Snowball even go with him? Nobody but Sofia had ever taken her for a walk before. Snowball did have some shade in her run and she would have food and water. But it wasn't enough for a dog used to being with her mistress every hour of the day.

Very well. This must be the last day she spent hiding in her room. She would have to persuade the doctor, and more importantly Aunt Agnes, that she had taken no harm from her unexpected dip in the lake and then summon up some courage from somewhere and go and face the other house guests.

And Oliver.

She'd thought she couldn't bear to watch him selecting any of the other candidates, if he really had thought better of asking her to marry him. But she rather thought that in future years, when she looked back on this week, she would feel far worse if she simply let him go without putting up a fight.

It was high time she stood up for herself instead of hiding away whenever anything got hard to deal with. Running away and hiding had never done her any good, had it? It was what she'd done when she'd overheard Jack, rather than facing up to the truth.

But if she'd faced Jack down, got it all out into the open...

She shuddered. There would have been a terrible scene.

But at least she wouldn't have ended up practically lying to her uncle and aunt, who didn't deserve that sort of treatment after all they'd done for her.

At least she had managed to tell them point-blank that she could never, ever marry Jack. It was only the *why* she'd shied away from bringing into the open.

And telling them even that much had certainly cleared the air.

She drew in a deep breath of air that was far from clear, as it struck her that in finally speaking up for herself, she was starting to grow up. She was no longer that frightened, lonely little girl who would have done anything to win the approval of the only people who'd been willing to take her in, even though she had looked such a disgrace.

As the word slipped into her mind, her thoughts diverted from herself, and directly to Livvy—a little girl who felt much the same as she'd done once and with far greater cause. Because someone in this household had told her, to her face, that she was a Disgrace.

She clenched her fist. If there was anything she could do while she was here to ease the plight of that poor little girl...

She could do it by marrying Oliver himself. That was what he wanted—or had wanted, before she'd made such an exhibition of herself.

But...he couldn't withdraw his proposal. It wasn't the done thing. It was for the woman in question to do that.

So, if she didn't let him...if she insisted he stuck to his word...

The others were prepared to fight for him. Why shouldn't she?

Because it would be to sink to their level, that was why.

She pounded the window frame with that fist. She'd hated him proposing simply because she could mother his child. It had hurt almost as much as hearing that Jack was only pretending to be interested so that he could feather his own nest.

She wanted...she wanted...someone to love her, for herself.

A man who loved her enough to defy convention, flout the rules of two religions and ignore the censure of his family, to make her his; who would think her such a fine woman that, should she die, he would never wed another.

In short, a man who would love her the way her father had loved her mother.

She sighed and pressed her head to the cool glass of the windowpane in misery. For how she was to achieve that goal, when she'd got entangled with Oliver and his daughter, she couldn't begin to imagine. If she went downstairs, for instance, and reminded him he was honour-bound to stick to his proposal, not only would she be just as bad as the others who'd stop at nothing to gain his title, but she'd never be sure he had any real regard for her at all. Let alone the kind of love she'd just discovered she truly wanted.

Still, she—

A knock at the door broke her train of thought. A knock unlike that of the maids, or the housekeeper. If anything, it sounded like a very timid attempt to attract her attention, as if whoever was on the other side of her door was hoping she wouldn't even hear it.

So instead of calling out to let whoever it was know they could come in, she walked to the door and opened it herself.

To see Lady Margaret standing there. Sofia's first shock at receiving such a grand visitor, before she'd even washed and changed out of her nightgown, soon gave way to concern when she saw the way Lady Margaret was wringing her hands and looking as though she was about to burst into tears.

'Whatever is the matter? Oh, you'd better come in,' she added, as Lady Margaret gave a little sob and tears began flowing down her face.

She pulled the sobbing girl over to a chair and went to her dresser to find a handkerchief, since Lady Margaret didn't have a reticule with her.

'Th-thank you,' she said as Sofia pressed the hanky into her hand. 'I n-never knew that you had been so ill,' she said, wiping her cheeks. 'I n-never thought you m-might die from some sort of infection. I n-never meant you to f-fall into the lake, c-come to that.'

'I know you didn't,' said Sofia soothingly. 'It was

all the most stupid accident. I missed my footing, that was all.'

'B-but everyone is saying I p-pushed you in out of spite! And this morning, at breakfast, your aunt was telling everyone how delicate you are, how you've been ill all w-winter and were at Burslem Bay taking the c-cure...'

'Well, that just goes to show how silly it would be to try to kill me by pushing me into the lake, even if that had been what you were trying to do, which of course you weren't,' Sofia responded, going to her drawer to fetch another hanky, since Lady Margaret had already soaked the first one. 'I mean, why should dunking in sea water be a cure, yet dunking in lake water be lethal?'

'Oh. Yes, I...' Lady Margaret sniffed. 'I never thought of it like that.' She took the second hanky and blew her nose.

'And to let you into a little secret,' she said, snatching up a shawl to drape round her shoulders since her summer nightgown was rather insubstantial, 'I have suffered no ill effects at all. The only reason I am staying in my room today is because...' She paused, feeling her cheeks heating up.

'You need not explain. I can quite understand how mortifying it must have been when everyone saw more of you than they should, what with your gown going completely transparent after its soaking, and how hard it must be for you to come down and face everyone.'

Oh. That was an aspect she hadn't considered before. Although they wouldn't have seen much more than her legs, surely? After all, her corset was a robust affair of canvas and whalebone, which wouldn't become transparent no matter how wet it might get. And Oliver had kept her close to his chest, and walked very, very fast to the carriage, so that people would not even have had more than a glimpse of her legs and that from a distance. And then he'd covered her with his own jacket.

Once more, she looked back upon a person's actions from a new perspective. Perhaps he hadn't been so angry with her that he wanted her out of the way as soon as possible. Perhaps he'd been trying to shield her from embarrassment.

Or, perhaps getting an embarrassing person out of the way?

She sighed. There was always two ways to look at everything he did.

'And with some people saying that you staged the whole thing to attract the Duke's attention, the way some sluts in town damp their skirts so that men can see their legs better.'

'What?'

'Of course, I know that cannot be true, since it was my fault you went into the water…'

'By *some people* saying I did it on purpose, you mean Lady Sarah, I suppose?'

A frown flickered across Lady Margaret's face. 'Well, yes, but I soon put her right, explaining how it was. Only now…well, I've begun to wish I'd never defended you, because everyone's saying I pushed you in out of spite, when I'm not spiteful. I'm not! I'd never have done it on purpose…'

Lady Sarah's work again. It must be.

'Oh, dear. You make me even more reluctant to leave my room and face all that gossip. But I shall,' she vowed. She'd already decided it was time for her to grow up and stop being such a coward; to become a woman her father—and Aunt Agnes, she rather thought—could be proud of. 'If the doctor permits, and Aunt Agnes agrees, I shall come down to dinner this evening and I will show everyone that I bear you no ill will over the incident.'

'You will?'

'Yes. Why not? Because, actually, just before you came to talk to me on the jetty, I had been thinking how hot and uncomfortable I was and how I wished I could take a swim.'

'Really?'

'Of course, I would have preferred to have had lei-sure to change into more suitable attire and done it without an audience, but...'

Lady Margaret, who now had a sodden hanky in each hand, stared at her. 'You...you are making a jest out of it?'

Sofia shrugged. 'Why not?'

'Because, if you chose, you could ruin me over this. You could play the victim and tell His Grace that I tried to drown you.'

'Why on earth would I wish to do that?'

'To eliminate me from the competition, of course.'

'Ah. No, that is not my way.'

'No, I can see that it is not,' said Lady Margaret, shifting in her seat. 'And in spite of what some people say, you are not ineligible at all, are you? Mama says your grandfather was an earl.'

'Yes, that's right. The Earl of Tadcaster.'

'I...well, if... That is... I mean, I am supposed to be in my room, consulting with my maid over the outfits

I mean to wear during the course of today. I...' She got to her feet. 'I ought not to linger here any longer. If I am missed, someone is bound to accuse me,' she said resentfully, 'of doing something clandestine...'

'Why don't you simply tell them,' said Sofia, full of evangelical zeal for her new outlook on life, 'the truth?'

'The truth?' Lady Margaret looked at her as though she'd said something obscene. 'You are a fine one to talk about telling the truth, when you kept the truth of your birth from us all, even when we all treated you as if you were just some country miss.'

Well, that was because there were other circumstances in her background which she had no wish to reveal.

'Nevertheless, it might help you if you simply told anyone who may question you that you stopped by my room to see how I fared.'

'Yes, I suppose I could do that,' Lady Margaret said grudgingly. She began to make for the door. 'And tonight, you will act as though you bear me no animosity?'

'I will. Because I don't. Truly,' she added when Lady Margaret looked as though it was hard to believe. 'Feelings were running high, yesterday. You all want to become the Duchess so much that you get things a bit out of perspective, occasionally, I think.'

Lady Margaret frowned. 'But don't you want to become a duchess, too?'

'I...' She blinked. 'Well, yes, I believe I do, although I didn't at first.' If only he loved her, even just a little bit, she could very easily agree to marry him. He was such a fine man. And he kissed like a...like a...well, since no other man had ever kissed her she had nothing with which to compare it. She only knew that his kiss had been much, much more than the touch of lips. It had set fire to every part of her person and made her yearn for more.

Lady Margaret, she noted, was scowling at her.

'But, I rather think I may have lost any chance I might have had with him,' Sofia continued miserably. 'He was very, very angry with me yesterday. Did you not see how he scolded me, before bringing me back to shore?'

'Yes,' she said, brightening up. As though Sofia's obvious misery over the incident was doing more for Lady Margaret than anything Sofia had said or done so far. 'We all did.' She cocked her head and looked at her assessingly. 'Very well, I shall see you at dinner where we will present an amicable front to the world. In fact,' she added graciously, 'if I should be fortunate enough to win the Duke's hand, you shall always be able to consider me your friend.' So saying, she lifted her chin, and swept out of the room.

Sofia was left open-mouthed. There was a girl who knew what she wanted and believed, what was more, she was entitled to go out and get it.

All of a sudden, Sofia felt an overwhelming need to get washed and dressed, because talking to people you hardly knew, when wearing only your nightgown, left you feeling very, very vulnerable.

And who could tell who might decide to drop by her room next?

## Chapter Twenty-Three

It turned out to be the doctor.

'Well, well, up and dressed today, are we?' He took hold of her wrist as he pulled out his pocket watch. 'Hmm, yes, good, clearly over the shock of the accidental immersion,' he declared, dropping her wrist and tucking his watch away.

'But she still looks flushed, Dr Cochrane,' said Aunt Agnes. 'And she feels hot to the touch.'

Doctor Cochrane placed his hand briefly against Sofia's forehead. 'We all feel warm today,' he said, pulling out a handkerchief and mopping his own forehead. 'But perhaps it would be wise for your niece to continue to rest today, just to be on the safe side.'

Aunt Agnes beamed at him.

'May I go down to dinner tonight?' Sofia asked, mindful of her promise to Lady Margaret.

'I see no reason why not, provided you do not feel unwell at any time before that. And I shall be on hand, of course, to make sure she does not overtire herself,' he said to Aunt Agnes.

'While you are here, might I enquire,' she said, darting a wary glance at Aunt Agnes, 'about Mrs Pagett?'

'Ah, yes, you are the young lady who rushed to her side and so very misguidedly threw your cloak over her, weren't you?'

'M-misguidedly?'

'Goose fat is what should have been applied first. So the cloth would not stick.'

He looked so stern that Sofia wanted to apologise for not having had the foresight to have been carrying a jar of it in her reticule that evening.

'But you weren't to know, of course,' he conceded graciously. 'And she is recovering nicely, so no real harm done.'

Having totally demoralised her, he bade her aunt a cheery good day.

'Well, that is good news,' said Aunt Agnes, the moment he'd gone. 'You have your embroidery by you? Oh, and some books, I see. Well,' she went on swiftly, before Sofia had a chance to reply. 'I'm sure you will be able to keep yourself amused until I come back.'

'Come back?'

'Oh, I won't be far away,' she said, startling Sofia by patting her on the cheek. 'His Grace has arranged a tour of his succession houses this afternoon. I am most anxious to discover how he manages to grow pineapples.'

Pineapples? Really? But from the look on her aunt's face as she left, she considered it a high treat.

Once she was alone, Sofia dragged a *chaise longue* to the window, which she opened, even though the air outside was too heavy to heave itself in over the windowsill. She then armed herself with a fan and one of the novels Aunt Agnes had noticed. For she would much rather lose herself in the improbable adventures

of a romantic heroine than do a single stitch of embroidery, even though her aunt was always insisting it was
a much worthier pursuit.

She was soon so deeply engrossed in the tale that
she had no idea how long she'd been sitting there before she became aware of a strange scuffling noise.
She looked up. It seemed to be coming from behind an
alcove that contained a set of shelves so shallow they
would scarcely hold an egg cup. She gave a shudder
of revulsion at the thought of rats coming out to play
whenever the house was quiet.

But then she heard another noise. A persistent
scratching that sounded just like a dog's claws when
it was trying to open a door. And then the unmistakable whine of a dog.

She sat up straight, the book falling from her lap as
the entire wall of the alcove swung open, as though it
was a door, and a white blur shot out and came streak-
ing towards her.

'Snowball,' she cried in delighted surprise as her
dog jumped on to her lap, knocking her fan from her
hand and frantically licking her face. 'How on earth did
you get here? I know you are a clever girl, but breaking
out of your kennels and making your way along secret
passages is more than I suspected even you could do.'

She looked across to what she could now see was
the entrance to one of the discreetly disguised servants' corridors Livvy had told her about. And saw
Livvy herself, standing there looking defiant and rather
grubby.

'Livvy, sweetheart, please come in,' said Sofia. As
if to add her voice to the invitation, Snowball jumped
off her lap and ran to Livvy. Then ran back to Sofia.

Then ran back to Livvy again, skidding across the rugs and rucking them up in the process.

'Thank you so much for bringing Snowball to visit me.'

'I didn't do it for you,' said Livvy mutinously. 'I did it for her. She wouldn't eat anything yesterday. She hated being locked up in the kennels, all on her own. I thought she'd like to come to the woods with me. That was why I let her out. But she made for the house instead,' said the little girl, looking askance at the dog.

'I see. She was lonely, most of all. She missed me. I'm so sorry, Snowball,' she said, ruffling the dog's ears, 'that I had to leave you in that nasty kennel. It was the rules, you know.'

'There's too many rules in this house, if you ask me,' said Livvy, sounding far more grown up than her height suggested.

'Are there?'

'Yes,' she said with a scowl, though she inched a bit closer. 'But the most important one is to stay out of sight,' she said defiantly, taking another step nearer to where Sofia and Snowball were sitting.

'Well, you can stay out of sight here, if you like. It is what I'm doing, after all.'

'You are? Why?'

'I'm in disgrace.' She pulled the corners of her mouth down. 'I fell in the lake yesterday, during what was supposed to have been a very respectable picnic.'

Livvy's mouth fell open. 'Did you drown?'

Ignoring the obvious answer, that of course she hadn't drowned or she wouldn't be here, Sofia said, 'Oh, no. Because I can swim like a fish.'

'You can? I wish I could.'

'Perhaps…' She'd been about to say that perhaps she could teach Livvy to swim in the lake. But she could only do that if she stayed, which would mean marrying the girl's father, and she wasn't sure his proposal still stood, after the way he'd spoken to her yesterday. And even then…

She wrenched her unruly thoughts away from Oliver to concentrate instead upon his daughter.

'That is, at home… I mean, where I come from, where I live with my uncle and aunt, I used to say I was taking Snowball for a walk so that I could go for a secret swim. I had a favourite pond. Nowhere near as big and fine as the lake here. And Snowball would sit on the bank guarding me. If anyone was coming, she would bark a warning, and I could hide under the jetty until they'd gone.'

Which was how she'd known Jack was approaching.

'That sounds like fun.'

'It was. But it was not fun yesterday. I lost my bonnet in the water and your father jumped in with all his clothes on because he thought I needed rescuing. He was very cross with me.'

'He's very cross with me, too,' said Livvy mournfully.

'Why? What have you done?'

She shrugged and started straightening out the rug which Snowball had rucked up. 'He's always been cross with me. The very first time he saw me, I thought he was going to…' Not only her mouth, but her whole face closed up.

Since Oliver had told her a little about the way he'd felt upon discovering he had a daughter, Sofia knew that if he had been cross, it hadn't been with Livvy.

And she also knew how easy it was for a child to mis-interpret the look on an adult's face, particularly after that child had been betrayed by an adult she trusted.

'I don't think he was cross with you,' she said.

'That's all you know. He was cross then and he's still cross now. He must be, else why would he have handed me over to Mrs Starchypants?'

'Well, perhaps he simply doesn't know how to be a father.' It was what he'd told her. 'Perhaps...'

'That's all well and good...' Livvy sniffed, a sus-picious sheen brightening her eyes '...but he keeps *on* scowling at me whenever he sees me. Which ain't often. And Mrs Starchypants says she's only surprised he has me in his house at all, rather than sending me back to the kind of people I belong with.'

It sounded to Sofia as though Mrs Starchypants had a lot to answer for. If she had any say in the matter, she'd send the horrid woman packing.

Before she could think twice, she'd leaned down and scooped Livvy up on to her lap, which wasn't easy considering Snowball already occupied most of it. But Snowball wriggled to make room and licked Livvy's face in welcome. Livvy put her arms round the dog and buried her little face in her soft fur.

Sofia was still racking her brains for something to say to ease the troubled little girl's mind when there came a brisk knock at her door, the knock which she recognised as belonging to Aunt Agnes.

'Quick,' said Sofia, pushing Livvy off her lap. 'Hide. You, too, Snowball. And mind, be silent.' She tapped the dog on the nose before shoving both her, and the little girl, under the low *chaise*.

Aunt Agnes, who rarely waited for Sofia to say she

could enter, came bustling in just as Sofia was arranging her shawl across her legs so that it draped down to the floor, concealing the miscreants under the *chaise*.

'I just came to see how you are doing,' said Aunt Agnes. 'And to tell you that the trip round the succession houses was rather a disappointment.' She flopped down on to a chair by the other open window and flapped her hand before her face. 'His Grace was not there. Instead, it was his head gardener who gave us the tour. I was rather disappointed at first, but at least I got some satisfaction from seeing Lady Sale and that dreadful daughter of hers being thwarted in their ambition to get His Grace alone.'

Ah. So he'd organised the tour of the pinery the same way he'd organised the stroll through his portrait gallery—as an excuse to spend time with one of his bridal candidates.

Which meant that he was still considering the other girls.

Which meant that he'd changed his mind about wanting to marry her.

Except that he hadn't actually gone on the tour.

Oh, lord. As usual, when wondering about Oliver's motives, she found her guesses had veered wildly from one extreme to the other.

'Did anyone say why he handed Lady Sarah and her mother over to the care of his gardener?'

'Only that some urgent business had cropped up which he had to attend to personally. You wouldn't expect him to explain his movements to anyone, would you?'

'No,' Sofia replied with resignation.

'Well, I'm glad to see you looking so very much better this afternoon. I will go and have a rest before dinner. Lord, but it is hot,' she sighed, getting to her feet. 'And even hotter in that pinery. Lady Sale's face was like a beetroot by the time we came out,' she tittered. 'Oh!' She peered out of the window. 'It is raining.'

Sofia followed the direction of her aunt's gaze and saw a few splashes of water strike the windowsill. In the far distance, a bank of almost bluish-black clouds hung low over the trees.

'It looks as though we will have a storm before the day is out,' said Aunt Agnes. 'Good thing, too. It will be much cooler after and we will all feel the benefit.' After a short discussion about what Sofia ought to wear to dinner, she bustled out of the room.

The moment the door shut behind her, Sofia twitched her shawl up off the floor. 'It's safe to come out now. Good girl,' she said, when Snowball snuffled into her lap for a petting. 'Just a moment, Livvy, I must just give her a treat for staying silent and not giving you away.' She got up and went to the dressing table in her bedroom where she kept a bag of the hard biscuits the cook at Nettleton Manor made especially for Snowball, while Livvy, too, crawled out from her hiding place.

'Sit,' Sofia commanded Snowball, who'd come running after her on hearing the word *treat*. Snowball sat and took her treat most politely.

Livvy ventured as far as the bedroom door to watch.

'You know,' said Sofia, 'I've been thinking about what you said about your father being cross. Please, won't you come and sit at my dressing table?'

As Sofia pointed in that direction, Snowball trotted over and looked at her expectantly.

'Oh,' said Livvy. 'She thinks you meant her.'

'She wants another treat,' said Sofia drily. 'Would you like to give it to her?'

Livvy needed no second asking. She was over at the dressing table in a flash, giving Snowball all the commands she'd heard Sofia use and giving the dog a treat every time she performed.

They were both delighted with the game and it had the benefit of getting the girl exactly where Sofia wanted her.

'Here,' said Sofia, who'd gone to fetch paper and pencil while the others were amusing each other. 'Sit at the stool, won't you, for a minute. I'd like you to do some sums.'

'Sums?' Livvy looked at her aghast.

'Oh, very well, not sums then. How about some writing? I'd just like to see what a clever girl you are. I'm sure you can write beautifully, can you not? And then, when you've finished, you can play with Snowball again.'

Livvy looked mutinous, but she took the pencil and wriggled round on the stool so that she was facing the mirror.

'What shall I write?'

'How about a poem?' Sofia suggested. 'About Snowball.' She wanted Livvy to have to think hard about what she was writing. And, just as she'd hoped, not long after she'd picked up the pencil, Livvy's brows drew down in concentration. Swiftly, Sofia tilted the girl's head up so that she was looking at her own reflection. 'How cross you look.'

'No, I'm not cross, I'm just thinking hard. I want to write a really good poem for Snowball.'

'Yes, you want to do your best. And that, I fancy, is what your papa was doing, whenever you thought he was angry with you. Wondering how to do his best for you.'

Livvy studied her reflection for a moment or two. Her frown faded. 'Do you really think so?' she asked, wistfully.

'Yes, I do. You are so very like him to look at. And sometimes your expression is very fierce, when I'm sure you are just thinking hard.'

Livvy nodded. 'Then, you think he might not be cross with me?'

'I'm sure he isn't...'

But then, someone else knocked on the door before she could get any further. And Livvy, with a squeak of fright, dived under Sofia's bed. Snowball, who looked as though she was starting to regard diving under various items of furniture as part of her daily routine, was only a split second behind her.

And just as well, because the person knocking did not wait for a response but came crashing into her rooms like a clap of thunder.

Sofia gasped. It was Oliver, breaking all the rules of etiquette by coming into her room. Doing what no host—or gentleman—should ever do.

And he looked furious.

## Chapter Twenty-Four

Oliver had not given a thought to how Sofia might react before coming here. But had he done so, he might have known she would be shocked.

Not afraid, though? Surely she must know he would never harm her?

But if she did, what had put that look of trepidation on her face?

'I know it is highly irregular, me coming to your room like this,' he said. 'Improper, even,' he added, shutting the door firmly behind him, lest anyone see him standing there. 'But I heard you intended to come down for dinner tonight and I may not be able to be there, and did not wish you to think that I was avoiding you.' He advanced across the sitting room but stopped on the threshold of her bedroom. It was one thing invading her private suite, but to set foot in her bedroom really would be crossing a line.

'Why,' she replied nervously, inching away from the bed, 'would I think that?'

'Because of the way we parted. I… I was harsh with you. Harsher than I should have been. Later, when I'd had time to reflect, I could see that you might have interpreted what I'd said as a criticism…'

'It *was* a criticism,' she said.

'Well, yes, but I didn't mean the half of it. Can't you see, Sofia, that I was out of my mind with fear? I thought you were drowning. I thought I'd lost you before you were ever truly mine and I could not stand it. And then, when you scolded me for thinking you might need me…' He ground to a halt. He'd used her given name without first securing her permission to do so. Even though she'd used his, she didn't appear to think he had the right to do the same, not to judge from the forbidding cast of her features.

'We both said things we did not really mean,' she said.

He breathed out.

'Or at least,' she added, making him hold his breath again, 'things that expressed our feelings in a very poor way.'

'Are you…is that your notion of an apology?'

'It's as good as the one you just gave me,' she retorted.

'I did not come here to quarrel with you again. The truth is…' Yes, what was the truth? 'The truth is that I want you more than is healthy. And I resent you for wanting you so much. You make me so angry with myself that I…'

The wounded look in her eyes struck him to the core. 'No, no, Sofia, sweetheart, I never meant it to sound as though anything is your fault.'

And then, because he could not help himself, he closed the distance between them and pulled her into his arms.

'The fault is all mine,' he said into the crown of her hair, since she'd lowered her head and would not look at him. 'I have always been afraid to love. Afraid of what it would do to me. And yesterday, at the lake, my worst fears came to pass. You were in danger and, instead of being what you needed, I lost my temper. That is the kind of man I am.'

But in spite of having just admitted, and shown her, the very worst of himself, her arms stole round his waist, like a benediction. 'You are no worse than any other man,' she said into his chest. 'You may have shouted a bit, but then you made sure that I was cared for. You carried me to the carriage so that I did not have to drip my way across the field and then you gave me your own coat to shield me from prying eyes.'

'Thank you for that,' he breathed in heartfelt gratitude. 'Thank you that at least I have not your rejection to worry about tonight. Because if I do not have you to come back to, if there is no hope left for us, then I do not know how I will bear...'

She reached up one hand to cup his cheek. 'What is it? What is the matter?'

And even though he knew it was the worst thing he could possibly do, he could not help himself. One kiss. He needed at least one, to see him through what he feared he was about to face.

And since her face was turned up to his, it was but a matter of lowering his own a fraction for their lips to meet. She gasped in surprise and tensed, as though she was considering pulling away. But after only a moment, she yielded to the passion that flared up whenever they were together, kissing him back like a woman who was putting her whole heart into it. And there was a bed nearby. It would be an easy matter to guide her over there and push her down and…

He wrenched himself away from her. Ran his fingers through his hair. 'I should not have done that.' That was what happened when a man yielded to feelings. It turned him into a beast. Disgusted with himself, he turned and paced away.

'Pardon me. But I am at my wit's end. No, no, that is no excuse for pouncing upon you like a beast.'

'I… I didn't mind.'

'Yes, you did. At first. I overbore your reluctance. It is in my blood. I once thought I had managed to conquer that side of me, but with you…' He paused to look at her, his pulse pounding.

'I had better go. Before the storm reaches us. I'm sorry, I'm not explaining myself very well. The truth is that Livvy is missing. Nobody has seen her all day. And they…' He stopped, clenching his fists, his chest weighted with a dread chill. 'We searched the woods this afternoon, but there was no sign of her. And with the storm approaching…' he swallowed '…I cannot bear to think of my little girl all alone out there in the woods, or wherever she may have run to.'

Sofia strode across the room to him and seized one of his hands. 'I am sure she is quite safe.'

'How can you be sure?'

She jerked her head in the direction of the dressing table, before widening her eyes, then blinking, then lowering her gaze to her feet. If it had been any other woman than Sofia, he would have thought she was showing signs of being touched in the upper works.

But it was Sofia, so, to be charitable, he would assume

she'd realised how silly her expression of sympathy had been and was hanging her head in shame.

'I know you are trying to make me feel better, but really, this is not the time to utter empty platitudes,' he said. 'You cannot possibly know she is safe. And even if she were, it wouldn't make me feel any better.'

Her head flew up. 'Why do you say that?'

'Because I've failed her so badly that she felt she had to run away.'

She regarded him thoughtfully. 'You do know,' she said rather sternly, 'that some dreadful woman has told her that she is a disgrace? That she ought not to be allowed anywhere near respectable people?'

'Yes, I...that is, you told me about it and I confronted her governess. Demanded she tell me who could have said such a thing. She promised to find out and have that person punished.'

She raised her eyebrows as though she was astonished. 'You...asked *her* to find out...don't you know that *she* was the one to say such things?'

'She was?'

'Well, yes, if her name is Mrs Starchypants. Although I suppose Livvy might have meant the housekeeper, for a more starched-up woman I have never met.'

'Livvy's governess is Mrs Stuyvesant. So it is...but, no, I cannot believe she would...'

Sofia gave him a reproachful look. 'Do you think Livvy is untruthful?'

'I do not know her well enough to judge...' He had to stop, for Sofia was looking at him as though he'd really disappointed her. 'That is, Mrs Stuyvesant came highly recommended.'

'By whom?'

'By…my secretary, Perceval.'

'And he has a lot of experience of bringing up children, does he?'

'No. And come to think of it, he was the one who suggested that I send Livvy away to some family in the country and pay them to have her brought up in secret. Perhaps that is what I should have done.' He sighed. 'After all, they might have known how to make her happy. And I *was* better off with my foster parents than I would have been had I stayed here.'

'In what way?'

He gave a bitter laugh. 'Well, at least they did their best to keep me alive. Even if it was only because I was their main source of income.'

When Sofia looked perplexed, he added, 'Look, I am wasting time standing here talking about my past and why I so badly wanted to keep Livvy with me. I have failed her. She is out there, lost and afraid, and there is a storm approaching. It has already started to rain. And now that I have explained why I must search for her, rather than attend to any of my guests this evening, I ought to go…'

As he turned, she laid a hand on his sleeve and shook her head. And then pointed at the dressing table.

He'd only glanced at it before, but now he examined the litter strewn across its surface more keenly. There was a hairbrush, various pots, and some notepaper and a pencil.

And scrawled across the top of the notepaper, in a childish hand, *A bome for Snowpall.* His heart kicked. Livvy was always getting her p's and b's mixed up.

'You have not really explained why you wanted to

keep Livvy with you,' said Sofia, firmly. 'Or why, since you have, you have allowed that dreadful woman to make her feel as though she is not fit to be seen.' She then jerked her head in the direction of the bed.

He was not fool enough to think it was an invitation to take her to it. Not with a sample of Livvy's handwriting sitting out in the open. This time, he was also certain she was not jerking her head like that because she'd developed some form of mania.

'Do you love her, Oliver?' If anyone else had asked him such an impertinent question he would have given them short shrift. But Sofia was not asking out of curiosity. No, what she was doing was providing him with the opportunity to explain his motives to Livvy, who was, if he was not mistaken, hiding under Sofia's bed. And she'd used his given name. The way she'd done in the summer house.

Before he could properly consider the significance of her doing so he heard a rumble of thunder from somewhere to the west. His mind flew back to a long-ago stormy night when he'd been the child hiding under a bed from his own father.

The comparison shook him so badly it took the strength from his knees. He just made it to Sofia's dressing-table stool before they gave out completely. He sat down hard and buried his face in his hands. How could he have turned into the very kind of monster he'd striven so hard to eradicate from his personality? And yet he must have done, or his own child would not be hiding from him this way.

Everything he'd done had all been for nothing.

'What is it?' Sofia laid a hand on his shoulder. 'Are you ill? Should I pour you a glass of water?'

'I...' He shook his head. He could not brush this off. Besides, if he answered her truthfully, it would also give him the chance to explain his behaviour to his daughter without betraying the fact he knew she was cowering under Sofia's bed. And he had to persuade her to come out of her own free will. There was no way he would get down on his knees and terrify her by trying to drive her out. By swiping at her with a poker.

'A glass of water would help,' he admitted. It would give him the excuse he needed to stay and talk Livvy out from under the bed without scaring her. Or scaring her further, anyway.

Sofia crossed to her bedside table, upon which stood a jug, and poured him a glass. She followed the direction of his gaze, which was riveted upon the small gap under her bed.

'Would it help,' she suggested, 'to talk about it? I know that men find it hard to speak of anything besides sport, or at least, the men in my family do. But in this case...' She gave another speaking look in the direction of her bed.

When she returned to him with the glass of water he gripped her hand, squeezing it in gratitude.

'I don't know where to start,' he admitted.

'Perhaps...' She bit down on her lower lip and frowned. 'Perhaps you could explain how it is you were so averse to having Livvy sent to a foster family and how you know so much about them.'

'Ah. Well, it isn't a pretty story.' He paused and took a sip of the water while he thought about how much he could reveal without damaging his daughter even further.

'I told you that my father sent me away to live with strangers after my mother died, did I not?'

There was a shocked gasp from under the bed and then a muffled bump, as though someone had jerked and bumped their head. He couldn't pretend he hadn't heard it. He turned his gaze to Sofia, his heart squeezing in a sort of anguish.

She threw back her shoulders.

'I suppose you heard that.'

When he nodded, she said, 'I have a confession to make. Please, do not be too cross with me.' She gave him another speaking look. He took it to mean that if he could demonstrate forgiveness for whatever she had done, then perhaps Livvy would have the courage to believe he could forgive her, too, for having turned his entire household upside down while searching for her.

'I don't believe,' he said a trifle hoarsely, 'that I could ever be really cross with you. Or not for long, anyway,' he concluded, for the sake of complete honesty.

Sofia's eyes welled up. She swallowed, then said in a clear, ringing voice, 'Snowball. Come.'

From under the bed came the wriggling, furry form of her pet.

'I know she is not allowed in the house, I know she should stay in the kennels but she was pining for me. And so...' She dropped to her knees and put her arms round her dog's neck and now there were two pairs of hopeful brown eyes gazing up at him, as though begging him for clemency.

To his knowledge, she hadn't stirred from her room since her impromptu swim in the lake and there was only one person in his entire household who might have been concerned enough about her dog to go and check, and decide the creature was pining for its mistress, then have the nerve to break her out of her canine prison.

But he could not let on that he suspected the true culprit was Livvy, rather than Sofia.

Not yet. Not until Livvy was ready.

'I think,' he said decisively, 'it is about time some of the rules in this household changed.'

## Chapter Twenty-Five

'From now on,' he vowed, 'Snowball will have the run of the house. I shall make sure of it.'

His heart swelled at the look of gratitude in her eyes. 'Thank you,' she said. 'Snowball is very well behaved and won't cause any mess, I promise.'

'The rule was not mine to begin with. I leave all aspects of managing the house, or at least I have done until now, to Mrs Manderville. And I think she is more concerned about preserving the Court's treasures than she is with the comfort of my guests.'

He glanced around the tiny rooms in which he found Sofia.

'I only learned today that she had put you here. Practically in the servants' quarters—' he indicated the ceiling '—rather than in the main house with all my other guests. This…' he waved one hand round the box-like proportions of her sitting room '…is no doubt her expression of displeasure at me for adding you to the guest list so late in the day.'

'It doesn't matter,' she said generously. 'It is a lovely set of rooms. Better than I'm used to, in most ways.'

'In most ways? In what way is it not an improvement on what you are used to?'

'Oh, it's nothing really. It's just that one of your servants appears to be having trouble sleeping. I keep hearing them pacing up and down at night.' And then it was her turn to point at the ceiling.

'Ah. I must apologise. You see, the room directly above this one is the schoolroom. It will have been me you've heard, pacing back and forth. I go in to look at Livvy every night, you see, while she is sleeping. And then I...well, I go to the schoolroom and think. And I tend to pace when I am thinking.'

'You wait until she is asleep,' she said with disapproval, 'before going to see her?'

'Well, I don't wish to intimidate her by summoning her to my study every day as though she has to give an account of her movements. But I do need to see, with my own eyes, that she is well.'

'But why all that pacing up and down?'

'Because, so very often, I can see tear-tracks down her cheeks. She isn't happy here and I don't know how to make things better. I often wonder if I should have found somebody who could care for her the way I seem incapable of doing. I...' He reached inside himself for the courage to expose his deepest, most private self. The weakness he was so vigilant about concealing from everyone else. 'I have no idea how to be a father. My own, you see...' He swallowed and rolled the water glass between his palms a few times while choosing his words, knowing that whatever he said, his daughter would hear.

And realising, with faint surprise, that for once he felt no need to weigh up the consequences of sharing this topic, not with Sofia. Because he trusted her. She would never, he knew, hold what he was about to tell her over his head. She would never use the knowledge she was about to gain to further her own ends. It was not in her nature.

'One night, when I was very young, my father dragged me out of bed in the middle of a storm. He was in a rage. He shook me like a terrier would shake a rat. I saw blood on the cuffs of his shirt, just before my nightshirt tore, so that I fell to the floor. I was so terrified that I wriggled under my bed and refused to come out, no matter what he threatened. The space was too small for him to get under and drag me out. So he went to fetch a poker.' He paused, drawing in a breath or two to steady himself.

'All the while,' he continued when he could, 'he was shouting at me, calling me foul names. *Bastard* among them. And *the Duke's Bastard* was how my foster family referred to me. That was what I thought I was. Just a bastard. A nothing.'

Sofia had pressed her hands together at her chest, as though trying to hold back some deep emotion, though he could see it on her face. Normally, he would have recoiled from such a look of pity. He was not an object of pity!

But…there was Livvy to consider.

'That is why, when you saw Livvy you…'

'I thought I knew exactly how she felt, yes. But more than that, you must see why I am so angry that somebody in my household has used words to make her feel bad about herself when she has done nothing wrong, any more than I did anything wrong, apart from being born. I brought her here specifically to shield her from that very kind of ill usage.'

Sofia's eyes filled with tears. He thought she was going to say something pertinent to Livvy's feelings or the treatment to which he had exposed her. Instead, she stunned him by saying, 'You must have been terrified.'

He shrugged one shoulder, as though it didn't matter. 'It was a long time ago. I could not have been more than three years old. But,' he continued, loathe though he was to remember that time, let alone speak of it, 'the very morning after my mother died, I was banished from Theakstone Court. I grew up believing my father had…had killed her, that night, in a fit of rage.'

'Oh, no! How awful.' She reached out one hand, then withdrew it, as though she could see how reluctant he was to receive any form of pity.

'Worse was the fact that he never paid for the crime. No charges were ever brought against him, probably because he was too powerful. And by the time I was old enough to do anything it was too late. You cannot imagine the difficulties inherent in attempting to investigate a crime that took place over twenty years previously. Besides…' He jerked his head in the direction of her bed, reminding her and himself that there was a more important issue at stake now.

'I was not precisely safe myself. You see…' he shifted on the stool, wishing he'd taken her hand, for then he could be pulling her on to his lap '…my father did not summon me home until some ten years later, by which time my half-brother had grown to an age where he was unlikely to succumb to any childhood ailment. And, tellingly, my father had given him the courtesy title of Marquess of Devizes, a title which is normally given to the heir to the Dukedom.'

'But...*you* were the heir.'

'Yes. But he did not believe it. He thought my mother had played him false and that I was no son of his. He did have what he believed was evidence. For one thing, my father had blue eyes. And my mother had blue eyes. But I have brown eyes. And, according to what investigations I could carry out, witnesses said that she discouraged him from visiting the nursery when I was awake. I don't know what her reasons were any more than I can guess what Ruby's motives may have been for concealing Livvy from me.' She couldn't have thought he would harm his own child, could she? The fear she might have was one of the things that had him pacing the schoolroom at nights. Had she seen something in him that was essentially the same as what resided in the depths of his own father's nature? Something dark and cruel?

'You know,' Sofia said, hesitantly, 'not many men are all that interested in visiting the nursery except when their offspring are washed and bathed and quiet. Perhaps you were a fractious baby. Or...'

'We will never know. The only thing of which I can be sure is that the sight of my brown eyes, when I started crawling and pulling myself up at his knee, came as a horrible shock to him.'

'I'm surprised she didn't do it the other way round, then.'

'Other way round? How do you mean?'

'Well, babies all have blue eyes when they are born, you know. So she could have shown you to him with complete confidence that he would not suspect a thing.

It was later she should have hidden you away, when your eyes darkened, if she was guilty of…of anything.'

'She was guilty of nothing,' he growled, setting down the water glass and getting to his feet. The next part was going to be even harder to relate than anything that had gone before. He'd never told another living soul what he was about to tell Sofia and Livvy. But Livvy had to know why he could sympathise with any child who went in fear of their own father. That he wouldn't hold it against her.

'No, of course not. I didn't mean to imply…'

'I need to tell you about the manner of my homecoming,' he said, making an impatient gesture with his hand to cut her off. He had to get the telling over with before his nerve failed him.

'One day, my foster father told me that the third Duke of Theakstone thought it was about time I learned to shoot a gun. And that he wanted to be the one to teach me. So, it was goodbye. He looked sad as he was packing me into the coach. Since I'd grown rather cynical by then, I assumed it was because he was going to miss the money he'd been paid for having me live with him. It was only later…'

Sofia clapped her hands to her mouth. 'You think… you thought…you said you weren't *safe*…'

'It is probably irrelevant now.' And probably best to gloss over it anyway, with Livvy's little ears no doubt straining to hear every word. 'The point is, the moment he clapped eyes on me his jaw dropped. He dragged me straight up to the gallery and stood me next to the portrait of my Aunt Mary, his sister.'

'Who has the eyebrows.'

'And, apparently, the brown eyes beneath them. He

went white as paper. I thought he was going to cast up his accounts. Instead, he sent for the housekeeper to have a room prepared for me.' Their eyes met at this significant point. And he could see she understood, because she was shaking her head, in horror rather than denial.

'That same day he banished my poor stepmother and her brood from the house.'

'What? Why?'

He shook his head. 'Who knew what possessed him to do anything? He was, not to put too fine a point on it, a touch unhinged. He would dote upon me one day, then fly into a rage with me the next. He was the same with his second family, from what I can gather. He cosseted and indulged my half-brother to a high degree and then, after he brought me back, not only banished him but hardly acknowledged him ever again. It created a rift that I have never been able to heal. Whatever I try to do for them, they believe I am doing it out of malice.'

'I'm not surprised. Not if they had no idea you existed until you showed up. Which must have been the case if your half-brother was brought up expecting to become the next Duke. He sounds like a perfect beast.'

'He was. I went in fear of my life every moment my father lived, lest he take it into his head to undo the decision he'd made to acknowledge me as his legitimate first born. Fortunately, I'd already learned how to keep my true feelings hidden. My foster family taught me that much,' he said, a wave of bitterness surging to the fore. 'I learned that there was no point in crying, for it only earned me a beating. No point in complaining, or asking for anything. By the time I returned here, I was like a little automaton. Not trusting anyone. Never confiding in anyone. When my father began to try to teach me that women in particular were not to be trusted, that I should never give rein to my emotions, he thought he found me an able pupil.'

Until Ruby. For a while, at least, she'd called to something in him that he'd thought life had extinguished. Every so often he'd even shared...

Which perhaps explained why she'd hidden Livvy from him. Perhaps she'd been afraid he might turn out like his own father. Especially since he'd told her he'd never wanted to father a child out of wedlock. Knowing what bastards went through, he'd never wanted to be responsible for making another innocent child feel the same. But had she mistaken his motives for urging her to make sure she didn't quicken with child?

Well, whatever her reasons for acting as she had, Livvy was here now and he needed to concentrate on coaxing her out from under the bed.

'My father encouraged me to behave with coldness, to weigh up everything everyone said to me. Always to question what a person's motive might be for approaching me, or attempting to befriend me.'

'You must have been so lonely,' Sofia said, reaching out a hand to touch his arm. This time, her gesture of sympathy seared into his soul like a brand. He wasn't sure if it was pain he felt, or something more beneficent. His instinct was to recoil from it.

And yet, another part of him, the part he'd been deliberately suppressing ever since his mother's death, put out its arms in the hope she would enfold him. Smother him with compassion.

'The point is,' he said stiffly, while the two parts

of himself were still wrestling for supremacy, 'I know what it feels like to lose my mother, to be sent to live with strangers and to be despised by those who had the task of raising me.'

He was past saving. But there was still time to prevent Livvy's soul from being stunted and warped, and crippled.

'When I first met Livvy, it all came rushing back. I knew just what she must have felt like when she saw me. I could see it on her face. My first instinct was to try to shield her from all that I'd suffered. Above all, I would not place her in the hands of people who would raise her only for financial gain. What would they care if she was ill? And if she wanted a puppy, or a pony, would they refuse, grudging the expense? And yet, it appears, that I *have* failed her. Somebody in my household is making her feel as though she is to blame for the circumstances surrounding her birth. And worse, she appears to be as afraid of me as I was of my own father.'

'Well, you know,' Sofia said, apologetically, 'you... you are a bit...stern in your manner.'

'I know it. And it tears at me, seeing how unhappy and withdrawn Livvy remains. Which is why I finally decided I needed to marry and provide her with a mother. Someone who could give her the...the...emotional care that I am incapable of giving her.'

'Oliver,' said Sofia, shaking her head. 'You have so much more to give her than you think. My own father...he made a *lot* of mistakes. But I never doubted he loved me. And you do love Livvy, don't you? Everything you have told me, all your struggles, all you have tried to do for her, it all proves it.'

There was the sound of a stifled sob from beneath the bed. Snowball whined and wriggled free of Sofia's arms, returning to the edge of the bed and sticking her head beneath it.

'You know,' Sofia said, 'you could simply hug her, once in a while. If you ever found her upset, or hurt…'

'Would she want me to hug her?'

'I am fairly sure she would. It sounds as if her mama was very affectionate and demonstrative. Livvy talks of all the hugs and kisses she misses…'

'But it is the hugs of her mother she misses. I am a stranger to her…'

'Hugs are hugs,' said Sofia simply. 'All little girls need them. And I'll tell you how I know it. The day I reached Nettleton Manor, dirty and dishevelled and defiant because I was so sure that these people, too, were going to let me down, I stood there glaring at my aunt and uncle. Because I was blowed if I was going to let them see how scared I was. If only my aunt had broken through all that bravado, and her own disgust at the verminous state of my clothing, to hug me, even though I'm pretty sure I would have stood stiff and sus-picious in her arms, at least I would have known that she cared; that she wasn't just taking me in on suffer-ance, because it was the right thing to do. Everything would have been so different,' she went on, a little teary-eyed. 'I certainly wouldn't have been so terri-fied of being sent away if I stepped out of line that I turned myself into a…total bore.'

She dashed a tear from her cheek in an angry ges-ture that made him want to take her in his arms and comfort her. But she shook her head.

'And you are not going to send Livvy away if she is

sometimes naughty,' she continued, 'are you? You don't even want to punish her for what she's done today, do you? For running away and hiding, and worrying you?'

'No. I would just be glad to know that she was safe. Though I would want to know what made her hide in the first place, so that I could see what I could do to make her want to stay here. And be happy here.'

'Perhaps it might help if you were to discipline her governess. It sounds as though she is at the root of Livvy's misery.'

'I think losing her mother is at the root of her misery. But that woman certainly has not done anything to alleviate it.'

Suddenly he knew what he had to do next. And it started with him going to the bell pull. Then, since Sofia's rooms were not in the best part of the house and servants were unlikely to come in answer to a summons very quickly, he strode to the main door to her suite and bellowed for a footman.

A young one appeared remarkably swiftly.

'Send for Mrs Stuyvesant,' he said to the puzzled-looking young man. 'Quickly!'

'Sir...er... Your Grace,' he said, his eyes sliding past Oliver, to where Sofia was standing, in the doorway to her bedroom. 'You want me to fetch her here?'

'Here,' he confirmed, before shutting the door in his face.

When he returned to Sofia's room, it was to see her on her hands and knees, next to her dog, her head under the bed, holding a frantic, whispered conversation with his daughter. And the most ignoble part of him couldn't help noticing that she had a very shapely bottom.

But now was not the time to be distracted by her

physical charms. He had a small, frightened child to coax out of hiding.

'She won't come out,' said Sofia, turning to look at him over her shoulder. 'When she heard you send for Mrs Starchy...that is to say, Mrs Stuyvesant, she got it into her head that you did mean to punish her, in spite of what you said before.' And then she mouthed, *please don't be angry.*

'I am not really surprised she does not trust me,' he said. 'After all, she is my daughter. And she has clearly inherited a suspicious nature from me. She needs proof that I mean what I say. And it will take time for her to learn that I never say anything I don't mean. I will be patient with her. I will give her the time she needs to learn that I am a man of my word.'

Sofia got up, dusted down her skirts and came up to him. 'You are not angry with her for not trusting you?'

'Trust has to be earned,' he said.

She frowned, then nodded. 'I see. And, having witnessed the behaviour of the other women you have brought here, to see if they could be good mothers to Livvy, I can understand why you needed to...test us all. You have been used to people betraying you, from as far back as you can remember.' She laid one hand on his cheek.

Finally, he yielded to temptation. He turned his face into her palm and kissed it.

'I admit I wanted to test you, to see if you were what Livvy needed. I needed to make sure that I was right about you. That you could be a mother to Livvy, that is true. And that I wanted to ignore the...other things I felt whenever I saw you. But...' Hang it, this wasn't the time to be making a declaration. He groaned. 'This is the trouble with you. I always try to behave like a rational, sensible man, but around you I have never been able to manage it. From the first moment I saw you, you…'

'Yes?' She was looking up at him with what looked like hope in her eyes. And she'd inched nearer. She was definitely standing closer to him than she'd been a minute ago.

'You…you got under my skin,' he admitted.

'Like nettle rash?'

'As welcome as that affliction,' he agreed. 'I try to keep reminding myself that it is for Livvy's sake that I am searching for a bride, and for someone who can become the fourth Duchess of Theakstone. But… I want you so much, for myself,' he grated. 'Thank God Livvy likes you as well, because even if she didn't, I…'

She moved her hand to stop his mouth and shook her head fiercely.

And that, right there, was why he…he loved her. She had a good heart. A kind, caring nature. Even when he was trying to tell her that she was more important to him than his own child, she would not allow him to say so. Not when that child might be able to hear it.

She was a woman in a million.

## Chapter Twenty-Six

When Mrs Stuyvesant arrived, the Duke urged Sofia to sit on the *chaise longue* by the window, while he took up a stance in her bedroom doorway. Snowball, as though sensing trouble brewing, shot under the bed to hide alongside Livvy.

Oliver was setting the scene, Sofia perceived. If his own memories of being a child, cowering under his bed while his father attacked him with a poker, had stayed with him all his life, then his daughter's would stay with her, too. And in years to come, she would wager that Livvy's abiding memory of this scene would be of watching the woman who'd been so unkind to her being given a rare trimming before being dismissed by her father—through the framework of his sturdy legs.

After today, Livvy would never regard her father as a man she needed to fear, but as a strong and protective figure, instead. Because he would continue, staunch and true. Because that was the kind of man he was.

The moment the governess had stalked out of the room, unrepentant in spite of being soundly denounced for her cruelty, Livvy and Snowball came out from their hiding place.

For a few moments father and daughter stood there, looking at each other warily.

'Livvy,' said Sofia, 'would you not like your father to hug you?'

Livvy thought about it. She raised her chin. 'Not if he don't want to. I'm not a baby.'

'No, you are a very brave and resourceful young lady,' said Oliver.

'You ain't cross with me? Truly?'

'No. I am angry with myself.'

'With yourself?'

'Yes. For not seeing through that vile woman sooner. For believing her word over yours. For not being a better father.'

Livvy took a step closer. 'You'll get better at it. You just need practice.'

'I…' His voice choked up.

'Oliver,' Sofia said gently, 'I can see that today has been very hard for you. Would it help if Livvy gave you a hug?'

'Only if she wishes to,' he said.

'Oh, for heaven's sake, come here, the pair of you,' she said, taking Oliver by one hand, and Livvy with the other and then, when they were close enough, putting one arm round each of them. Livvy leaned into her, though she kept her eyes upon her father, who put his arms round the pair of them.

'We need you, Sofia,' he said. 'You are going to marry me and make us a family, aren't you?'

'Please, Miss Sofia. I don't want none of those others to be my mama.'

Sofia didn't blame her. Oh, she could see why Oliver had considered each and every one of them. Lady Sarah would have made a magnificent duchess and both she and Lady Margaret were so ambitious they would have swallowed any condition Oliver imposed upon them regarding Livvy, if it meant getting their grasping claws on his title. Lady Elizabeth would have defended Livvy from wagging tongues as a matter of principle, judging from the way she'd reacted to Lady Sarah's machinations.

Only Lady Beatrice might have genuinely liked Livvy. Though that relationship could well have foundered if it turned out that Livvy didn't love horses.

'And I,' said Oliver firmly, 'do not want any of them to be my wife.'

'I know you could teach him how to be a good father,' said Livvy. 'Not that I'm sure what a father oughta be seeing's I never had one before I come here, but...'

'We will find out together,' put in Oliver, 'what a father should be, I think, Livvy. I am not altogether sure myself, you see, having had such a bad example set for me.'

Livvy looked up at him, her little face wearing a very grown-up expression of sympathy. 'You got a lot to learn about being a husband, too, I reckon. None of Mama's beaux would ever have said she was like nettle rash.' She shook her dark head in reproof.

'Your father,' said Sofia, a smile tugging at her heart, 'may not have a smooth way with words, it is true, but I do think he could be the perfect husband for me.'

Oliver's arm tightened round her waist. He looked at her warily. 'You do?'

'Oh, yes.'

'But you…accused me of…and said you needed more time…'

'Which you very generously gave me. So that I could think things through. Which I needed to do. Even though none of the other ladies you invited here would have done. And I know it must have been very hard for you to understand, but then they wanted very different things from you as a husband than I want.'

'But—' his face tightened '—you want me to love you, Sofia. And I don't know how to do that…'

'Yes, you do,' she said gently.

'I wish I did, but…'

He looked so baffled she wanted to hug him, then realised she already was hugging him. Which meant she would have to explain it to him in very simple words.

'You mean, I think, really, that you wish you didn't, because you think love is a weakness. Otherwise you wouldn't refer to it as suffering a form of nettle rash. And I can see why you have resented the process of falling in love with me. It has made you break so many of your resolutions. You told me you were never going to be alone with any of your Duchess candidates, yet the moment I arrived, you took me to the kennels to visit Snowball.'

'You looked so worried.'

'You looked so cross,' she countered with a smile. 'And then, when I said I couldn't marry you because I didn't know how to be a duchess, you wouldn't accept any of my reasons, would you? Not even when I said I wouldn't know how to defend Livvy from spiteful gossip.'

'Well, your aunt can teach you how to do that,' he said with a touch of impatience. 'Don't forget, I was there when she crossed swords with Lady Sale. She is a force to be reckoned with.'

'Oh, Oliver, you don't need to try to persuade me you want me to be your wife for practical reasons. I know you are wary of giving way to emotions. But not all emotions are bad. Just consider…out of all the married couples who are here this week, which is the happiest, would you say?'

'Your uncle and aunt,' he said without hesitation.

'Exactly. And they married in the teeth of opposition from my family because they were in love. And that love has lasted and sustained them throughout all their years together.'

He searched her face.

'Oliver, you don't need to worry that succumbing to love will make you a lesser man.'

'But what of you,' he said, avoiding the issue. 'You said you didn't love me, either. Have you…changed your mind?'

'Yes,' she said simply.

He frowned. 'When? What changed it?'

'It was after I fell in the lake. When you were so cross with me.'

'You decided you loved me because I was cross with you?'

'No, not exactly. It was because I started to worry that you were so cross you might have changed your mind about marrying me. The thought of you with any of those others…' She shuddered. 'I couldn't bear to so much as leave my room in case I saw you seeming to favour any of them.'

He squeezed her and dropped a kiss on the crown of her head. 'I will never change my mind about wanting to marry you.'

'I know,' she said, her heart soaring. 'I knew it the moment you called me Sofia, today, without asking my permission.'

'Ah,' he said, looking a touch uncomfortable. 'I do apologise. I never manage to behave with complete propriety whenever I get within two yards of you.'

'No, no, that is a *good* thing,' she assured him. 'Because while I was thinking about what kind of husband I wanted, I worked out that I wanted a man who would love me the way my father loved my mother—so much, that he flouted all the conventions by marrying her in spite of her being a foreigner and a Catholic. It caused *such* a scandal.'

'Did it?' He looked worried. 'You wish me to cause a scandal, to prove how much I love you?' He took a deep breath. 'I suppose I could—'

'No...' she laid her hand across his mouth '...you do not need to do anything further. You have already flouted enough conventions, for a man of your principles, to prove your love to my own satisfaction.'

'I have?'

'Yes. You broke all the rules that you apply so strictly to others. You used my given name without permission. You invaded my bedroom...' He flushed a dull crimson. 'But most of all, you trusted me with the truth about Livvy. Trusted me to be a mother to her, when she is your most precious treasure.'

He tore his intent gaze from her, to glance down at Livvy.

'She is,' he grated.

'And just now, you know, when you weren't thinking about it, you said you would cause a scandal to prove how much you love me.'

'You did,' cried Livvy.

'Yes, I did,' he said slowly. And then one side of his mouth curved up. 'I've lost this particular battle, haven't I? I ought to feel defeated, but I don't.'

'Don't you?' She smiled up at him.

'No,' he said, his smile growing wider. 'I feel about ten feet tall. Because you love me back. It makes me feel as if I could take on the world.'

And then all of a sudden he swept her into his arms, and whirled her round and round, to the delight of Livvy and the bewilderment of Snowball, who gave vent to a volley of barking and jumping.

'We will announce our betrothal tonight, at dinner,' he said, setting her down.

'Oh, and will I be sitting next to you, then?' she couldn't resist asking. 'By rights it should be the turn of Lady Beatrice. She is, after all, the daughter of an earl…'

He gave her a mock glower. 'And to think I was expecting you to want me to start flouting conventions.'

'Not if it is going to mean hurting anyone.'

His severe lips curved into a knowing smile. 'I don't think Lady Beatrice will care. She is well on the way to reaching an understanding with Captain Beamish, if I am not very much mistaken. And once I announce our betrothal, her mother will stop pushing her in my direction.'

'Then I shall not mind sitting by your side at dinner tonight,' she conceded.

'And for the rest our lives,' he said firmly.

Oh, that sounded good. So good. Finally, after all the years of trying so hard to fit in, she'd fallen into a niche that could have been carved out especially for her. A place where she truly belonged.

In the hearts of these two dear people.

But most importantly in the arms of this one man.

\* \* \* \* \*

*If you enjoyed this story check out the
Brides for Bachelors miniseries
by Annie Burrows*

The Major Meets His Match
The Marquess Tames His Bride
The Captain Claims His Lady

*And also be sure to read*
The Debutante's Daring Proposal